A SHAMWELL TALES NOVEL

OUT!

JL MERROW

RIPTIDE
PUBLISHING

Riptide Publishing
PO Box 1537
Burnsville, NC 28714
www.riptidepublishing.com

Out!

Cover art: Natasha Snow, natashasnowdesigns.com
Editor: Carole-ann Galloway; Alex Whitehall
Layout: L.C. Chase, lcchase.com/design.htm

ISBN: 978-1-62649-610-1

Second edition
June, 2017

Also available in ebook:
ISBN: 978-1-62649-609-5

A SHAMWELL TALES NOVEL

OUT!

JL MERROW

RIPTIDE
PUBLISHING

With thanks to Penelope Friday, Blaine Arden, Cleon Lee, Susan Sorrentino, and Kristin—and to Patricia for introducing me to New Rocks. This is for everyone who asked me after Played! *whether Patrick would be getting his own story!*

To stay in, you've got to not get out.
—Geoff Boycott, former England cricketer

TABLE OF CONTENTS

CHAPTER ONE

Mark clenched and unclenched his hands in his lap—fortunately hidden by the large oak table they were all sitting around. This should *not* be at all nerve-racking. He'd spent twenty years building a successful career as a tax advisor in the City of London. He'd faced down boards of directors and pointed out the errors of their ways. He'd brow-beaten so many inspectors of taxes on behalf of his corporate clients it was a wonder the country hadn't gone bankrupt.

He should be able to face a meeting of the Shamwell Spartans Fun and Funds Foundation.

The trouble was, there was no hiding behind his professional persona here. This was a social situation, which had never been his forte. Mark couldn't help being reminded of his school days. He'd changed schools on an almost annual basis, and he'd always hated being the new boy. Having to negotiate all the little cliques that inevitably formed wherever two or three were gathered together. Everyone here knew everyone else here—except him.

The upstairs room of the Three Lions pub was fairly large, with white-painted walls that made the best of the light coming in through small, many-paned windows. The ceiling beams, black with age, stood out in stark contrast. There was a mingled aroma of beer, furniture polish, and somebody's enthusiastically applied aftershave tragically failing to cover his stale sweat.

The website had said the Spartans was open to all villagers of the male gender (was that even legal these days?) between the ages of twenty-one and forty-five. Mark was comforted to find he wasn't the only one there who was edging towards the upper end of that range. Several heads were greying to greater or lesser degree—unlike his own,

Mark was happy to say with *almost* complete truth—and he strongly suspected Barry the chairman's thick, dark head of hair of being a dye job. There were also a couple of early receders who'd made the best of it by shaving the lot off.

Barry knocked on the table with an actual, old-fashioned gavel. "Right, you lot, if you can shut your gobs for a moment, I want you all to welcome our new member, Mark Nugent. He's just moved in to the village. Mark, you want to introduce yourself?"

"Thank you, Barry," Mark said with a confident smile. He stood, realising even as he did so that what might be right for the boardroom might, in this context, just make him look like a self-important prick. But sitting straight down again would make him look like an idiot. He had a split second to decide: sessile fool or erect . . . prick?

Mark decided that, on the whole, he'd rather be a prick.

"Not a lot to tell," he began self-deprecatingly. "I'm a chartered accountant and chartered tax advisor, formerly based in practice in London and now taking a career break to concentrate on my family. I'm a single father with a daughter of fourteen who's just started at . . ." Damn it, what was the bloody name of the place? ". . . one of the local schools. She was the one who encouraged me to come along here, in fact."

Actually, her words had been more along the lines of "For God's sake, Dad, get some bloody hobbies. You're driving me mental hanging round the house all the time."

"And I hope I'll be able to use my professional expertise to further the aims of this excellent group. Thank you, gentlemen." Mark cleared his throat again. *Yes, thank you, and I hope you enjoyed this evening's order of pomposity. Plenty more available at a very reasonable hourly rate.*

Mark hoped he was imagining the variety of amused, incredulous, and horrified looks that had turned his way. The one saving feature of the evening was that Florrie—no, *Fen*, damn it—wasn't here to witness it. He could hear her exasperated *Daaa*-aaad in his head, even now.

"Right, well, thanks for that, Mark. I'm sure we'll be able to find . . . something for you to do. Anyway— Oh, hang on. We oughta tell you who we are, don't we? Me you know, and that's—" Barry rattled off a list of names going round the table, most of which Mark immediately forgot. "Right, now we all know each other—" He was cut off by the door opening.

A man walked in, his gait the confident, easy swagger of young, good-looking men everywhere. Clearly on the younger end of the Spartans' age scale, the newcomer might have just stepped from the pages of a fashion shoot. Or out of one of those adverts for online dating agencies Mark had been trying to ignore lately. He was dressed in a pale-blue casual shirt that Mark was ninety-five percent certain wasn't designer but looked it anyway on his slim, fit figure, paired with jeans that hugged him, if not lovingly, then certainly with lust in mind. His eyes, set off by the shirt, were a startling blue, lively and bright. Cropped in close at the sides, his sandy hair was styled up on top with gel—was that why he was late? Maybe he'd needed the extra time to do his hair—bringing his height up to a level that, if it wasn't six foot, wasn't far off either. Just an inch or so shorter than Mark, in fact.

He was . . . hot. *And*, Mark reminded himself hurriedly, even in the statistically unlikely event that this young man was attracted to (a) men and (b) older men in particular, *firmly off limits.* Mark had his daughter to think of. The thought filled him with a heady mix of pride, purpose—and insidiously creeping depression.

The newcomer flashed them all a cheeky smile, and now apparently Mark had a heart arrhythmia to add to his woes. What the hell was the matter with him tonight?

"Patrick. *Finally*," Barry said with good-humoured reproof. "We'd just about given up on you."

Patrick's reply was pitched low, with just a hint of roughness under the light Essex accent. "All right, lads? Sorry I'm late—total bastard of a day at work, and then when I get home, Mum's got it into her head she's gonna put up a shelf in the kitchen. Managed to drill into a water pipe. So there's me stuck with my thumb in the hole like a little Dutch boy while she calls that plumber she fancies."

There was a collective wry chuckle, accompanied by the odd muttering of "Women, eh?"

"Anyway," he carried on. "By the time this plumber bloke gets there, I'm soaking wet, which, from the way he eyes me up, makes me think Mum could be barking up the wrong tree there, so I had to go and get changed."

Mark was mesmerised by the image of Patrick, soaking wet and peeling off his clothes. So much so that he almost didn't catch Barry's reply: "What, and you didn't stay to chat him up?"

That was interesting . . . Except no, it wasn't, because young, fit fashion models didn't look twice at middle-aged men. And responsible fathers didn't shock their troubled teenage daughters by getting mixed up with boy-toys.

Damn it. Mark's mood crashed again.

The blue eyes twinkled. "What, and step on Mum's toes? I'd never hear the last of it. You never know, maybe he swings both ways."

"Go on, admit it," the better looking of the shaven heads—Roger? Rodney? Roderick?—said loudly. "You just needed the time to do your hair."

Patrick's response was a hearty laugh. "Rory, mate, you know you're just jealous."

Barry cleared his throat. "We were just getting to know our new member. Mark, this is Patrick."

Caught by surprise, Mark stood once more—*damn it, legs, why do you keep doing that?*—and offered Patrick his hand.

Patrick raised an eyebrow, making Mark feel even worse, but took his hand and shook it firmly. His grip was warm and smooth, and all sorts of thoughts Mark should *not* be thinking started to run through his head like an X-rated earworm.

"Good to meet you," Patrick said. "New in the village? I don't think I've seen you around."

"Ah, likewise." Mark's mind wasn't really on his response. The room was stiflingly hot. It couldn't be good for the ancient timbers, not to mention the environment. Why the bloody hell didn't someone turn the heating down?

And was Patrick implying that if he'd seen Mark, he'd have noticed him?

No, surely not.

Was he? Mark realised he was still holding Patrick's hand and dropped it like a hot potato. Fortunately nobody seemed to have noticed. He sat down hastily as Patrick took a seat at the other end of the long oak table.

Oh God. Mark's life had just turned into the classic midlife crisis.

This young man was apparently attracted to men, gorgeous, and sharp in just the right way. His smile set Mark's stomach in turmoil, and his voice had a similar effect on . . . other areas.

And he was young enough to be Mark's *son*, for God's sake.

Mark was doomed.

Barry banged on the table once more, and the susurration of murmurs that had sprung up abruptly ceased. "Right. Three-legged sponsored pub crawl—who's up for it?"

CHAPTER TWO

"**W**hat's the story with the new bloke?" Patrick asked Rory as they leaned on the bar downstairs, far enough away from Mark that he wouldn't be able to hear, although he kept his voice down just in case. After the meeting had finished, they'd all headed down for the usual pint or three. Mark, Patrick had noticed, had seemed a bit doubtful about it and kept checking his watch, but he'd come along after a bit of persuasion. So, not a hot date he wanted to get off to. Maybe he had someone waiting for him back home?

Patrick reckoned he ought to find out about that.

Barry had steered Mark over to one side—the bloke took his responsibilities as chairman seriously—and was leaning back against the bar, clearly in full flow about the Spartans, his beer gut jiggling as he went overboard with the hand signals. Mark, a head taller and light years fitter, was nodding along and doing a reasonable impersonation of a bloke who wasn't desperate to escape. Patrick smiled to himself. Yeah, that looked familiar. Poor sod would get home tonight and wonder how the hell he'd managed to sign himself up for the pub crawl, the fun run, and to be an elf in Santa's sleigh come December.

Not to mention the induction ceremony. Which, obviously, Barry wouldn't. Not until the bloke was well and truly hooked.

Rory smoothed a hand over the five-o'clock shadow on his mostly bald head. He was in his early forties, so wouldn't be long for the Spartans, which was a shame. Couldn't be easy, facing the prospect of being told he was too old for something he'd given so much of his time to. At least Patrick had a couple of decades before he'd have to worry about that.

"Uh, I think he said he was a chartered accountant or something? He's got a teenage daughter, I remember that. Doesn't look old enough, does he?" Rory's kids were seven and five, the youngest just started at the local primary school. "Why, you interested?"

Not sure, but I think he *is.* "Not if he's married I'm not," Patrick said firmly.

"Nah, single dad. Must be divorced." Rory winced, maybe because his own divorce had only just gone through. He'd had a few gloomy pints to "celebrate" after the last Spartans meeting. Then he frowned. "Oh. So he's not gay. Sorry."

Patrick laughed. "Bisexuals really are invisible as far as you're concerned, aren't they, mate?"

Rory made a helpless gesture that nearly had him spilling his pint. "Well, it's a bit confusing, innit? I mean, don't get me wrong, I got no problem with people being gay, and obviously I got no problem with people being straight, but bisexuals, I just don't get it. Why can't they just pick one and stick with it?"

He was a good bloke at heart, Rory was. Just not very up on issues and stuff. "They do," Patrick said patiently. "Then when that one goes tits up, they pick another one and stick with it. Just like anyone else, except they're a bit more open-minded about who they go out with. It's not that difficult a concept, mate. It's not even that uncommon. I've been out with girls in my time."

"Yeah?" Rory looked at him doubtfully. "You sure it wasn't just a phase?"

Patrick let that one go, because he reckoned if he started having a serious discussion about bisexuality versus sexual fluidity, Rory's head would probably explode. "And there's Sean. He used to go out with Heather from the Sham-Drams."

"The rat bloke? Yeah, but he's just got engaged to Lucy's teacher. She made 'em a card and everything. So he's gay now, right?"

"No, he's just in a relationship with a bloke. He used to go out with Heather, and that didn't make him straight. Love's not that simple, all right?"

"Which is what I'm trying to *tell* you, innit? It's all so bloody confusing." Rory shook his head and scratched the beginnings of a beer gut. "No wonder it didn't work out, me and Evie."

Poor bastard. Patrick clapped him on the shoulder. "You oughta give the lads a go."

"No fear. With my luck, I'd just chat up the wrong bloke and end up getting a kicking. Nah, give me women any day. They're . . . soft. And they smell nice. And they know about stuff like curtains and sewing name tags on the kiddies' clothes."

"You're a real Renaissance man, aren't you?" Patrick said with a grin. "Gotta go. There's a mate over there all on his tod—I'd better go and say hi." He picked up his pint and left Rory to join in a spirited discussion on whether the under-eights in the local kiddies' football club were going to win the County Cup or not this year. Given what Patrick had heard about their performance as under-sevens, he wasn't holding his breath.

Con, who Patrick knew from the local amateur dramatics society, was sitting at a table in the corner. He was wearing a soft bottle-green shirt that made his shoulders look about six foot wide—having a bloke had definitely smartened him up a bit. "All on your own tonight?" Patrick asked as he dropped into a chair.

"Nah, I'm here with Heather. She's just nipped to the ladies'."

"Your bloke off wowing them in the West End?"

Con nodded. "Yeah, it's been going really well for him. He's got another gig lined up as soon as this one finishes its run."

"Yeah? Good for him, but seriously, mate, I know you and Tristan live together now, but do you ever get to see him? Your sex life must be almost as tragic as mine."

"Self-employed, aren't I?" Con grinned. "I can choose my own hours. Good to see you, anyway. Spartans night tonight?"

"Yep. We've just been having a meeting upstairs. You ought to join us," Patrick added. Con was a handyman studying to be a carpenter—those sorts of skills could come in, well, handy. And he was a good bloke. With some free time in the evenings, what with Tristan's unsociable hours.

"Not sure it's really my thing," Con said with a shrug. "Isn't it all about lads' nights out, getting pissed, and putting on really bad drag?"

"Well, some of it is," Patrick admitted with a laugh. "Then there's the induction ceremony, where they make you put on a leather skirt and helmet and drink half a yard of ale. Don't think anyone's mentioned that to the new bloke yet."

"New bloke?"

"Mark somebody." Patrick cast a glance over at the bar, meeting Mark's gaze head-on. The guy flushed and looked away. Patrick grinned as he turned back to Con.

Con was peering at the bar. "Which one's he? There's a couple of blokes over there I don't know."

"He's the one talking to Barry. Tall, fit, light-brown hair, dark-brown sweater . . ." Patrick paused, but what the hell. "And if I'm not mistaken, he fancies the pants off me."

Con frowned. "Isn't he a bit . . . old?"

"Well, he'd have to be under forty-five to be in the Spartans. Unless he's telling porkies, of course. It's not like Barry ever asks to see anyone's birth certificate before he lets them come to a meeting."

"Yeah, but even forty-five . . . That's old enough to be your dad."

"So? Nothing wrong with a bloke with a bit of experience, is there?" Patrick said it mostly to wind Con up. From the way Mark was acting, Patrick reckoned experience was one thing the bloke didn't have a right lot of. At least, not with men.

Still, that could be fun too.

A bit wide-eyed now, Con took a slow swallow from his pint, then put the glass back on the table. "You always go for older blokes, then?"

Amused, Patrick raised an eyebrow. "What do you think?"

Result. Con blushed. Yeah, he hadn't forgotten that time Patrick had tried to chat him up. Course, what with the broken leg and being in hospital, Patrick had been a bit off his game at the time. More to the point, he'd been too slow off the mark—Con had already fallen for Shamwell's biggest drama queen. Sorry, professional actor.

"Oi, what've you said to Con? His face is clashing with his shirt something chronic." Heather sat down with a wicked smile and pushed up the sleeves of her sweater, showing off her slim, tan forearms. She was a pretty girl, in a natural sort of way—she didn't wear much makeup, and she never straightened her hair—and a decent actor. Patrick had been in quite a few Sham-Drams productions with her. "Hope you're not talking dirty to him while his bloke's not here."

"Nah, just telling him about Mark."

"Mark?" Heather raised an eyebrow at Patrick.

"New Spartan," he explained.

"New *gay* Spartan, Patrick reckons," Con threw in. "And he fancies him."

"Oh my God! So who is he, then? And hang on, he fancies you, or you fancy him? Or both?" She peered at the bar. "I can't see anyone I don't know except that tall bloke talking to Barry . . . Oh my God, is it him? Isn't he a bit, well, *old* for you? When did you get into daddy kink?"

Patrick laughed and gave her a one-fingered salute. "Just cos he's a bit older than me doesn't make it a kink. That's ageist, that is."

"Yeah, but I mean, what is he? Late thirties? Forty? That's like your mum's age. Actually, you know what? I could totally see him with your mum. You should introduce them. Maybe he's bi."

"Mum's forty-four. And she can find her own blokes, all right?" And frequently did—a bit too frequently for Patrick's liking.

Maybe Heather was thinking the same thing. "Yeah, but they're all such total losers. I mean, no offence, but your mum's taste in men is bleedin' tragic. So what's he doing in Shamwell, then, this not-a-daddy-kink bloke?"

Patrick shrugged. "Dunno. I missed the start of the meeting where he introduced himself."

"So go chat him up now and find out, then."

"Nah. I think I'll wait. I'll be seeing more of him anyway." He laughed. "If he makes it to the induction ceremony, I'll be seeing a *lot* more of him."

Heather giggled. "Make sure you tell me when it is, all right? I don't want to miss it."

"Why—you got a thing for older blokes in leather skirts?"

"It's not the skirt that does it for me. It's the fact that'll be all he's wearing. He looks like he's pretty fit, for an old bloke."

Con frowned. "That's all they get to wear, is it? Gonna be a bit nippy, this time of year."

"He'll have a cloak on too," Patrick said, a bit distracted himself by the image. Yeah, this Mark bloke would look a damn sight better than most of the lads did in the Spartan getup. He'd had nightmares about some of the beer-guts . . . "And there's the helmet."

"Ooh, yeah, don't forget that," Heather said. "I'm looking forward to seeing his helmet."

Con choked on his pint.

Patrick grinned. "And his six-foot weapon. Don't forget that."

"Is he gonna be poking people with it?" she shot back.

"Fancy a poke from him, do you? Even though he's old enough to be your dad?" Patrick added pointedly, and took a mouthful of beer.

"Oi, I thought you said he was gay?" Con interrupted. "Sorry, Hev, looks like you're out of luck."

"Bum." Heather made an exaggerated frown face.

Patrick put his glass down on the table. "What I *said* was, I reckon he fancies me. Maybe he goes for women too. Course, if you want to have to explain to Chris you're planning on cheating on him with some bloke you've never even spoken to . . ."

"*And* who's old enough to be her dad," Con put in, a bit unhelpfully to Patrick's mind. He'd already said that, hadn't he? There was no need to keep going on about the bloke's age.

She pouted. "Hey, maybe me and Chris have got an open relationship?"

Patrick laughed. "So that was some other girl I heard the other night threatening to cut his bollocks off with a spoon if he didn't stop looking at the new barmaid's tits?"

He glanced over at the bar automatically—and caught Mark's gaze on him again. There was something in the bloke's eyes Patrick couldn't read, not that he got more than a nanosecond before Mark looked away. Did he know they'd been talking about him? Nah, he couldn't have heard anything.

Still, Patrick felt a bit bad about it, somehow. It had to be hard, starting fresh in a new place—especially such a small village, where everyone knew everyone else. Maybe he should do a bit more to make the bloke feel welcome.

Maybe he'd suggest they pair up for the pub crawl. Yeah, that was it. He'd do that. Now would be a good time. Patrick took another swallow of his beer and put his glass back down. He was just about to tell Con and Heather he'd be back in a minute, when Heather glanced up, surprised. "Your bloke's leaving."

"Yeah?" Patrick looked round again. Mark was already halfway to the door, shrugging his overcoat on as he walked. It was a classic style and looked good on him—he had the height to carry it off.

And Patrick had just lost the chance of going over to talk to him. Well, if he tried to catch him now, he'd just look daft.

He could wait.

"Um," Heather said, looking worried. "You don't think he knew we were talking about him, do you?"

Patrick frowned, then shrugged. "Not a lot we can do about it now, is there?"

Still, he'd make a point of asking the bloke about the three-legged pub crawl next time he saw him. Make sure he felt welcome here.

They ended up staying until closing time. It was ten minutes' walk back to the little house Patrick shared with his mum on the edge of the Hillside estate—just long enough for the night-time chill to seep through his leather jacket and almost make him wish he'd worn that naff woolly scarf his mum had made in her one and only attempt at knitting and had wrapped up for him as a gag gift for Christmas.

Even the neighbour's cat's fur felt cold as he stroked it with one hand, fumbling for his keys with the other. They had a brief stare-off when he opened the door—the cat knew it wasn't allowed in, but it never stopped chancing its paw—then it flicked its tail and stalked off. For some reason, it reminded him of Mark, and an unwelcome surge of guilt made Patrick kick off his Nikes on the doormat with a bit more force than necessary. He hadn't *meant* to make the bloke feel uncomfortable. Ah, what the hell. He'd make it up to him.

Patrick hung up his jacket and padded into the living room, where his mum was snuggled up on their squashy yellow sofa in her penguin pyjamas with a glass of wine, her bobbed, straw-blonde hair all damp at the ends. She smiled as he walked in.

"Hello, love. Have a good evening?"

"All right." Patrick threw himself down on the sofa next to her, then frowned as the comedian on the telly let out a massively annoying, braying laugh. Fingernails down the blackboard of the nation's souls, that laugh was. "What are you watching that git for? He's that one who was in the papers for not paying his taxes—earned millions and tied it all up in offshore trusts so he could cheat the rest of us poor sods."

"Yeah, but it's not like he did anything illegal," Mum said, gesturing with her glass. "And, anyway, he's funny."

"You won't be laughing when they close down your department because the hospital budget's been slashed. *He's* the one laughing, with his one percent tax bill, and the rest of us are the bloody joke. Bastards like that don't give a toss about anyone else." Patrick grabbed the remote and changed channels.

"You're all grumpy. What happened at the Spartans? They didn't vote to let *women* in, did they?" she added sarcastically.

Mum could be a bit funny about all-male things. Patrick blamed his dad, which was easy cos he never saw the bastard and hadn't since he was thirteen. Hadn't wanted to either.

"I'm not grumpy." Patrick realised he was frowning and made an effort to stop. He was way too young for Botox. "It just pisses me off when people don't pay their way, that's all. All these MPs moaning about benefit cheats and making people jump through hoops to get the money they need to live on, when it's a drop in the ocean compared to all these rich bastards and corporations making millions and paying no tax at all."

"There *are* some people who cheat the system, as you well know." Mum gave him a pointed look and took a sip of wine.

"Yeah, and you can leave Dad out of this. I'm talking about the innocent majority who get tarred with the same brush."

Instead of arguing, Mum just gave him a sympathetic smile. "Bad day at work, love?"

Trust her. She always could read him like she'd downloaded him onto her Kindle.

"Yeah. Sorry." He sighed. "You know I've been trying to get sponsors for this fun run? I rang up that big pharmaceuticals company in Stortford, and they were all keen on helping out the disabled—until they found out SHARE's a charity for the *mentally* disabled and, worse, adults. Then all of a sudden it's 'Sorry, I'm afraid we've exhausted our budget for this year, but we'll definitely keep it in mind for the future.' Load of bollocks. He's fine with helping cute kids in wheelchairs—or even cute kids with Down's—but once they grow up, they can just sod off. Don't fit the corporate image."

"Poor love. Didn't Spartans cheer you up, though?"

"Well, yeah, but then I get home to find that smug git on the telly," Patrick teased, leaning back and stretching out his legs. "There was a new bloke at the meeting tonight. Think he's into me."

Mum sighed dramatically. "What it is to be young and beautiful. Where's all the decent straight blokes gone? That's what I want to know."

Patrick grinned. "No such animal. You told me that years ago."

"Yeah, but that was when I was young and bitter."

"Instead of old and bitter like you are now?"

She chucked a cushion at his head. Patrick caught it with a smirk and tucked it behind his neck.

Mum *humph*ed. "I'll have less of that, my lad. I'm not old. I'm just . . . less young. And less bitter. Mellow and mature, that's me."

"What, like a lump of cheddar cheese? Yeah, you keep telling yourself that, Mum." Patrick paused. "Hypothetically speaking, what would you think about me going out with a bloke who was *mature*?"

"I'd think he was a dirty old man leading my little baby boy astray. Hypothetically speaking." She gave him a sharp look.

"Mum, I'm twenty-five. I haven't needed *leading* astray for years."

"Maybe not, but what d'you want to go out with some old fart for? I know it's been a while since you've had a proper relationship, and I *know* I go on at you for being too picky, but that doesn't mean you have to drop your standards completely. You just need to get out more. Have a night out in London or something. Go on Grindr—"

"Mum! First, I dunno what you think you know about Grindr, but it's not about finding a *relationship*, okay? And I'm not dropping my standards. Just cos he's a bit older than me doesn't mean he's a loser." Shit, Mum had that glint in her eye that meant an interrogation about the "hypothetical" old fart was coming. Patrick decided it'd be safest to go on the attack. "Anyway, you can talk. What about that dustman you went out with just because he asked you? That bloke was *rank*."

"There's nothing wrong with working in refuse collection."

"I never said there was. Just, next time pick a bloke who actually bothers to have a shower once in a while, okay? I still can't believe you let him get within five feet of you."

"We didn't kiss much or anything. I had a cold at the time, all right?" Mum topped up her glass. "It took me a while to notice."

"It took me thirty seconds. *And* I was standing upwind." Patrick stood up and stretched. "Gonna get an early night. Today was a killer."

"Not so fast, my lad." Mum shot out a leg covered in mini penguins to bar his way.

True, he could have stepped over it, but . . . Patrick gave in. It usually saved hassle in the long run. "What?"

"This mature bloke. You going to tell me about him, or do I have to start stalking you online again?"

Patrick laughed. "I hope you're better at it now than when I was fifteen. That was embarrassing, that was. There's nothing to tell. Seriously. He's a bit older than me, and he's just come along to the Spartans for the first time."

"How much older? And what does he do for a living? He'd better not be married," she added darkly.

"Don't know, don't know, don't think so. His name's Mark. And now you *literally* know as much as I do." Patrick yawned, hoping she'd get the hint.

Mum's leg didn't budge. "Well, if you really like him, flippin' well ask him out before someone else snaps him up. There was that bloke you liked last year—that one with the muscles, remember him?—and you missed the boat on that one."

Patrick smiled despite himself. "You mean Con, right? Nah, it wouldn't have worked out, me and him. Just as well I never got around to asking him out till it was too late. Him and Tris are a great couple."

"You always say that, but just cos they find someone else doesn't mean it wouldn't have worked with you. It just means they got fed up waiting."

"Worried I'm going to end up left on the shelf? Well, I can see your point. Not a very safe place to be—not if you put it up, anyhow."

Mum glared at him. "I'll have you know I'm very good at putting up shelves. Not my fault they put the water pipe in the wrong place."

Patrick laughed. "Yeah, right. Anyhow, I'm off to bed. Don't go starting any more DIY projects, will you?"

"What, at nearly midnight? No chance. I'll get you up nice and early in the morning for it, all right?"

"You do and you can expect a few choice words from your little baby boy. Night, Mum."

"Night, darling. Sleep tight."

Patrick padded up the stairs and pushed open his door. He'd been fifteen, nearly sixteen, when they'd moved here, Mum wanting a fresh start, so there wasn't a lot in his room to remind him of his childhood. He'd been old for his years, anyway, he reckoned, what with Dad being... the way he was. Mum had let him decorate the room how he liked it, so it was in rich, deep blues. Made a good contrast to the rest of the house, which she'd done in bright, aggressively cheerful tones.

They'd toned it down a bit since then, but the first year they'd lived there, the place had looked like it was on acid, all lime green and orange.

She'd even let Patrick get a double bed, the twin of hers down the hall. Not that *his* bed had seen a lot of action over the years. Patrick hadn't taken a vow of celibacy or anything—far from it—but he didn't bring anyone home if he wasn't one hundred percent certain about them.

As he laid his head on his pillow, Patrick wondered what it'd be like to have Mark lying next to him. Then he laughed silently.

Mum'd probably tar and feather the poor bloke for taking advantage of her little baby boy.

CHAPTER THREE

Mark left the pub early after the Spartans meeting. He wasn't entirely happy leaving his daughter alone for too long—and if he was honest, Patrick's little group of friends over in the corner wasn't making him feel any more relaxed, what with all the laughter and the frequent glances in his direction.

He hadn't, of course, been disappointed to see Patrick make a beeline for the tall and ruggedly handsome young man sitting on his own. To have been disappointed would have implied he'd had some hopes in Patrick's direction, which, obviously, he didn't.

And equally clearly, once the pretty, mixed-race girl had joined them, Mark *hadn't* listened to Barry with only half an ear as he tried to work out who, if anyone, was with whom. Patrick and the other young man certainly hadn't seemed to be acting like a couple—at least, not like the couples Mark had seen in his few furtive forays into London's gay scene after splitting up with Ellen.

They—the forays, not the couples, about whom he wouldn't presume to judge—hadn't been particularly successful, either in terms of romance or of coming to terms with his "new" identity. Most of them had left him feeling like that schoolteacher—usually the PE teacher, for some reason—who tried to be cool by dancing with the kids at the school disco, while everyone laughed at him behind his back. Not to mention, he'd been paranoid he might bump into David, his PA. It'd been a revelation, though, seeing young men in their teens and early twenties casually kiss one another on the street after a night out. Had things really changed so much in the last twenty years? Mark couldn't imagine daring to kiss a boy on the street at a similar age. Of course, he'd still been trying to make a go of it with girls back then.

If kissing boys had seemed more acceptable, his whole life might have been different. He might never have gone on holiday with Ellen—the holiday that turned out to have such lasting consequences.

He couldn't regret the way his life had gone—after all, it had brought him Florence. But it would have been nice not to have felt so alone. Even now, Mark's gaydar seemed to be perennially on the blink. In his youth, coupled with a crippling lack of self-belief, it had been nonexistent. The only gay man he'd been reliably certain he'd known had been so stereotypically camp, he'd been known locally as Ray the Gay.

Mark winced at the memory. Yes, a bit of generally accepted on-the-street kissing would definitely have helped there. At least, if it could have taken place without upping the hate-crime statistics. Not, of course, that *hate crime* had been a recognised offence back then. Sometimes Mark felt like he'd grown up in the Dark Ages.

In a village like Shamwell, though, there were probably a lot of conservative types around even now. Public displays of affection between those of the same gender were probably frowned upon. It was one of the reasons he'd chosen the place—it'd help him stand firm in his determination to put his daughter first and avoid looking for hookups while she was living with him.

Of course, he hadn't expected to meet anyone like Patrick.

Mark and his daughter had been living in Shamwell for precisely one month, having found a house in the centre of the village. Or rather, *Mark* had found it, as Florence's sole contribution to the house-hunt had been a sullen "What*ever*" every time he'd showed her the latest wodge of details that'd come through from the estate agent.

Florence wasn't happy about moving to a country village. She wasn't happy about changing schools and leaving all her friends. She wasn't happy about *anything*, at least as far as Mark could tell. Reminding her it was all her own fault just didn't seem to have the desired positive effect.

It'd all started with the phone call from Ellen three months ago. Mark had been halfway through his Lean'n'Mean chicken curry and a bit annoyed to be interrupted. "Ellen, I'm eating. Can I call you—"

"Do you *know* what your daughter's done now?" Ellen's voice was shrill and a bit painful to listen to over the phone, so Mark moved the receiver an inch or two away from his ear.

"Not being a mind reader, no, I don't." Mark cringed at his tone. He'd tried to keep it light, but he had a nasty feeling he'd only managed supercilious.

That was what usually happened when they spoke on the phone these days. Or off the phone. Mark had hoped the lingering bitterness might have faded after more than a year apart, but apparently he'd been wrong about this—as, indeed, he'd been about so many things, at least if you listened to Ellen.

Looking on the bright side, though, since they'd split there had seldom been any occasion to leave passive-aggressive notes for one another. Mark hadn't, of course, kept any of Ellen's notes, but he was fairly sure the course of the marriage breakup could have been charted by the increasing spikiness of her handwriting.

"Oh, it's all right for you, isn't it?" she was saying. "You with your warehouse bloody flat and your lack of responsibilities and your bloody *career*. You can *afford* sarcasm. Go on, make your little jokes. I've got all day."

"Ellen . . ." Mark looked sadly at the remains of his curry as it congealed on his plate. It hadn't been that nice to start with. He doubted letting it cool to room temperature would improve the flavour.

"And if you bloody tell me to bloody calm down, I'm warning you . . ."

"Sweetheart, what is it?" Damn it. That was the second thing that always seemed to happen.

"Don't you *dare* call me *sweetheart*. Don't you *dare*." There was a loud sniff.

And there went the third. "Ellen, I'm sorry." For everything. "Please, just tell me what she's done."

There was a pause for audible nose-blowing. "She's been excluded."

It didn't quite register at first. "Wait—you mean she's been expelled?"

"They don't call it that these days. They call it *excluded*. But I suppose I can't expect *you* to know anything about schools."

"Now that's not fair, Ells. Look, will you just tell me what happened?"

"She and a group of friends got together," Ellen said, enunciating her words with bitter clarity, "and they vandalised a teacher's car."

"*What*?" Mark stared, horrified, at the phone in his hand, then hastily put it back up to his ear. "What kind of people have you been letting her hang around with, for God's sake?"

"Letting her? *Letting* her?" At Ellen's ear-piercingly shrill tone, Mark moved the phone farther away again. "I'd like to see you bloody well try and keep her away from them. She's *fourteen*, Mark. What do you want me to do? Lock her in a playpen?"

"You just need to be firm with her. Let her know the boundaries—"

"You know what? *You* do it, for once in your life. *You* have a go at getting her to behave. You live with her and see if you do any better. I've had enough of being the one who has to say no all the time. You try it and see how you like it."

"Ells, sweetheart—"

"Don't you say another *word*. I'm serious, Mark Nugent. It's about bloody time you took some responsibility for your only child."

"Ellen—"

"I can't, all right? I just *can't*, not anymore. You don't know what it's like, worrying about her being out all hours and doing God knows what with God knows who." Her voice, which had been getting higher and higher, broke into sobs.

Mark had been getting ready to remind her of all the twelve-hour days he'd worked when Florrie had been little, building up his career—what the bloody hell was that if not taking responsibility for his family?—but all at once, a new plan had popped, fully formed, into his head. It wasn't just a plan. It was a *good* plan.

"Right," he said firmly. "Pack her things—she's moving in with me."

"*What*?"

"That's what you want, isn't it?"

"Well . . . But . . . How long for? Next weekend? A week? Until I find her a new school?"

"No, of course not. Indefinitely. *I'll* find the school."

"You don't know anything about schools! And I'm not having her in some inner-city comprehensive full of girl gangs and drug dealers—"

"Of *course* not," Mark said soothingly. "I'll get a new place. Somewhere in the country. Somewhere it'll be safe to raise a teenager. The centre of London is no place for Florrie to grow up."

"That's what I keep *telling* you. You *always* do this. You take what I say and you make it sound like it's all your own idea and *I'm* the one being unreasonable. You always have to bloody well know best—"

"Ellen, I really think it's what's best for Florence that's important here."

There was a pause. Mark wasn't certain, but he thought he could hear Ellen counting under her breath. Her voice was definitely a semitone less shrill when she spoke again. "But you *hate* commuting. *And* the country."

She had a point. Then again . . . Hadn't he been feeling already that he'd gone about as far as he could in Whyborne & Co? "I'll give up the job," he said decisively. "Florence is more important."

"*What*?"

"I'll take a year out from work. And once she's back on track, I'll look for something new."

"And just what are you planning to live on? Don't think I'm paying for this. You *know* I don't earn much, not after all those years out looking after your daughter."

"Oh, you needn't worry about money. Bonuses have been excellent for the last few quarters." Not to mention, without Ellen to insist on family holidays—a total waste of money as far as Mark was concerned, seeing as he always seemed to spend half of them on the phone or on his email dealing with things that had come up at the office—he hadn't been spending a great deal.

"What?" Ellen sounded bewildered.

"This *is* what you want, isn't it?" Mark said cautiously.

"Well, yes, but I never thought you'd actually agree! Mark, you barely even *know* her these days."

That, Mark thought, was unfair. He'd done his bit by Florence—he was never late with the child support payments, and he'd bought her everything she'd ever asked for. He was damned if he'd let *his* child suffer the disappointment of being promised the earth and then thrown a lump of mud. "All the more reason to do this, then. I'm not having my little girl grow up a stranger to her father."

There was a strange snorting sound down the telephone. "Your little girl? Oh, just you try calling her that. Just you *try* it."

Mark wasn't entirely sure what she was getting at there, but it would probably be safer to let it go. For his eardrums, if nothing else. "Anyway, it's decided," he said firmly. "I'll let them know at the office tomorrow, and start looking for a house. A proper home for her to grow up in."

"We had one of those," Ellen muttered. "Until you broke it."

Mark slept soundly that night, his dreams full of idyllic walks in sunlit meadows with his daughter—whom his subconscious seemed to have aged down to about eight, but that was just a minor detail. When he woke, he found his resolve had only strengthened. He was going to do this.

He expected his announcement at the office to meet with a certain amount of surprise and (he hoped he wasn't flattering himself unduly) some dismay. He'd underestimated the amount of sheer, uncomprehending disbelief he'd face, however.

First thing in the morning, Mark strolled into his office with an airy step, hung up his trench coat and considered how to go about breaking the news. The correct thing, he knew, would be to speak first to Charles, senior taxation partner and his immediate superior. However, for several reasons, Mark thought he'd speak to David, his PA, first. Should he call him into his office? Mark stared for a moment out of his window at the magnificent view of the Thames, stretching down to the London Eye. Damn, he was going to miss that view . . . *Focus.* No, a more casual approach would be better.

David would undoubtedly milk every drop of drama out of the situation however Mark dropped the bombshell, but at least this way he'd be able to escape if things got too overwrought.

He could see David through the open door of his office. He'd hung up his long, full-skirted military coat, unwrapped the vast lengths of a cashmere scarf from around his neck, and removed his slim-fitting dark-grey suit jacket, and now sat looking like an advertisement for tailored shirts in deep purple. Mark couldn't see his computer screen from here, but the rapidly changing expressions that flitted across his sensitive, finely boned face suggested he was checking his Twitter feed.

Not for the first time, Mark wondered why he didn't find David attractive. He was undeniably beautiful—but it was the sort of beauty Mark could admire only in an abstract manner, like a pre-Raphaelite painting or the Taj Mahal. Mark would hesitate to call David's beauty *feminine*—for a start, if David heard him, he'd probably launch into a sulk epic enough to dwarf even the Great Stationery Order Debacle—but there was a certain fineness to his features and grace to his movements that might have had something to do with it.

Nevertheless, it had been David's arrival as his PA two years ago that had first prompted a no doubt long-overdue self-examination on Mark's part and led, finally, to the breakup of his marriage. Which, come to think of it, had probably also been long overdue, given that the results of Mark's soul-searching had been the ninety-nine percent certainty that he was queer as a three-pound note.

Ellen hadn't taken the revelation particularly well, even though Mark had been at particular pains to point out she should be relieved to hear their dismal sex life wasn't her fault.

Anyway, it was time now for action, not introspection. Checking that no one else was in earshot, Mark ambled casually out of his office and perched on the edge of David's desk in what he hoped came across as a relaxed attitude. "David, I've got something I need to tell you."

David raised a dark, and possibly plucked, eyebrow, a worrying gleam in his eye as he leaned in just a little too close. "Really?" he breathed.

Mark cleared his throat. "Yes. I've decided to take a career break. For at least a year, maybe longer."

David startled back and almost knocked over his skinny vanilla latte. What was more, Mark was ninety-seven percent certain it wasn't just one of his usual melodramatic gestures. "Give up work?" David squeaked, now gripping the edge of his desk as if he needed something solid to hold on to. "You? But you *live* to work."

"What? Nobody lives to work." David was making it sound like he had absolutely zero outside interests, which was patently untrue. There was the running, for a start. All right, he'd let that lapse a little of late, but he hadn't had time to find a good route since he'd moved . . . a year ago. And there was the theatre, which had been part of his decision to move into the centre. There were *dozens* of shows he'd been meaning to see. He just hadn't had anyone to go with, that was all.

"Not unless they're called Mark 'Weekends are for Wimps' Nugent. Were you aware that when polled, fifty-seven percent of junior staff were under the impression you don't even *have* a home to go back to? A further twenty-two percent thought you have got a flat, but it's so long since you've seen it, you've forgotten where it is. A small but significant five percent think you're actually a robot who never sleeps and just plugs himself in to charge overnight."

"What? That's ridiculous. I don't come into the office *every* weekend," Mark protested.

David cocked his head and pursed his lips. "No, of course not. It's the paperwork fairies that leave a neat stack of correspondence for me to find in my in-tray every Monday morning."

Charles waddled past with a sour expression and a muttered, "Thought *you* were the paperwork fairy. Isn't that why they call you Camp David?"

Mark winced. There was more than one reason why he wasn't out at work. *Sorry*, he mouthed to David behind Charles's broad, retreating back. Thank God the man hadn't come by a couple of minutes earlier.

"Oh, I don't mind *him*. He's just tetchy because the Hausfrau's put him on another diet. *Ve haff vays of making you thinner.*" David broke off and stared at Mark, wide-eyed. "Oh. My. *God*. That's what this is all about, isn't it?"

Mark frowned. "Diets? Charles's wife? What's The Trout—I mean, *Traute*—got to do with me giving up work?"

"Not Charles's wife. *Yours*. You've found another one, haven't you?" The eyes turned sorrowful. "You're leaving me for another woman," he wailed.

And that was the *other* reason Mark wasn't out at work. David's flirting, bad enough when Mark had been safely married to Ellen, had increased exponentially once he'd become single. If David ever got wind of the fact that Mark wasn't as straight as he seemed . . . Mark shuddered. "No. There's no other woman. No woman at *all*, I mean. I simply want to spend some time with my daughter."

"Who is not a woman?"

"Not in that context she isn't!" Mark was frankly appalled at the thought of Florence being counted as a woman in *any* context. She was practically still a baby, for Christ's sake. She wouldn't be a woman for . . . for *decades*, if he had anything to do with it. "She's a child, and she needs my guidance."

"Really? Isn't she a bit young to be filling in a tax return?"

Mark flushed. "Tax isn't the *only* thing I know about."

"Oh really? Let me see. Mark Nugent: his limits . . ." David started to count on slender, well-manicured fingers. "One, knowledge of popular culture: nil. Two, music: nil. Three, sport: nil, so how you manage to stay so trim is beyond me. Four, tax: immense. Can spot a loophole at twenty paces and tie a tax inspector in knots with it, presumably to the satisfaction of all concerned but, most of all, to that of the client." He paused to bat disconcertingly lush eyelashes at Mark. "You can ensnare me in one of your loopholes anytime. What are we up to now? Oh, yes. Five, sex: well, one would have to presume a basic working knowledge, given that you apparently managed to produce a daughter, although—"

"*Thank* you, David," Mark cut him off. "That'll do."

"Are you sure? I've got *loads* more appendages to count on." David waggled his fingers suggestively.

"Quite sure, thank you," Mark said firmly, not wishing to see anything else waggled. "Anyway, I need to go and give Charles the bad news." Mark stood up and was about to walk off, determined to get it over with, when David's soft hand landed on his arm.

"You're serious about it, then?" David's solemn expression was disconcerting on a face seemingly designed for frivolity.

Mark nodded, although not without a curiously empty sensation in his belly. "I am. Look, don't worry. You'll be fine. Charles would have to be an idiot to let you go—you'll be needed to help out whoever takes over my clients." He gave David an awkward pat on the shoulder.

"Oh, it's not that. But you were my one constant in life. I always thought you'd be sitting at that desk until the day you keeled over from a heart attack and the cleaners had to cart you off with the rubbish."

Mark stared. David sounded worryingly serious. "All the more reason to take a break, then, surely?"

"If only to spare poor Mrs. Patel the shock. But what are you going to *do* all day? I presume the little moppet will be spending her days at school. Are you *sure* you've thought this all through?" David's soft brown eyes were doing a passable impression of saucers, and his hands fluttered anxiously.

"Calm down. It's all going to work out. I'm selling the flat and moving to the country. We'll get a house, a proper home. Somewhere with a sense of community. So I'm sure I'll get involved in . . . community things. You should come and visit, once we're settled," Mark went on hastily to forestall any demands for specifics, and crossed mental fingers David wouldn't take it as a sign of interest. "Bring your boyfriend," he added as insurance.

He was sure that David would, one day, make someone a wonderful wife. But Mark had had one of those, and it hadn't worked out.

David wasn't looking happy. "It's a midlife crisis, isn't it? Next we know, you'll be dyeing your hair and getting a trophy girlfriend who's younger than your daughter."

"I hope not, seeing as Florence has only just turned fourteen. And what do you mean, dyeing my hair? My hair doesn't need dyeing." Mark ran a hand over his head. The touch of grey at the temples just made him look distinguished, didn't it?

"Of course not. You don't look a day over forty-five."

"I'm thirty-nine!"

David looked momentarily startled, then flashed him a winning smile. "Figure of speech?"

"Right. Anyway, I need to talk to Charles." He strode off purposely, pretending he hadn't noticed David had opened his mouth to say something. Mark might not have been having a midlife crisis before, but he was beginning to think their conversation was about to spark one. He knocked on Charles's door for form's sake, then walked straight in.

Charles looked up with a dyspeptic expression. Too late to back out now, though.

Mark plastered on a smile. "Charles? Have you got a moment?"

"Do I have a choice about it?"

Assuming the bad-tempered question was rhetorical, Mark grabbed a chair from the side and sat down on it in front of Charles's desk. Best just to rip off the plaster—or, as David would no doubt put it, the waxing strip—as quickly as possible. "I'm handing in my notice."

Charles's expression seemed to congeal. "Do I look like I'm in the mood for jokes?"

"It's not a joke. I want to spend some time with my family."

"Oh, for God's sake. You're not a Tory politician. No need to resign. Just pay the bloody rentboy off and buy the wife a bunch of flowers."

Mark blinked. "You do remember I'm divorced? And . . . rentboy? Seriously?" Mark was more than a little insulted at the implication he'd have to pay for it. He'd never paid for it in his life. The fact that he'd never actually had *it*, if *it* meant gay sex, was, he felt, a minor detail.

"So what is it, then? Drink? Cocaine? Gambling?"

"It's my fourteen-year-old daughter, actually. Florence has been having a . . . difficult time. She needs more of my attention than I'm able to give her at the moment."

Charles *humph*ed. "Drugs? Or boys? Just promise her a new iPhone if she gives it up, that'll do the trick. Works with my girls, anyway."

Mark had always looked up to Charles, in a professional sense. He was beginning to suspect, however, that as a parenting role model, the man lacked a certain something. "No, I really feel this is something that requires personal attention."

"So take a week off. God knows it'll be bloody inconvenient with Goldsmith's year end coming up, but Norton has been pushing to get involved with their account. About time I gave him a chance to make an arse of himself."

Mark winced. Norton was an ex-public school boy, all mouth and expensively tailored trousers. Chances were he *would* make an arse of himself. Mark's certainty, already slightly dented by his conversation with David, wavered further. Could he really justify leaving all his clients in the lurch?

Florence's sweet, childish face, as portrayed by her final primary school photo, flashed into his head. Yes. She was worth more than all the multimillion-pound clients in the world. "No, my mind's made up. I'll work out my notice, of course, but with accumulated leave built up . . ."

"You'll be leaving the day after tomorrow? Bloody marvellous."

"Well, Wednesday week, actually, but close enough."

Charles's expression, already sour, turned positively acidic. "Thank you for making my Monday complete. I was just thinking I needed another ulcer. I hope you realise what you're doing. You've been with this firm all your working life and always been the one man I could count on. Never let your personal life get in the way of the job. Until now. I suppose this is the point where I'm supposed to say that I'll be keeping your job open in case you have a change of heart? I won't be. Now get out."

Mark swallowed and got out.

On the whole, that had gone rather better than expected.

CHAPTER FOUR

Mark had perhaps not fully taken account of how his daughter might feel about the proposed upheaval.

The weekend after the fateful telephone conversation, he gazed into Florence's sullen face—still heart-shaped and plump from childhood, but now accessorised with thick black eyeliner and multiply pierced ears—and wondered exactly what had happened to his sweet little girl. And *when*.

While he was at work, of course, his conscience told him. But . . . it wasn't as if he hadn't kept in contact. He'd seen her every other weekend—at least, as long as she didn't have other plans, and there wasn't something urgent at work to see to . . .

Dear God, how many months had it *been*? He'd definitely seen her at Christmas. He'd dropped round to Ellen's on Christmas Eve, taking presents . . . Except, Florence had been out with her friends, hadn't she? And she'd cancelled on him the following weekend, saying she had a party to go to.

With a jolt like a thousand volts hitting him straight in the conscience (it appeared to be located directly beneath his sternum and, moreover, excessively tender), Mark was suddenly aware of what an appalling father he'd been. How had he let this happen? He hadn't *meant* it to happen. He'd gone into fatherhood with a steely determination that no child of his would ever want for anything.

How had he managed to forget that in a child's eyes, a very big part of *anything* was an actual, physically present father?

He was going to make it up to her, Mark told himself, stricken. He was going to make it all up to her. He smiled at her hopefully.

"Florrie—"

"*Don't* call me that. I hate it."

"Florence, then," he conceded with good grace.

"I hate that too. It's a stupid name to start with, and Dad, I'm not thick, all right? I worked it out. Born nine months after you and Mum went to Tuscany?"

Mark nodded.

"You named me after the place you had a shag, didn't you? Have you got *any idea* how *gross* it is being reminded of that all the bloody time?"

Mark winced. Now he came to think of it, *he* wasn't all that happy at the constant reminder of sex with Ellen either. "So, well, what should I call you, then?"

"Fen. It's what all my friends call me. Well, what they call me *now*, anyway. Before *you* drag me off to the butt-end of nowhere and I won't be able to see them anymore." She folded her arms and glared, looking disconcertingly like her mother. She'd inherited Mark's brown eyes and dark hair—now made several shades darker with dye—but that was very definitely Ellen's chin.

Fen. Mark supposed it made sense, for a girl he and her mother had (lovingly) named Florence Esther Nugent.

"Okay . . . Fen," he said in a tone he hoped would make him sound reasonable and conciliatory, rather than a total pushover.

The glint in her eye suggested he hadn't succeeded in that endeavour. Mark broke the silence hastily, before she could start demanding motorbikes and sleepovers with boys. "It could have been worse, you know. You were very nearly Siena Isabella, until we realised we'd got the dates wrong, and that would have left you with the initials SIN—"

"*Daaa*-aaad!" Florrie—*Fen*—had her hands over her ears.

He shut up, which gave her the chance to go back on the offensive.

"Why do I have to go and live with you anyway? Why can't I stay with Mum?"

Mark hesitated. He had an instinctive feeling *because she can't cope with you any longer* wouldn't go down well. "Don't you think it's fair we should share parental responsibilities?"

"I s'pose."

"And don't you think it'll be nice to spend some time together?"

She didn't answer.

"Flor—*Fen*?"

"*S'pose.*"

"Well, then. Why don't you take a look at some of the houses I've found—"

"But it's not like you ever wanted to spend any time with me *before*."

Mark's conscience appeared to be on the move; it was now wrapping itself painfully around his intestines like a boa constrictor with a grudge. "I was working. You know that."

"Yeah, and what's it going to be like when I move in with you? *If* I move in with you. You'll just be working all the time again."

"Didn't your mother tell you? I've given up my job." Mark smiled, his conscience relaxing its hold on his digestive organs and slithering away, presumably to bide its time for his next big parental cock-up. "We're going to spend all our time together, when you're not in school."

For some reason, Florence—*Fen*—didn't look as delighted as he'd expected.

It took another couple of months, but eventually Mark found both a house that would suit them and—this being the more difficult task—a school that would accept Florence, and might even be the making of her. Saint Jude's was a former grammar school with old-fashioned values and discipline. It even had a Latin motto and school song. School uniform rules were strictly enforced—the visit to the school outfitter's provoking another outburst of epic proportions.

"It's *all pink*!" Florence wailed as she stepped out of the changing room in her matching kilt, sweater, blazer, and school tights.

"Ah . . . I think they call it maroon," Mark said cautiously. She might just possibly have a point, but there was nothing they could do about it now.

"It's not maroon. It's fuc—" she caught Mark's frown and checked herself "—*fuchsia*. I look like a Disney princess."

"You used to love dressing up as a princess," Mark reminded her.

"When I was *three*. This is *horrible*. Why do I even have to wear this? The boys' uniform is so much better."

The boys' uniform was utterly unlike the girls' and consisted of black trousers paired with a grey tweed blazer that looked like it had been made from an old horse blanket that'd been left out in the rain. It even *smelled* like that. Nevertheless, Mark would have to concede that, once again, she had a point. "I think you look very nice," he lied smoothly.

"I hate you," she muttered, and disappeared behind the curtain once more.

The boot of the BMW was packed full of carrier bags by the time they left the outfitter's, and Mark was reeling from the expense. Why exactly did his daughter need *two* PE kits? If gym skirts (with matching maroon over-knickers, presumably to spare the girls' blushes on windy days) weren't suitable for all activities, why not just let them wear the shorts from the other kit for *all* sports lessons? Were maroon tracksuits essential equipment? Mark was quite certain the girls at his school had, like the boys, just toughed it out in T-shirts on winter days. The lacrosse stick, however, he found strangely comforting, even though he was only familiar with the sport from the pages of his mother's old 1950s girls' school books. *St. Jude's is far too elite to play common games like hockey*, it seemed to say.

He made the mistake of mentioning this to Florence—Fen, damn it. Apparently to her, it just said, Ha, you thought you were crap at hockey? Here's another sport you'll be even worse at cos everyone else has done three years of it already. But Mark had every confidence in her.

If all else failed, there was always the option of private coaching.

"And I'm not gonna know *anyone*. It's going to be *horrible*."

"You'll soon make friends," Mark promised her. "Just . . . join some clubs or something."

"Like *you've* joined anything since we moved here. God, what are you even going to *do* all day? Just sit around and watch daytime telly in your underwear?"

"Oh, don't you worry about that." Mark beamed, pleased to get the chance to talk about his new pet project. David's concerns about him having nothing to do while Fen was at school had sparked some serious thinking on Mark's part, and he flattered himself he'd come up with the perfect solution. "I'll be writing."

"*You? Writing? Like, what?*"

"A book. I'm going to call it *The TAX-idermist: Telling HMRC to Get Stuffed.*" He was rather proud of that one.

Fen's kohl-rimmed eyes were that curious mix of confused, irritated, and pitying he was coming to know all too well. "That's just *so lame*. What's HM-whatsit even *mean*?"

"It's short for Her Majesty's Revenue and Customs." Her look remained blank. "The tax man?" he tried. "I suppose I could put it in full, but it'd make for a rather crowded cover. And I wanted to avoid having *tax* in there twice."

"Dad, it's already lame. You're not gonna make it any *worse*." Her frown deepened. "I thought you worked for them, though? Like, doing taxes and stuff?"

"Well, more or less—except I'm on the other side. Poacher, not gamekeeper." He smiled.

"Isn't that against the law?"

"Only if you don't do it properly," Mark said firmly. "Tax *avoidance*, not tax *evasion*."

"Whatever. That's like saying stealing's not a crime if you call it, I dunno, extreme borrowing, or something. So instead of watching telly all day in your underwear, you're going to sit at a computer all day in your underwear. *Big* difference."

"The difference, young lady, is that watching telly achieves nothing, whereas writing a successful book can make a great deal of money."

"What do you even *want* more money for? It's not like you ever spend it on anything. Mum said you've got loads in the bank, and it all just *sits* there cos all you ever want to do is work. *God*. Could you *be* any more of a sad old loser?"

"Ahem. Excuse me, madam, but I happen to have spent quite a lot of money recently. And all of it on one rather ungrateful young lady."

"On what? On that stupid uniform for that stupid school you're making me go to?"

"Well, houses don't exactly grow on trees!"

"Yeah, like this house is all for me. And anyway, Mum said you must have made *loads* selling your flat."

Mark was beginning to wish Ellen had been a little more taciturn on the subject of him and money. "Anyway, the point is—"

"I mean, you don't even go on holiday anymore. Not, you know, like you ever did holiday stuff even when we used to go away. I remember that time in Corfu when I wanted you to go on the waterslides with me, and you were all 'Yes, darling, just as soon as I've made these phone calls,' and I waited and I waited and *you never came*."

Oh God. He'd *wanted* to play with his daughter. Of course he had. But that idiot they'd had on secondment from Manchester had made such a god-awful mess of things, Charles had been about to burst a blood vessel, and it had only been supposed to take half an hour . . . He'd taken her out on a speedboat trip the following day to make it up to her and thought it had all been forgiven and forgotten.

He'd been wrong.

Telling himself firmly he was in the process of making amends, Mark rallied. "And that's what this is all about. You and me, together. And that's why I'm not working now, so I can focus on you."

"I'm not a *baby*. I don't need you watching me all the time."

Mark blinked. Hadn't she just been telling him he hadn't spent enough time with her? "I thought we could do something fun together."

"Like what? There's *nothing to do* here."

"We could go bowling. There's bound to be somewhere near—"

"*Nobody* goes bowling with their dad. That's just *so lame*."

"Well . . . there's the cinema."

"*Boring*. There's nothing good on. They show all the good films at Christmas, and then it's just crap until the summer."

"Language, young lady." Mark brought out the big guns. "All right, what about shopping? For clothes. Fun clothes, I mean."

For a moment, she looked tempted . . . Then the shutters closed again. "No. You'll only try and make me buy stuff that looks *pretty*."

"Free choice. I promise. Within a set spending limit," Mark added hastily at the beginnings of a gleam in her eye.

"I *suppose*." Fen heaved herself to her feet as if the weight of the world were upon her narrow shoulders. "It's not like there's anything *else* to do."

The shopping trip, Mark considered, went remarkably well in the end. All he had to do was close his eyes to his daughter's purchases and remind himself firmly that black was a good, serviceable colour that didn't show the dirt. And he made sure she was stocked up on all essential toiletries—at least, she disappeared into Boots the Chemist with an unlikely amount of money and strict instructions to Mark to "Wait here. I'm not buying this stuff in front of *you*," and came out with a laden carrier bag, so he hoped she was now well supplied.

Ellen had always handled this sort of thing before. Mark wondered if *she'd* had to kick her heels out in the cold while Fen stocked up, or if female sisterhood extended as far as mothers.

From the way Ellen had been at her wits' end with her daughter, he rather suspected not.

Once they returned, however, Fen disappeared to her room with her phone, leaving him with her bags full of Goth chic and unmentionables, leaving Mark feeling somehow more alone than he'd ever felt in his London flat. Her room in the new house, in fact, appeared to be the one thing about her new life his daughter *did* approve of, at least judging by the amount of time she spent in it.

The house Mark had chosen was at the end of a modern terrace right in the centre of the village, set back from the high street in a cul-de-sac opposite the church. It was a three-storey town house with a postage-stamp garden that consisted mainly of patio, which was Mark's sort of garden. The sort a man could relax in, rather than being nagged at to labour in on a rare day off. After all, if he or Fen wanted anything bigger, they had the whole of the surrounding Hertfordshire countryside to play in.

It had three bedrooms and two bathrooms—the estate agent had warned that with a teenage girl in the house, an extra bathroom would be less of a luxury and more of an essential, at least if he ever planned on showering again. The ground floor was spacious, with a well-equipped kitchen and a light, airy open-plan living room-cum-dining room that faced the garden, plus a study and a small cloakroom. It was, Mark had considered, as close to perfect as he was likely to get. Not so large that he and Fen would be rattling around in it, but not so small they'd be tripping over one another all the time either.

Huh. Tripping over one another, he'd discovered, was *not* likely to become a problem. Fen seemed to consider the prospect of coming out of her bedroom with the sort of wary caution with which Mark had always regarded the idea of coming out of the closet. They'd moved into the new house at the start of the Easter holidays, which Mark had fondly imagined would give them two weeks of getting to know one another again before term started. He hadn't anticipated the current level of difficulty in just getting to *see* his daughter.

When he'd spoken to Ellen on the phone about his frustrations, she'd sounded oddly smug. "Not so easy, is it, when you're actually there with her all day?"

"Am I?" Mark groaned. "I wouldn't even know. She comes down for meals, but for all I get to see of her in between times, she could be abseiling out of her window and going God knows where." He'd never really understood the way Ellen had used to complain about the school holidays being too long, back when they were married, but he was beginning to have an inkling. "And she *hates* me, Ells," he added. "You haven't . . . well, you haven't said anything to her about why we split, have you?"

"What, because I thought telling her that her father's a homosexual would be just the thing to straighten her out and get her back on the rails?" Ellen wasn't sounding quite so smug now. "This is *typical* of you. *No*, I haven't said a word about your dirty little secret. As far as she knows, Mummy and Daddy just grew apart, and that's the way it'll stay from *my* end, at least. Have you found yourself a *dirty little secret*, now, by the way? You'll have to introduce us. I'm sure we'd have *so* much in common."

Mark winced at her cutting tone. "I'm hardly likely to be seeing someone, am I? Not with Fen living with me now," he said patiently. At least, that was how he hoped it would sound.

"And I see she's got you calling her that made-up name."

"I like it," Mark said. It wasn't *precisely* a lie. If it made his daughter a little happier, then he liked it, all right?

"Oh, you *would* take her side. Of course, she gets it from you. You always did insist on putting your initials down in full. *M.A.N.* It's like you're trying to convince people."

Ouch. Mark bit back a sharp retort. "My middle name's 'Anthony' after my grandad, remember? I have very fond memories of him. So you've no idea why she's so set against me?" he added with very little hope he'd get a useful reply.

"Probably for the same reason she hates me right now and has done for most of the last year. She's a teenager, and we're her *parents*." Ellen sighed, a staticky rasp down the phone line. "Look, I don't want to seem ungrateful for you having her—although why I should be grateful for you finally taking an interest in your own daughter, I don't know—but you can't keep ringing me up with problems." Her tone sharpened. "I thought the whole *point* of all this was that you thought you knew best."

He had done, hadn't he? Well, more fool him. "Yes, but you must have known I was wrong. As usual," Mark added wryly.

There was silence from the other end of the line.

"Ells?"

"I hate it when you do that," she said in a small voice. "Go all reasonable."

"Sorry. Won't happen again. Or at least not before I've completely redressed the balance, I'm sure." He hesitated. "How are you doing?"

There was the faintest of sniffs. "I'm fine. You?"

"I thought we'd already established I'm drowning, not waving."

"*Is* there someone else?"

"No. And there won't be. Not before Fen's settled down a bit. A *lot*," Mark amended and hesitated. "How about you?"

"No. There was someone I thought . . . But no."

"Well . . . Look after yourself, won't you? Enjoy the peace—although if she spent as much time in her bedroom when she was with you as she does now, I'm surprised you can tell the difference, to be honest."

"The *peaceful* times are the ones you need to watch out for. But I'd better go. Bye, Mark."

"Bye," he said, but the click of her hanging up had already sounded.

Dauntless, Mark had scanned village notice boards and done internet searches for local clubs and societies, trying to find things they could do together—and when that met with scorn, he'd tried to find activities Fen could do without him. Something to at least get her out of the house, to exercise her body and direct her mind away from destructive impulses. But after the first few suggestions were met with the sort of derision that could wither an oak tree—"Ballet, Dad? *Seriously*? Like I'm *five*?" and "Horse riding? Yeah, right, because I *really* want to spend my weekends shovelling *shit*."—he'd given up and found his attention straying to things he might like to get involved in. After all, there was only so long he could spend at the computer typing his magnum opus.

Mark ignored the fact that so far there was very little *magnum* about it or, for that matter, *opus*. That would change when Fen started school. He was certain of it.

The Shamwell Spartans Fun and Funds Foundation, despite an acronym that, to Mark's mind, sounded like the sort of noise a balloon might make if you blew it up and let it go before tying the end, had piqued his interest immediately. It had looked like the sort of thing he'd be able to bring his financial acumen to. And it had looked, as the name suggested, like *fun*. So he'd emailed the chairman, Barry, who'd been encouragingly keen to tell him when and where they'd next be meeting.

Mark hadn't thought getting ready for his first Spartans meeting would be in any way difficult, time-consuming, or challenging.

He'd reckoned without his daughter. He knocked on her door to say he was going out, and to please *try* not to burn the house down with her hair straighteners, to be met with a horrified cry.

"*Daaa*-aaad. You can't go out in *that*."

Mark frowned at his daughter, recumbent on the bed, phone in hand, surrounded by an unlikely amount of pillows, cushions, and stuffed animals. He wasn't very up on modern teenage tribes, but whatever Fen was—Emo? Goth?—it seemed to necessitate black clothes, black hair, and, whenever she could get away with it, black nails and lips. Oh, and tight T-shirts and skirts so short they probably had a complex about shrinking into nothing and disappearing. In the matter of unsuitable clothing, Mark felt he had very good grounds for considering she didn't have a ripped-stockinged, Doc Martened leg to stand on.

"What's wrong with it? I thought it fit rather well," he added, smoothing the sweater down over his (thankfully still flat) stomach.

Fen actually put her phone down and sat up straight. A stuffed frog tumbled unheeded to her sheepskin rug. "It's grey. Worse. It's sludge-brown grey. It's horrible. *And* it matches your hair. You look like you need dusting."

"It's taupe, actually," Mark corrected, crossing his sludge-brown grey arms defensively. "And what do you mean, it matches my hair? My hair isn't grey."

"Yeah, right. You keep telling yourself that, Dad." She gave him a searching look that made Mark feel acutely uncomfortable. "You need . . . I dunno. Warm colours or something. Red, or purple maybe." For some reason, she blushed. "Haven't you got *anything* that's not boring to wear?"

"Does it matter? I'm not going on a date. It's just going to be a roomful of men who like the odd drink while raising money for charity."

"So it's just an excuse for a piss-up?"

"Language. And no, they raise a lot of money for local causes."

"So why's it all men?"

"Probably because they all have daughters or wives who got fed up with them hanging around the house and told them to go and *do* something?"

Fen flushed. "Yeah . . . I didn't *mean* that, Dad. Not really . . . It's just, you never used to just sit and watch telly. It's weird, that's all. Like you're not you anymore."

Mark thanked God once more he hadn't told her he was gay. "Of course I'm me. Just . . . a more relaxed me."

Fen eyed him for a moment, something of a speculative look in her eye, then with a breezy "Okay," she turned her attention back to her phone. "See you later, yeah?"

Dismissed. Mark blinked, then roused himself to go and change his sweater.

CHAPTER FIVE

When Mark got back home after his first Spartans meeting, the house was silent. After calling out, "Hello?" and receiving no answer, he ran up the stairs with a certain amount of trepidation and knocked on Fen's door.

Thankfully, there was a surly call of "What?" from within, so she hadn't sneaked out for a spot of underage drinking or vandalism, or whatever young people did for amusement in the village.

"It's me. Dad. I'm home."

Silence.

"Can I come in?"

"I'm on the phone."

"Oh. Anyone I know?"

"*Daa-aad.* I'm *on* the *phone.*"

"Oh. Right." Mark hovered for a moment outside his daughter's bedroom door, then knocked again.

"*What?*"

"Don't forget it's your first day of school tomorrow."

"*I know. Duh.*"

Mark bit back the admonition to get an early night and crept back downstairs. It was natural, he told himself, that Fen wouldn't be interested in how his meeting had gone, or if he'd met anyone worth talking about. Not that he'd have told her about Patrick in any case, of course. There was nothing to tell, not really, and there wouldn't *be* anything.

But it might have been nice just to exchange a few words, now he was no longer living alone.

When he came back up to go to bed an hour or so later, no light seeped under the bottom of Fen's bedroom door, so he had to hope she was asleep. He set his alarm—two weeks had, it transpired, been just long enough get out of the habit of early rising—and turned out his own light.

Did Patrick talk to his mum when he got back home? Did he mention meeting Mark? And, oh God, how pathetic was Mark that he was—perhaps, in some *very* mild way—obsessing over someone who still lived with his *mum*? Still, house prices in the village were surprisingly stratospheric. Perhaps she didn't have a very highly paid job and needed him to help with the mortgage.

Perhaps *Patrick* didn't have a very highly paid job and needed help with the mortgage? Mark wondered what he did for a living. He should have asked Barry. If he'd tried a little harder, he was almost certain he'd have been able to get a word in edgewise. Not that Barry's history of the Spartans and all their worthy deeds hadn't been *interesting*. It had just been a little long. And perhaps not the sort of thing Mark could have interrupted without risking making his interest in Patrick mortifyingly clear.

No, on reflection, it was better he hadn't asked. Because he wasn't interested in Patrick. At least, no more than in a purely academic sense.

A faint glow from the streetlamps outside limned Mark's curtains with cold, white light. A few cars still crawled over the speed bumps on the high street, the noise of their engines barely audible through the double glazing. Occasional passing youths shouted and laughed. All around Mark, here in the heart of the village, his neighbours slept, watched late-night television, or did their bit to ensure the continuing growth of the village population.

Odd, how in the midst of humanity, one could feel so alone.

Mark turned over. Eventually he slept, and dreamed of nothing he could remember in the morning.

The next day started so promisingly. Mark was up in plenty of time to get Fen to St. Jude's, and when he knocked on her door, she responded with "I'm getting dressed, all right?"

Apparently, for teenage girls, getting dressed was something that took upwards of half an hour. Mark was prepared to concede that a pair of tights might be fiddlier to put on than the average pair of trousers, but surely it shouldn't take *this* long. What the hell was she *doing*? He knocked on her door again, a little more sharply.

"*What*?"

"You're not going to have time for breakfast at this rate."

"I'm not hungry."

Was this the first sign of anorexia? Fen seemed, if anything, a little on the plump side, but did that mean anything? "It's going to feel like a long time until lunch," he cautioned.

"So I'll take a snack. Jeez. I'm not *five*, Dad."

He had to call her three more times before Fen finally emerged, stomping down the stairs with sulkiness evident in every step.

"Finally," Mark said, glancing at his watch more to telegraph his impatience than to actually tell the time, which he knew to the minute already. "You'll be lucky . . ." He trailed off, staring at his daughter.

Fen now had purple hair. Mark was ninety-five percent certain this hadn't been the case last time he'd seen her. He'd have remembered.

"What the— What on earth have you done to yourself?"

"I dyed it. Last night. *Duh*."

Ye gods. Mark was never going out for the evening again. Combined with the fuchsia—no, maroon, damn it—school uniform and the early morning, Fen's hair was making his eyes water. "They're not going to let you go to school looking like that."

"Why not?"

"The uniform rules said 'hair of a natural colour.'"

"Yeah, but it's not like they're gonna send me home once I've got there. They'll just have to deal with it." She folded her arms, the mulish expression Mark was becoming all too used to marring her pretty face. "And anyway, if I try dyeing it back, I'll be well late. You don't want me to get a detention on my first day, do you?"

Mark sighed. "Put your shoes on. I'll go start the car."

The roads between Shamwell and Bishops Langley, which had seemed so quiet whenever Mark had driven along them before, were practically gridlocked at eight fifteen in the morning. By dint of tailgating the car in front and speeding ruthlessly through the thirty-mile-an-hour zone, Mark managed to roar up in front of St. Jude's at the dot of eight forty, which was when school started.

"Right, you'd better run. Have a good first day, and I'll see you at—"

The slam of the car door cut off his words. Fen had already gone.

Mark had just inched his tedious way back home through the rush-hour traffic when he got a phone call.

"Mr. Nugent? This is the secretary at St. Jude's. I'm afraid we're having to send Florence home. She'll need to do something about her hair. The school rules are quite clear about permitted colours."

He sighed and got back in his car.

Neither of them was very chatty on the way home. Fen's face was as sullen as ever, but it had at least lost all trace of smugness, as well it might. Mark had, in a few choice words when he picked her up from the school office, made it quite plain to her how immature she was being, risking her second chance for the sake of fashion.

Fen had, in a few even choicer words, made it plain that fashion was *nothing* to do with it: *"It was a statement, God, you just don't get it, do you?"*

Mark had explained that her actions reflected on him, her father, for whom this was all rather embarrassing.

Fen had pointed out that her hair was, like, *literally* nothing to do with him, *God*, and why was it always about him and not her?

Mark had had quite a few other things he'd have liked to mention, but the Teenager Taming website he'd been looking at had said to remember he was the adult and act accordingly. Mark wondered, though, if the author of the site had ever been subjected to such overwhelming temptation to say *I told you so*.

Arriving back at their house, Mark parked the car and pulled the handbrake on with a jerk that was perhaps a little harder than necessary. "We're going straight to the chemist, and we're going to get something to dye your hair back with. Which you will do *straight away*."

"Whatever."

"*Not* 'whatever.'"

"Jesus, I *said* I'd do it, all right?"

They walked—or, in Fen's case, stomped—towards the chemist's shop, which proudly proclaimed its existence in the village since the 1800s and still seemed to have the original window display. Their route led them past the village baker's shop, from whose open door emerged an enticing aroma of iced buns and coffee, the chatty sounds of a business doing a brisk trade—and Patrick.

He was carrying a takeaway cup and something in a paper bag, and Mark all but walked straight into him.

Patrick smiled, his eyes bluer than ever in the weak spring sunshine. "Whoops. Nearly got you, then."

Mark flushed.

Fen narrowed her eyes.

Damn it. "Oh, hello. Fancy meeting you here," Mark said weakly, and God, could he sound any more ridiculous?

Patrick raised an eyebrow. "All right, Mark?"

"Uh, how are you? This is my daughter," he added. "Florence. Fen. I mean, her name is Florence but she likes to be called Fen." Oh God. He was babbling like a *complete* idiot.

From Fen's muttered "*Daaa-aaad*," she thought so too.

"Nice to meet you. I'm Patrick. Gotta go now, but maybe I'll see you around, yeah? Like the hair," he added as he left.

"Who's that?" Fen asked sharply.

"Oh—just someone I met last night. One of the Spartans." Mark held the door of the chemist's open for his daughter.

"He's a bit young, isn't he? I thought it'd all be old people like you."

Mark sighed, following her into the shop. "He is, isn't he?" Then the rest of what she'd said sank in. "Wait a minute! I'm not even forty!"

"Yeah, but he's well young. I can't *believe* you made me come out in my school uniform," she added, tugging angrily at her maroon skirt.

Mark decided firmly to ignore the implications of this and tried to concentrate on searching the shelves for hair dye. "You're supposed to be *at* school right now," he reminded her. "*Not* trying to impress young men who are, in any case, *far* too old for you."

Ah. Bit of a fail in the ignoring-implications area.

"Boys mature later. *Everyone* knows that."

"Not *that* late they don't." Mark tried not to give in to the misgivings causing his stomach to flutter. Had he seriously overestimated Patrick's age? He'd thought the man to be in his mid-twenties—might he, in fact, be barely out of his teens? Mark glanced at the teenager slouching beside him and swallowed. "How old do you think he is?"

"I dunno? Twenty-five?" Her shoulders lifted in an exaggerated shrug.

The tightness in Mark's chest eased with a flood of heady relief—which promptly evaporated when he remembered those implications he'd been trying to ignore. "Which is *far* too old for you," he said sharply.

"I was only *looking*. I didn't say I wanted to have *sex* with him or anything."

She just *had* to come out with that in the middle of the shop, didn't she? The young, white-coated assistant behind the counter smirked, while the old lady she'd just served, who'd already been eyeing Fen with disapproval, gave an outraged *tut*.

Mark flushed again. "Could you *please* just find some hair dye?"

"All *right*. Jesus."

"Language." Mark watched as she rummaged through packets of hair dye, all of which seemed to have the same model on the front, her hair photoshopped into all colours of the rainbow. He wasn't sure how that was supposed to give you confidence they'd achieve the "natural" results they promised.

"No, wait, that's black," he said as she grabbed one. "Your natural hair colour is brown." At least, he was fairly sure he remembered her having brown hair. Back in the days when her age had been measured in single digits.

"The rules say *a* natural hair colour, not *my* natural hair colour. Black's natural." Fen's expression could have been used to illustrate the Teenager Taming website, under mood swings: sullen.

"If you're Indian or Afro-Caribbean. Which you're not," Mark gently pointed out.

"That's racist."

It was?

"Anyway," Fen continued with an air of triumph, "brown won't cover the purple. So I'll have to get black."

She didn't actually say *so there*, but there was a definite *so there*-ness in her expression. Mark decided to let it slide. "Come on, let's get it paid for."

It was only as they walked back up the road that it occurred to him to wonder how Fen had gone from black to purple, and why that method couldn't have been used to go from purple to brown.

CHAPTER SIX

Patrick chuckled to himself as he made his way back to his office in River Lane, which SHARE got at a special rate on account of (a) being a charity and (b) taking a philosophical view of the occasional rat that wandered up from the river to sniff at the bins.

Looked like Mark had his hands full with that one. Purple hair with a burgundy school uniform? There was a girl who knew how to get noticed. Mark had been looking good, though. Although his clothes were a disaster, poor sod. Someone really ought to take him in hand.

And didn't that conjure up some wicked images? Thing was, did Patrick really want to take on the job? From the way Mark was acting, it looked like he'd be a shoo-in for the role. But there was the age difference, the teenage daughter . . .

Yeah, there was all that. And then there was the guy's smile, the way he genuinely didn't seem to know how attractive he was, and, well, the fact he was prepared to be a single dad. Patrick liked a man who faced up to his responsibilities.

Sod it. He liked *Mark*.

When he opened the office door, Patrick was glad to see Lex, his admin assistant, had got in now, and was looking cheerful, so the medical appointment must have gone all right. Lex was nineteen but a bit more mature than your average teenager. Well, they'd had a lot to deal with growing up. Still did. "All right, Lex?"

Lex smiled, lip piercings bobbing. "Good weekend?"

"Not bad. You?"

"Met someone." Lex swung around happily on their swivel chair, which squeaked even though Lex couldn't weigh much more than the chair itself. Not that you could tell for certain, what with the baggy clothes Lex always wore, but nobody had wrists that bony if they had an ounce of meat on them anywhere else.

"Yeah?" Patrick's smile was cautious. Lex was forever meeting someone, but it didn't always end well.

"We just sort of got talking. And then we sort of got snogging. He's a metalhead. Rides a Harley. Wants to take me to Bloodstock— did you see Corpse Grinder are playing this year? It's gonna be well good."

"Yeah? You gonna camp? Tell you what, you wouldn't get me doing that. It's en suite or nothing for me."

Lex grinned. "Yeah, you'd be more into glamping. You oughta try it. Get out of your comfort zone."

"I like my comfort zone. I like *comfort*, full stop. Do I look like Bear Grylls? No. So don't expect me to go sleeping in a puddle of mud and washing in front of ten thousand strangers."

"It's not that bad. Well, not if the rain holds off. Anyway, it's fun. Get a few beers down you and you won't care what your hair looks like."

Patrick grinned and ran a hand over his hair, which stayed reassuringly in place due to just the right amount of product, ta very much. "If I ever don't care what my hair looks like, you'd better run, cos it means the zombie apocalypse has happened. So what's he like, this biker bloke? Apart from the musical tastes?"

"He's sweet." Lex grinned. "Got really soft lips."

"Oh yeah? No beard?" Patrick made an obvious show of examining Lex's pale skin for stubble rash.

Lex backed off, laughing. "Oi, get outta my face. Course he's got a beard. He's a metalhead, in't he? His beard's really soft and all. He's gonna set me up on his League of Lorecraft server so I can play with him and his mates." Lex paused. "Haven't met his mates yet."

"Yeah, well, if he likes you, they'll like you, won't they? If they're proper mates." Patrick crossed mental fingers. People could be gits. Lex's last bloke had been best mates with a total tosser who'd called Lex "it" and asked about all kinds of stuff that was none of his sodding business. And yeah, maybe the fact that the boyfriend hadn't called him on it had been a quick way of finding out whether he was a keeper, but it hadn't been a *good* one. Not for Lex, it hadn't. "Anyway, you're not going out with his mates, are you?"

"Nah. S'pose. So what about you? Anything happening in your love life?"

"Not exactly."

"*Oh* yeah? That's not a no, that ain't. C'mon, tell us all about it."

Patrick leaned back and stretched. The chair back added its protests to the squeaks of Lex's swivelling—seriously, the furniture in here was shite, but Patrick wasn't gonna complain when the people SHARE was set up to help needed every penny. "Nothing to tell. Seriously, nothing. It's just there's this new bloke at the Spartans, that's all. And I'm pretty sure he's into me."

"Yeah, but so's lots of people. You wouldn't even be mentioning him if you weren't into him back."

Shit, sometimes he forgot how good Lex was at reading him. "Yeah, well. Maybe. Got baggage, though."

"Yeah?"

"Single dad."

"How old? The kid, I mean. Out of nappies yet? Cos I've done babysitting, and that shit's gross."

Patrick laughed. "Hope so. She's about fifteen."

Lex's eyes went wide. "Fuck, how old's *he*? Oh my God, has he got all his own hair? Teeth?"

"Shut up. He's not a bloody geriatric. Dunno how old, 'cept he's in the Spartans, so he's under forty-five, all right?"

"So he's *probably* not older than your mum. So what, you after a sugar daddy now? Can I have your job if you go off to be a kept man?"

"Jesus, why does everyone have to make such a big thing about his age?"

"Cos it is a big thing. Like, twice as big as yours. Nearly." Lex caught Patrick's look. "All right, shutting up. Sorry. Jeez. You touchy or what?" They mimed zipping their lips, then mumbled, "Happy now?" sounding like a bad ventriloquist.

Patrick had to laugh. "Yeah, well. Maybe it is a bit of a touchy area. Shit, I don't know. I've never thought about getting involved with someone that much older, all right? Think it could ever work?"

God knew why he was asking Lex, whose record with relationships was only a bit better than Patrick's mum's.

Then again, none of it had been Lex's fault.

Lex frowned, their eyebrow piercings drawing closer together. "S'pose it depends, dunnit? What's he like?"

"I dunno, really . . . Sort of shy. Like he's only just come out."

"Sure he *is* out?"

Patrick thought about it. And frowned. "S'pose I just assumed."

"Might wanna find out before you start planning the wedding."

"Sod that." Patrick sat up straight and pulled his chair back in at his desk. "Come on, break's over. We've got a fun run to organise."

"Gonna get your bloke to sign up for it?"

Patrick nodded. "I might just do that."

"Better make sure we've got St. John's Ambulance in, then. Wouldn't want him keeling over with a heart attack before you get your leg over."

Lex laughed as Patrick stuck up a finger.

"It's funny, innit?" Lex said out of the blue as they were eating their lunch—a roll from the baker's for Patrick, and some weird homemade vegan rabbit food for Lex. They were eating at their desks today. Sometimes they took their lunch out to a park bench, or even just stood by the river and watched the ducks go mental hoping for freebies, but the wind had got up, making it a bit too nippy today.

"What is?"

"Well, you'd think it'd be better, knowing the other person likes you, wouldn't you? 'Cept, like, it's not, cos it messes with your head, dunnit?"

Patrick had his mouth full, so he just raised an eyebrow.

"Well, see, if you know they like you, it makes you think of 'em different, dunnit? Like, maybe you wouldn't've thought about fancying 'em if they hadn't fancied you first. So maybe you ask 'em out, or you say yes when they ask you out, and you think, 'Did I do that cos I wanted to, or cos they wanted me to?'"

Patrick swallowed his mouthful. "Yeah, but if nobody ever said they liked anyone else, nobody would ever go out with anyone. We'd all be sad, lonely bastards sitting at home watching telly." He frowned. "This about your metalhead? You know you don't have to settle for—"

"*No.* And yeah, I do know that, ta very much. I was talking about you and that bloke of yours. I been thinking about it, that's all."

"Yeah, well, why don't you wait until there's an *it* to think about, all right? *If* there ever is."

Patrick had thought about it too, on and off. Him and Mark. Could it work?

Could it work with a stroppy teenager in tow? She'd looked like a good kid, though. Trying her hardest to strike out her own path and prove she was totally different to her dad—but didn't all kids do that? Patrick ran a hand over his hair. Course, some had more reason than most.

Still . . . if Mark wasn't out to her, that'd be a problem. And not just cos Patrick wasn't planning on being anyone's dirty little secret. The thought of being part of a lie Mark was telling to his own kid left a bad taste in Patrick's mouth.

Shit. Why had Lex had to bring that up and throw ice water on all the warm and fuzzies? Patrick did a mental eye roll at himself. Yeah, because blaming the messenger was so bloody mature. Not to mention productive. He'd just have to tread carefully, that was all. Make sure Mark understood his position from the outset.

Yeah, that was the way to go. He'd sound the bloke out during the pub crawl. Patrick chuckled under his breath. If he couldn't get Mark to give up his secrets while they were half-cut and tied to each other, he was losing his touch.

Lex chased the last few nuts and . . . whatever around the corners of their lunchbox. "You're thinking about him now, aren't you? When are you gonna see him again?"

"Saturday night. The Spartans are doing a three-legged pub crawl."

"Saturday? That's ages off. Why don't you ask him out before then?"

Patrick crumpled up his paper bag and chucked it in the bin with a thud. "Because *I* don't jump in with both feet the minute I meet someone, all right?" Shit. That'd come out sounding a bit harsh. It wasn't just him thinking that, either—Lex's head was down, back hunched. "Sorry. But I like to get to know people a bit before I get involved. What's wrong with that?"

"I just think you never see what people are really like before you go out with them, so you might as well get on with it. Saves time, dunnit?" Lex looked up, face earnest. "And well, before you go out with someone, you sorta build them up in your head, don't you? Like, you start thinking they're all brilliant and well fit and stuff. So when you finally go out with them, yeah, and they're just like a normal person who farts in bed and picks their nose, right, you're gonna be way more disappointed than you would've if you'd just gone out with 'em straightaway."

"Bollocks. I don't go putting blokes on a pedestal."

Lex looked at him thoughtfully. "Nah, s'pose not. You're more the *he's a wanker until proven innocent* sort."

"Oi, I don't think all blokes are wankers." Patrick grinned. "Well, 'cept in the literal sense. Nah, I dunno. Just, you meet a few tossers"— most of 'em, in Patrick's case, hanging around his mum—"and you start to get a bit wary, that's all." Still, maybe Lex was right.

Maybe it was time to take a chance on someone.

CHAPTER SEVEN

Friday, Mark felt, was the welcome end to a rather halfhearted week. Somehow, by the time Fen had finished dyeing her hair back to something resembling a natural colour on Monday, it had been too late to take her back to school that day. Which had no doubt been her intention. However, Mark had been encouraged by her managing a whole day on each of Tuesday and Wednesday. She'd come home tired and snappish, which Mark had supposed was only natural. He'd spoiled her a bit, providing dinner from her favourite fast-food drive-throughs. They'd eaten in the car, which had been unexpectedly companionable compared to Fen's usual sullen silence at the dining table.

Mark had considered it entirely worthwhile, even if he did now have a BMW that smelled like the bins outside a burger bar. And had ketchup stains on the passenger seat.

Thursday, however, brought a text from the school about a fault with the boiler, which apparently meant that not only did the children have to be sent home early, the school would be closed Friday as well. What with the dyed-hair debacle, Fen's first so-called week at her new school had turned out to be barely two and a half days.

While Mark appreciated that the school didn't exactly *plan* these things, it was a little irritating that they couldn't have got it all out of the way during the Easter holidays. He'd gone to considerable trouble to find Fen another school. He felt the least the wretched place could do was actually let her in the door occasionally.

Still, he wasn't sorry to have an excuse to step away from the computer. Writing, which had seemed the ideal solution to keeping him occupied while Fen was at school, was *not* going as well as he'd expected. He'd thought working from home, in the peace and quiet of an empty house, would be ideal. After all, he'd always cursed the constant interruptions that were an unavoidable feature of office life. Somehow, though, the very lack of distractions was distracting in itself. Either that, or there was something in the Shamwell water that had reduced his attention span to that of a gnat.

He'd managed forty-seven words of the introduction so far. And he wasn't sure how many of them were actually *good* words.

Damn it. Still, at least it meant he could enjoy the unexpected pleasure of his daughter's company all the more.

If she ever came down from her room.

Mark was just debating the best way to entice her from her fortress of solitude (Television? Snacks? Television with snacks?) when the doorbell rang. Who the hell could that be? Postman? Someone to read the meter? Right now he'd even welcome the Jehovah's Witnesses. Mark strode to the door and threw it open, to be greeted by a cry of "Surprise!"

Well, he'd got that right. Through the foliage of an obscenely large bouquet of flowers, Mark could just make out David's sensitive features, stretched into a beaming smile.

Mark found himself smiling back, his mood soaring from subterranean to stratospheric in an instant. "David? Shouldn't you be in the office?"

The smile pursed up into a pout. "Work's been just *awful* since you left, so we thought we'd take a day off and come and see you."

We? Mark blinked. Maybe the boyfriend was locking up the car or something. David certainly looked like he was dressed for a date, in an alarmingly tight burgundy T-shirt—didn't he feel the cold? His nipples certainly begged to differ—and wet-look black jeans.

"It's great to see you," Mark said, guiltily conscious just how much more sincere his welcome was than it would have been a few short weeks ago. "Come on in. Just you, is it?" he added, the boyfriend still being nowhere in sight. Mark doubted anyone capable of hiding behind David's svelte-to-a-fault figure would have the strength to stand up.

"Au contraire." David thrust the flowers at Mark, who found them heavier than he'd expected and nearly dropped them. He hadn't realised they'd come already in a vase of water.

Nestled in the crook of David's arm, Mark could now see, was a teddy bear, nattily dressed in a trench coat, fedora, and dark glasses. David held up the bear and waggled one of its little paws at Mark. "This is Gregory—well, you *did* say to bring my boyfriend, and he's the only man who shares my bed at the moment. Ooh, would that be the little moppet? Shouldn't she be at school?"

Mark turned to find a wide-eyed Fen staring at them, clearly too startled to protest at being called a *moppet*. Or *little*, for that matter.

"This is my daughter, Flo—*Fen*."

David arched an eyebrow. "Floffen? Rather avant-garde."

Unexpectedly, Fen giggled. Mark stared. He'd had no idea she was still capable of doing that. "It's Fen," she said. "But they named me Florence."

David made a *tch* sound with his tongue. "Parents. What are they *like*? Come and say hello to Gregory."

Mark blinked again at the sight of his sullen, overly mature teenage daughter eagerly shaking a furry paw.

"So are you a friend of my dad's?" she asked. "Seeing as *he's* obviously not going to introduce us properly."

"I used to be under him—at the office, that is. Not anymore, though." David made an exaggeratedly sad face. "David Greenlake. You can call me Davey. So go on, tell me *all* about yourself."

Fen reverted to sullen type. "Nothing to tell. My life is *so boring*, stuck out here with no one I know."

"Don't believe it for a second. I bet you have the boys queuing up at your door."

"The boys in my class are just *so lame*."

"The girls, then?"

"*No*." Fen flushed.

"Stray cats and dogs?"

Her eyes went momentarily wide—then she giggled. "Not yet. But we've only just moved in. Dad, can we get a cat? Can we?"

"Um . . . I'll think about it, all right?" Mark wasn't sure where he stood on the question of cats, having always thought of himself as a dog person.

Not that he'd ever owned a dog, but he'd wanted one, as a child. His father's response had always been "Course you can, son—just not right now. Soon as the business is up and running," or *"Just give it six months or so, when I'm not so strapped for cash. I promise."*

He'd still been saying it when Mark left home.

"Only I couldn't have one before cos Mum's allergic, but now I'm living with you there's, like, *no reason* not to, is there?" Her eyes shone with an almost religious fervour.

Next time Mark looked, there'd probably be a shrine to the goddess Bast set up in the hallway. "I said I'll think about it, okay? Having a pet is a big responsibility." If a cat was what she really wanted, then they'd get one, but it wouldn't hurt to give it a couple of weeks to see if this was just a six-day wonder.

"Oh, *Daaa*-aaad. Don't be so *boring*." Her eyes raked him up and down, as if to say, *You even* look *boring, you fuddy-duddy old fart*.

Although if her eyes were to verbalise, they'd probably do it with a few more interjections of *like* and *totally*.

Mark was willing to admit he might have been reading too much into a glance—but there was nothing ambiguous about the way David's gaze had followed hers and was now examining him with a kind of fascinated horror, as if seeing him properly for the first time. "Oh. My. *God*. Is this what you wear when you're not in the office? We have *got* to sort out your wardrobe."

Mark frowned down at his shirt, which was a perfectly decent brushed cotton with a tweedy check. "What's wrong with what I'm wearing?"

"Nothing at all, if you were in your dotage. Put it this way, I'm no longer surprised there's yet to be a second Mrs. Nugent."

"I *told* him," Fen put in, more animated now. "Everything he wears is brown or grey. It's horrible. *Totally*. Like he's someone's grandad. Someone's *dead* grandad. In, like, a programme on the History Channel about rationing or something."

"Well . . . brown can work," David said, his head on one side as he stared at Mark's lower half with disconcerting intensity. "He does have rather lovely brown eyes."

Mark smiled, flattered—not to mention relieved to discover David's gaze did apparently lift above crotch level, if only occasionally.

"And brown will bring out the remaining colour in his hair," David added.

Mark stopped smiling.

"Not, however," David continued, "*that* brown. And *really* not in corduroy." He placed Gregory on a comfy chair and rubbed his hands together. "Now, take me to your wardrobe."

"Is this really necessary?" Mark asked in a valiant attempt to regain control. "I'm sure you've got things you need to be doing—"

David waved airily. "Oh, things, people . . . but this is *much* more important. And it's going to be such fun! Come along now." He offered an arm to Fen, who took it, giggling, and led him upstairs.

Mark followed in resignation. It could have been worse. Much worse. After all, if Fen's school hadn't closed for the day, David might have inveigled his way into Mark's bedroom *without* a chaperone.

"You know, you're really very different out of the office." David chatted away as, gleefully assisted by Fen, he pulled clothes out of cupboards and drawers, flinging some of them on the bed and others in the direction of the wastepaper basket, which had now largely disappeared from sight. "You always used to be so . . . masterful. Of course, as they say, clothes maketh the man." He fixed Mark with a sorrowful gaze. "And those clothes do not maketh a man. *Those* clothes barely maketh a hamster."

Fen giggled.

Mark rolled his eyes. "Just call me Penfold."

Two unnervingly similar blank stares were turned on him.

"From *Danger Mouse*? Originally voiced by Terry Scott?" Mark winced as the looks turned, if anything, even blanker. And a touch pitying.

"He's a hamster," Mark muttered, picking up a sweater from the reject pile. "In a cartoon. What's wrong with this one? It's not grey *or* brown."

"Dad, it's puke green."

"It's *moss*. And if you ever have vomit this colour, be prepared for a swift trip to hospital."

"Moss? More like some kind of diseased algae." David leaned his head so far on one side Mark was tempted to warn him it might fall off. "How can I put this? Green, in its place, can be acceptable. The *right* green, which this is not. Certainly not for you. *Who* did you say used to buy your clothes? Were they visually impaired in some manner?"

Mark *tsk*ed under his breath—not quite daring to do it audibly. "I've been buying my own clothes for some considerable time now," he said drily.

"Really?" David's eyebrows shot up far enough to conclusively disprove the rumours he'd had Botox. "In that case, why aren't you better at it?"

Fen giggled. Again. "I tried to tell him."

David looked sorrowfully at her. "Somebody is *well* overdue for an intervention. You're not busy right now, are you?"

She shook her head. "We got a day off school cos the boiler exploded yesterday."

"Ooh, were there any casualties?" David asked eagerly.

"*What*?" Mark's heart appeared to be developing arrhythmia again. "What do you mean, exploded? The text from school just said there was a fault. *Exploded*?"

Fen rolled her eyes. "It was, like, the least exciting explosion in *history*. There was just this really big bang, and when we looked out the windows, there wasn't even any smoke or flames or *anything*. Nathan Ibrahim was saying Mr. Anderson, that's the caretaker, got half his face blown off, but it wasn't even true, cos Serena saw him later, and he was fine."

"Well, *that's* disappointing. Not for Mr. Anderson, of course," David amended halfheartedly.

Fen matched his glum expression. "I *know*. Boring or what?"

"Wait a minute." Mark felt rather strongly that they were more than missing the point here. "You're telling me you and all the other children were in *mortal peril* and the school didn't see fit to inform the parents even after the fact?"

"Oh, *Daa*-aad. I just *told* you nobody died." Fen gave David a sharp look. "Was he like this when he was at work?"

Mark's "Like what?" was ignored in favour of David's "Hmm, no," as he cocked his head to the other side this time. "I think it's retirement that's done it. You see it a lot. Too little to occupy their brains, so they just sort of shrivel up."

"I am *not* retired!" Or, Mark felt strongly, in any way *shrivelled*.

"Then *why*, pray tell, do you dress like it?" David folded his arms with an air of triumph. "Come on, we're going out. There must be department stores even out here in the wilds of Hertfordshire, mustn't there?"

"Yeah, there's a decent one in Bishops Langley. Dad took me there to get stuff for my room when we moved in. Come *on*, Dad. We've only got a few hours before it shuts."

She grabbed one of Mark's arms. David, who was apparently a *lot* bolder when freed from the constraints of the workplace, grabbed the other.

Mark sighed. "Fine. We'll go shopping. If that's what'll make you happy." In fact, he hadn't seen Fen with a smile this wide since . . . Since primary school, probably. It made the prospect of becoming a fashion victim for an afternoon seem a very small price to pay.

And, well. If they did manage to come up with something decent between them, it wouldn't hurt to wear it to the next Spartans meeting. Not that anything was ever going to happen between him and Patrick, obviously. But it'd be nice to feel that the attraction wasn't *totally* one-sided.

As Fen, still smiling, chivvied him into his car and David climbed into the back with her, Mark wondered for a moment whether he might be overdoing the caution. After all, Fen had clearly taken to David, an obviously gay man. Maybe the revelation that her father was also gay would ruffle fewer daughterly feathers than he'd thought?

That evening, after David had departed, leaving Mark with a significantly fuller wardrobe (and with a significantly emptier wallet) Mark decided to sound Fen out about the subject. He managed to catch her before she'd disappeared into the black hole of her bedroom.

"Fen?"

"Mm?" Fen looked up from her phone.

"It was nice, David coming to visit, wasn't it?" Not the most scintillating conversational opener, but damn it, it *had* been nice. Fun, even, despite the constant denigration of Mark's sartorial choices. Fen hadn't seemed to feel the need to be constantly at his throat with David there. She'd been, well, much more like the daughter he remembered from rare days out with Ellen, back when they'd still been at least trying to be a family.

David had stayed for a fish-and-chip supper bought in the village, and Mark had, for once, bowed to Fen's demands to be allowed to eat it in front of the telly and, more specifically, the latest reality show. The cast had consisted of overly made-up and cosmetically enhanced young people, every detail of whose personal lives both David and Fen seemed to be intimately acquainted with. Despite the fact that some of these details were things Mark would personally have hesitated to disclose to his doctor. He'd been somewhat relieved to find David's and Fen's chief enjoyment seemed to come from ruthlessly mocking what they were watching. At least Fen didn't seem to show any signs of wanting to *be* one of them.

"Well *yeah*," Fen answered. Mark struggled for a moment to recall what he'd been talking about. "Least boring day we've had here. He's all right. I can't believe he used to work for *you*."

Mark frowned. "Why not?"

"Well . . . he's funny. And he knows about fashion and music and stuff. He told me I should make you take me out to shows and stuff in London."

"We could do that," Mark began.

"Nah. It'd be boring with just you."

Okay, that stung. Mark tried not to let it show. "We could invite David to come with us," he suggested.

"Can we? That'd be brilliant." Her face lit up like the London Eye at midnight on New Year's Eve. "Thanks, Dad. I want to see *Wicked* and *Sweeney Todd*, and David says *Kinky Boots* is really good too. And we need to see *Les Misérables* too, even though it's lame cos, like, *everyone's* seen that except me. When can we go?"

"I'll talk to David and see when he's free, all right?"

"Soon?" Fen persisted hopefully.

"We'll see. David does have a job to go to, you know."

"Well *duh*. The theatre's on in the evening, so that doesn't even *matter*."

"Yes, but I don't think it'd be appropriate on a school night."

"*Daaa*-aaad. We're like, literally half an hour out of London here."

"*And* the rest. Look, I said I'd talk to him. And the shows may be booking months in advance."

"So get on with it, yeah?"

"I'll email him tonight. Is that soon enough for you?"

"S'pose." Then she broke into a beaming smile. "It's going to be *brilliant*."

Fen hadn't forgotten about it the following day. First thing Saturday morning, Mark was met with a demand to know if he'd sent the email. (He hadn't, so sue him, it'd been late and he'd been tired. Also, he hadn't wanted to give David the wrong impression by seeming too keen to see him again.) Then she'd pestered him until he'd sat down at the laptop and done it. It was, Mark found, extraordinarily difficult to come up with a coherent sentence with a teenager tutting over his shoulder.

Finally he hit Send. And Fen disappeared back to her room.

One headache dealt with, the universe apparently decided Mark was due for another. Ellen rang. Mark took a deep breath before picking up the phone. "Ellen?"

"Well, who else would it be?"

Mark couldn't tell if she was being tetchy or playful. Which was a fair commentary on what their marriage had been like. "Everything all right?"

"Fine. Is Florence there?"

"Ah, yes. She's upstairs. Has she not been answering her phone?"

"She's been answering. *Most* of the time. I wanted to talk to you."

There was a silence. "What about?" Mark prompted.

"Oh, you know. How she's settling into her new school. That sort of thing." Ellen's voice sharpened. "She's not been getting into trouble, has she?"

"No, no. Far from it." The hair thing had just been a misunderstanding and really didn't count.

"Making friends?"

"It's a bit early to tell, to be honest. But I'm sure she will." Mark's tone was, without even consulting him, getting heartier and more patronising by the minute. He winced at the sound of his own voice.

Ellen, however, didn't appear to have noticed. "And . . . is she *happy*?"

"She . . . Well." Mark wasn't at all sure what she wanted to hear. She sounded sad—did she want to be reassured Fen was missing her too? "We had a good day yesterday, actually," he said quickly. "The school was closed because of boiler issues, and I had a friend from work come round. They got on like a house on fire."

"A friend?" Ellen's tone could have been used to cut glass.

"*Yes*, just a friend. I do have them, you know."

"Don't *start*." Ellen was definitely tetchy now. She spoke again before Mark had time to retort that he wasn't starting anything. "Are you in tomorrow?"

"Er, yes?"

"I'm coming over to see Florence. If that's *convenient*." Her tone made it clear that nothing short of a minor apocalypse would be accepted as an excuse.

"Fine," Mark said shortly. "But make it after twelve o'clock," he added, remembering it was the pub crawl tonight. "Fen will probably want a lie-in."

"Lunch, then," Ellen said decisively.

Mark froze in horror. Sunday lunch with Ellen had always meant a roast dinner, *"because that's what Sunday lunch is* supposed *to be."* Would she expect him to manage roast beef, Yorkshire pudding, and gravy? Apple crumble for afters? How did one even *make* gravy, anyway? Could you buy it at Waitrose? "Lunch?" he queried, a bit croakily.

There was an audible *tsk* down the phone line. "Don't worry. I'll take her out somewhere. I'm not expecting *you* to cook."

"Your mother's coming over tomorrow," Mark said over dinner. He'd made pasta, feeling a good lining to the stomach was probably called for in anticipation of the night's revelry.

Fen looked at him, then down at her half-eaten macaroni cheese (packet mixes were a godsend). He'd thrown in a few mushrooms, peas, and cherry tomatoes so she'd get something healthy, and there was now a sad little vegetable graveyard on one side of her plate. "She's coming here?"

"That is what I just said, yes."

"She's not staying, is she?"

Mark blinked. "I don't think that would work, sweetheart. She's got to be able to get to work."

Oddly, Fen seemed to brighten at that. "Oh. Okay. Can we have ice cream for pudding?"

"*If* you put some fruit in it." Mark gave her a stern look. "I don't think your mother would be too pleased if you came down with scurvy."

"*Daaa*-aaad. Nobody gets scurvy these days. They put vitamins in everything."

"Apart from teenage girls, by the look of it."

"*And* they're bad for you if you eat too much. People *die*." Fen seemed to relish the prospect. It was her next question that really floored him, though. "Dad, do you wanna watch a DVD after dinner?"

Of course, the one evening Fen actually wanted to spend some time with him one-on-one just had to be the evening Mark had arranged to go out. He grimaced with genuine regret. "Sorry, darling, but I've got to get ready for tonight. I'm going out."

"Why? Where are you going? Oh my God, you're not going *out* with someone, are you? Like, *on a date* out?"

"No. It's a—" Mark coughed. Announcing he was going on a pub crawl didn't seem like the sort of example he should be setting his child. "Charity fundraising event with the Spartans."

"That sounds *so boring*."

"Um. Yes. Probably. So what do you think I should wear?" It had slipped out before he could stop it.

Fen made a face that seemed to imply serious doubt of his sanity. "What, to get people to give you money? Who *cares*?"

"It's psychology," Mark said quickly. "People are more likely to contribute to the cause if we make a good impression."

"I dunno. Aren't they more likely to give you money if you look like you need it?"

"No, because I'm not collecting for myself. It's for the charity."

"Oh. Which one?"

Damn it. Mark didn't have a clue. "It's a children's charity," he lied, making a mental note to send a conscience-salving donation to ChildLine when he got a moment.

"Oh. Cool. Well, wear some of the stuff David chose, yeah?"

CHAPTER EIGHT

Patrick wandered into the bar of the Three Lions, where the Spartans were meeting up so everyone could get a drink down them before starting on the pub crawl proper. From the state of them, he reckoned Barry and Rory had turned up early. *Well* early. They were perched a bit precariously on stools at one end of the bar, collecting buckets at their feet, cackling away at something or other. Patrick gave them a nod and went to say hi to a couple of the lads.

Mark walked through the door on the dot of eight, so either his mum had brought him up proper or he was worried about having to risk either standing around on his own in the pub or getting left behind.

He was looking good.

Really good. Like he'd hired a personal stylist to give him a makeover or something. He was wearing new-looking black jeans that fit him really well, and a casual shirt in a rich, dark red under a tan leather jacket. It made him look younger and more confident somehow.

Patrick felt like that time he'd been on his way home from Tenerife with a wicked tan and a hangover and had stepped onto a travellator at the airport thinking it was moving. Except it hadn't been, so his stride had been all wrong and he'd almost gone arse over tit. It wasn't that he didn't *like* Mark's new image—he liked it a *lot*, ta very much. But it didn't quite fit with the shy, nervous, older bloke he'd been preparing to have fun with, wind up a bit, and maybe sweep off his feet in a less literal sense.

Made him think maybe he was gonna have to up his game a bit.

Mark's welcoming smile turned uncertain. "Er, I haven't come out with something on my face, have I?"

Patrick pulled himself together. The bloke underneath it all hadn't changed, had he? "Nah, looking good, actually." He gave Mark an easy smile. "Been shopping?"

"Oh God, is it that obvious? My, er, ex-PA ganged up on me with my daughter and they insisted on dragging me out to the shops. Please tell me they haven't made me look ridiculous."

"No worries. You can tell your PA from me, she's got good taste."

"Er, *he*, actually."

Patrick *really* wanted to know why Mark had blushed at that. "Gay?" he guessed, keeping his tone neutral.

"Oh God, yes. I mean, yes, David is. Very." He smiled like he was remembering something in particular about the bloke.

Patrick's gut twisted, just a bit, at that smile. "Gets on well with your daughter, does he?"

"Oh God, yes." Mark said it like he wasn't sure it was a good thing, which was reassuring. "Then again, Fen seems to get on well with everyone, just as long as they're not in any way an authority figure."

"Teenagers, eh?" Patrick sympathised. "Right, what are you drinking?"

"Have I got time for a pint?"

"And then some. We won't be getting going for another half hour at least."

"Are you sure? The email said 'eight o'clock sharp, be there on time or be Billy-no-mates drinking alone all night, you sad, pathetic old loser.'"

"Yeah. That's Barry-speak for 'if you're very lucky, I'll shift my arse by half past.' You get used to it. So what are you up for?"

"What's good? I tried the Brock Bitter after the last meeting, but I wasn't so keen. Bit on the sweet side for me."

"Nah, Barry raves about that stuff, but if you like it dry, you're better off with something like the Hedgehog. Or the Ridgeway—that's what I'm drinking." Patrick raised his glass. "Wanna try it?"

Mark blinked. "If you're sure you don't mind . . ." He took the glass and sipped at it like he was worried it might be hot.

Patrick gave an exaggerated roll of his eyes. "Go on—have a proper drink."

He was delighted when Mark looked him straight in the eye and downed half the pint in one long swallow. "Happy now?"

"Yep, because I know the next words out of your mouth are gonna be 'Buy you another?'"

"I really walked into that one, didn't I?"

"Yeah, mate. Yeah, you did. Still, good beer, innit?"

Mark just raised an eyebrow and headed off to the bar, but when he came back, Patrick noticed he was carrying two pints of Ridgeway.

By that time, a few of the other lads had turned up, so Patrick didn't get a chance to talk to Mark on his own. Shame. Still, the night was young. And so was at least one of them. Patrick smirked to himself and filed that one mentally under *jokes NOT to make in Mark's hearing*. It wasn't like he meant anything by it anyway—Patrick *knew* there was an age gap, but when he was talking to Mark, it didn't seem all that important.

Did it look different, seen from the other side? Patrick reckoned he was pretty mature for a twenty-five-year-old, but did he seem young to Mark? Still, what was he supposed to do about it? Start smoking a pipe and wearing reading glasses he didn't need? Sod it. If it didn't work out between him and Mark, it didn't work out, and trying to pretend he was someone he wasn't wouldn't make it any better.

"Oi, Earth to Patrick?" That was Alasdair, leaning forward so his bushy red beard was right in Patrick's face. "You still with us, mate?"

Patrick blinked. "Yeah. Sorry. Zoned out for a bit. What did I miss?"

"Only Alasdair talking a right load of old cobblers, as usual," Si said with a fond smile. Si was a bear of a man with a cuddly disposition and a beard to match Alasdair's, only in a brown so dark it was almost black. He looked like he'd just come down off a mountain. Course, with his Welsh accent, it was possible he actually *had* come down off a mountain. "So who's this young man, then?"

He was looking at Mark, and now Patrick came to think about it, Si hadn't been at the last meeting, had he? "Mark. New recruit. Be nice to him. Mark, this is Si. Lives up on The Hill. He's a roofer."

Now Patrick came to think of it, there was a definite theme of high places going on with Si.

"Pleased to meet you," Mark said, putting out a hand for Si to shake with his bloody great calloused paw.

Barry interrupted them, his arms full of those weird stretchy elastic things people used in the gym—resistance bands, Patrick had heard them called—and a wicked grin on his round face. "Right, lads. Bondage time." Barry tossed a band to Si, who started tying his ankle to Alasdair's, then looked between Mark and Patrick. "You two tying the knot together? You're about the same height."

Patrick grinned, mentally thanking the bloke for bringing up the subject. "All right with me. All right with you, Mark?"

Mark didn't look quite so sure, but he did his best to hide it, bless him. Patrick started feeling a bit more sure-footed. Christ, he was being ridiculous, getting jealous over Mark's PA. *Ex*-PA, even.

Still, it wouldn't hurt to make a move sooner rather than later, would it?

"All right, give us one of them things, Barry. Where'd you get 'em, anyway? You started going to the gym?"

"Give over! The missus uses 'em in that exercise class she does. *Booty Burner*, she calls it."

"Sounds painful." Effective, though. Barry's wife was half his size—literally; last time Patrick had met her, she'd proudly announced she *and* the two kids together weighed less than her husband.

"I reckon it bloody is and all. I watched her once, and you wouldn't catch me doing it. Why'd anyone want to put themselves through all that when they could be sitting at home in front of the telly and just exercising their right arm?"

Patrick raised an eyebrow. "Yeah? Well, I guess we know what sort of stuff you watch on the telly while your missus is out, then, don't we?"

"What do you— Oi, I didn't mean *that*. I *meant* this sort of exercise, you wanker." Barry mimed lifting a bottle to his lips.

"Yeah, right. I think we all know who's the wanker here."

"Shut it, Owen, or you're on Bud Light all night."

"Like to see you try and make me, Thompson." They squared up to each other, then broke away, laughing.

Mark cleared his throat. "I'm, er, fine with teaming up if you are."

"Good man. Here you go." Barry handed Mark one of the bands. "You know what? We should've made tonight your induction. Would've been a right laugh."

"Oh yes, I've been meaning to ask—what does induction actually involve?"

Barry clapped him on the shoulder. "Patrick'll tell you all about it. I gotta get everyone tied up, yeah?" He waddled off, the bands swinging from his arm.

Mark gave Patrick a suspicious look. "So what's this induction, and why would it have been a laugh to have it tonight?"

Patrick grinned. "Tell you when you've got a couple of beers inside you. Trust me, it'll go down easier. Right, are you okay if I go on the left?"

"Fine—are you left-handed, then?"

"Nah, I just had a bad break on my left leg last summer. The ankle's still a bit swollen, so tying it up with big rubber bands probably wouldn't be the best idea."

"Oh? What happened—if you don't mind me asking, obviously."

"What, like you're worried I did it during some kinky sex session?" Patrick laughed. "Nah, half the village saw me come a cropper, and I'm not that much of an exhibitionist. It was during a cricket match. The other team went in to bat first, so I was fielding in leg gully. Rob bowled—you met Rob yet? He teaches in the village school. Good bloke, although he dresses like he just walked out of a P.G. Wodehouse adaptation. Talks like it and all. Anyway, you'll know him when you see him. If you wanna make a good impression, just tell him you think his bow tie's cool. Where was I?"

"Leg gully." Mark's eyes were wide, his attention so rapt it was almost off-putting.

Patrick took a deep breath. "Right. Okay, Rob bowls, and the guy in bat hits the ball straight at me, near as. Total gift. All I have to do is run back and jump for it. So I jump, and I catch it, and just as I'm thinking Man of the Match is in the bag, I come down with my foot in a rabbit hole. Course, I don't know that at the time. All *I* know is I'm lying on the ground with my whites turning red from what I don't yet know is my actual shinbone having sliced through my skin and poked its head out to say hello. My leg's feeling like someone just lopped it off with a blunt hacksaw, and Rob's looking down at me going, 'Oh dear, that doesn't look very good, does it?'"

"Ouch." Mark was wincing. "I take it that was the end of your cricket season, then?"

"Just a bit."

"Did it scar badly?"

Patrick shrugged. "That and the surgery. It's not so bad, though." He pulled his jeans leg up to show Mark, who crouched down and even ran a finger along the still-red line where the surgeon had made the incision.

Funny thing, scars. See, Patrick could have sworn the area around it was still numb, but then why was his whole leg tingling and the hair on the back of his neck standing up? He swallowed. "Right. Better get into bondage, like Barry said."

"Yes. Yes, of course." Mark stood up. "So . . . you'll be all right doing this? I mean, it's not still painful?"

"No. I'm good." Patrick felt a bit weird, with Mark being all concerned like that. *Good* weird, mind. He brushed it off and put his right foot next to Mark's left—huh, big feet, fancy that—and bent to tie the band around their ankles with a half bow. "There we go. With a bit of luck, that won't be too hard to undo even half-cut. Us, that is, not the band. Barry's missus would probably throw a right fit if we damaged any of 'em, and you don't wanna be on the wrong side of that."

"Oh? Large woman, is she?" Mark was probably thinking of Barry's size.

"Christ, no. Just imagine being stung to death by an angry hornet." Patrick straightened, not without a bit of a wobble, and found Mark's arm slipping around his shoulders. Nice. Yeah, that felt like it belonged there.

"All right there?"

"Ta, I'm good." Patrick returned the favour, slinging his arm around Mark's waist. Oh yeah. That *definitely* felt like it belonged. "Wanna try walking? On the count of three, middle leg first: One, two—"

Mark's grip tightened. "Wait—do we walk *on* three, or *after* three?"

Patrick blinked, a bit distracted by Mark's closeness and the way he'd felt the bloke's words rumble through him. He was wearing some kind of aftershave, sort of woodsy and dry. It suited the new look and did wicked things to Patrick's libido. "What? Oh—right. Walk *on* three. Ready? One, two, *three*."

They walked. Well, for a given value of *walk*. They quickly got out of sync and only just managed not to face-plant. Patrick laughed. "Let me guess—three-legged pub crawls not been much of a feature in your life before now?"

"Hey, I'm not doing so badly." Mark nodded his head in the direction of Barry and Rory, who were staggering good-naturedly back to their feet after a close encounter with the carpet. "But no, not as such. I think the last time I did this must have been sometime in the 1980s."

"Yeah? I wasn't even born in the eighties," Patrick said without thinking. "Hey, did you have one of those early mobile phones that looked like a brick?"

There was a pause. "Not when I was in primary school, no. How old do you think I am?"

Uh-oh. Mark sounded a bit miffed. "Er . . . late thirties?" Patrick guessed, revising his estimate down a few years so as not to put the bloke's back up any further. Why the hell had he even said all that stuff anyway?

"Close enough." He huffed a laugh. "Although I'm fairly sure if you asked my daughter, she'd say I've got one foot in the old folks' home."

"Yeah, but that's teenagers, innit? She probably thinks I'm past it and all."

"Believe me, that's *not* what she thinks about you," Mark said darkly.

Patrick gave him a sharp look. "Do I wanna know?"

"I hope not. She's only fourteen."

"But reckons she knows it all already? Good luck with that one, mate." Patrick paused. "Course, as long as everyone's all grown up, I've got nothing against a bit of an age gap. Rather have it in the other direction, though." He gave Mark a bit of a squeeze, just in case that pint he'd just downed had impaired his ability to take a hint.

Mark drew in a sharp breath. "I think we're heading off now."

Patrick looked around. Bloody hell, when had he stopped noticing what was going on around them? Most of the lads had already gone, and the last two, Barry and Rory—no surprise there—were halfway out the door. "Right. Okay, on three again?"

Good job they both had long legs. They caught up to Barry and Rory with no trouble.

"All right, lads?" Barry asked, looking round at them and making Rory stumble. "Oo-er . . . steady as she goes."

"The engines canna take it, Cap'n," Rory said in a Scottish accent bad enough to have actually come from *Star Trek: The Original Series*, then gave Patrick a knowing grin. "We weren't sure you two were coming. Thought you might've decided to get a room instead." He and Barry cracked up.

Bastards. Mark went rigid beside him. "Ignore 'em," Patrick said quickly. Their pace had slowed by some sort of unconscious telepathy, letting Barry and Rory surge on ahead.

"It's fine," Mark said even quicker—much too quick for it to actually *be* fine. "Just a joke."

Shit. He wasn't out, was he?

If he were out, he'd have laughed it off. Told 'em they were just jealous or something. If he was straight—but he *wasn't* straight, Patrick knew he wasn't. He was gay, or bi, and he was into Patrick. It was fucking *obvious*, unless you were terminally stupid or straight or both.

And he didn't want anyone to know.

Shit.

"Patrick? It's not . . . I mean, I haven't got a problem with, um . . ." Mark trailed off. Patrick wondered just what his expression was saying.

"Yeah. Forget about it, all right?" Fuck knew *he* was gonna have to. They'd reached the Tickled Trout, thank God. "C'mon. Let's get the beers in."

CHAPTER NINE

The doors of the Tickled Trout were well narrow, so Patrick needed his full concentration to get him and Mark in the pub without getting stuck. Some of the Spartans managed it better than others—Rory and Barry seemed to be finding the logistics of turning side on a bit beyond them.

"You know, this could be an excellent way of avoiding binge drinking," Mark murmured under his breath after a few minutes watching and laughing.

Patrick laughed. "Yeah—if you can't work out how to get in the door, you're too pissed to go to the pub. Nice one." And thank God, Mark seemed to have relaxed a bit. "So what are you drinking?" he asked as they made it over the threshold. "My shout."

"I haven't been in here before. What do you recommend?"

"I usually go for the Tea Kettle. That's a stout. Pretty bitter. If you want something a bit lighter, there's the Mansion Mild. I'd steer clear of the Death or Glory, though. At least for tonight. That stuff's lethal."

The Tickled Trout was pretty busy, mostly with people eating in the restaurant. It wasn't the sort of pub that was anyone's local—that was what the Three Lions was for. Barry had tipped the bar staff off they'd be coming round, though, so the Spartans got waved through to shake their buckets at the diners while trying not to fall over and face-plant in anyone's fish and chips.

They made a fair haul, Patrick reckoned, but it was a relief to get back into the pub part and start propping up the bar. There were only a few people in this area—a family clearly waiting for a restaurant table, and a couple of blokes in suits who looked like they were having a business meeting.

"Jesus, it's Friday night. Get a life," Patrick muttered under his breath.

Mark followed his gaze. "That was me, ten years ago." He made a face. "All right, it was me six months ago too."

Patrick turned to look him in the eye, which involved a bit of neck strain in their current positions. "Yeah? Workaholic, were you? What happened—take the ten-steps programme?"

"More in the nature of a short, sharp shock. So, a pint of Tea Kettle?"

Okay, so *that* discussion wasn't going anywhere. "Cheers," Patrick said, and leaned on the bar while Mark ordered two pints of Tea Kettle.

Barry and Rory, he noticed, were on the Death or Glory.

"What's the food like in here?" Mark asked as he handed Patrick his pint.

Patrick took a sip of the dark, malty beer. Perfect. "Well . . ." He glanced up at the barmaid, who was still in easy earshot. "Tell you what, wanna take a look at the beer garden?"

"In the dark?"

"Well, yeah, but they have lights on the river. It's pretty," he added a bit defensively.

Mark took a swallow of his pint. "Okay, well, you didn't lead me wrong on the beer. Good stuff, this. Let me just drink a bit more so I don't spill it en route."

"Good idea." Patrick gulped down about a third of his pint while Mark did the same, then they headed out the back door.

If anyone noticed them going, at least they didn't make any loud comments about it, to Patrick's relief. It wouldn't have bothered him if they had, but he had a feeling Mark would've been embarrassed.

Tables—empty right now, of course—were set up close by the door, but Patrick took Mark around to the side, where they'd get a good view of the river. It wasn't too cold here, seeing as they were sheltered from the wind at least.

"You're right, it is pretty," Mark said, gazing down at the clear water that bubbled under the bridge to sparkle in the lights from the Tickled Trout.

"Better in daylight, obviously. The ducks all went to bed hours ago. You'll often see kids fishing from the bridge—more in summer, obviously."

"You're a fisherman?"

"Me? No. You?"

"Always wanted to try it when I was a kid." Mark sighed.

He didn't say anything more, though, so Patrick didn't ask. "Maybe you could give it a go now," he suggested instead.

Mark laughed. "My daughter already thinks I'm old, sad, and boring. I don't think taking up fly-fishing is going to improve matters."

"So what would impress her, then?" Patrick asked with a grin. "Skydiving? Bungee jumping? Or there's always Morris dancing. That's so uncool, it's probably all the way round to hip and trendy again."

"God, she'd be horrified. It's almost tempting." Mark chuckled under his breath—Patrick felt it more than heard it. "Is this leading into a confession?"

"What, that I like to prance around with a bunch of blokes with flowers in their hats, beating our sticks together and jingling our bells? Sorry, mate. I'm not *that* bent."

Patrick held his breath for a heartbeat, because there was an obvious lead-in if ever he'd heard one. Mark didn't take him up on it, though—no teasing questions as to just how bent he was.

He was pretty sure the bloke had tensed a bit, though. He was choosing to believe that was a good thing.

"So . . . You never did tell me about the food here," Mark said with the air of a man who was going to change the subject if it killed him. "What was so bad you couldn't say it in the bar? Suspected salmonella?"

Fair enough. Patrick could skirt around elephants in the room as well as the next man. "Nah, it's nothing like that. Just, it's gone downhill a bit since the old chef left. More stuff brought in frozen and microwaved, you know how it goes. Just a bit bland, that's all. You're better off going up to the Sticky Wicket these days." Now he came to talk about it, it seemed a bit of a weak excuse for getting the bloke out here on his own.

Mark was nodding, like he thought so too. Not that Patrick was paranoid or anything. "That's the one opposite the cricket ground?"

"Yeah. Take you up there for lunch one day, if you fancy. We could do it on a weekday—it's always a bit busy at weekends anyway." Patrick had nothing against Fen, but he'd rather have her dad to himself given half a chance.

"Oh, do you work in the village, then?"

"Yeah, I work for a local charity. SHARE—stands for Shamwell Regional Enterprise for Adults with Learning Disabilities." He caught Mark's look. "Yeah, well, SREALD didn't make for a snappy name, all right? Anyway, it's what we stand for. Sharing. People with disabilities ought to be part of the community."

"I wasn't questioning the name." Mark paused. "It's just . . . You're a professional charity fundraiser. And for relaxation, you join an organisation that raises funds for charity?"

Patrick couldn't help bristling a bit. "Yeah, so?"

Mark backed off—at least, he tried to. Seeing as he had his arm around Patrick's waist and their legs were tied together, he made it about a millimetre. "Er, that's very commendable?"

Patrick had to laugh. "Good save, mate. Yeah, well. I like to give something back, you know? And the day job, yeah, that's all good stuff, but I get paid for that, don't I?" He gave a tiny shrug. "Actually, they're not totally separate. The next thing the Spartans are doing is a fun run for SHARE. I'm organising it—can I sign you up?"

"Oh, absolutely—um, it's not going to be a marathon or anything, is it?"

"Nah, don't worry. You get to choose between 2K, 5K, and 10K. Course, the 2K's really only for the under-fives."

"I may not be in training for a marathon, but I'd hope I'd be able to stagger a bit further than two kilometres," Mark said drily. "Are you running?"

"Wish I could, but there'll be too much to coordinate." He smiled. "Happy to train with you, though, if you like."

"Thanks."

That wasn't taking him up on the offer, but it wasn't rejecting it either. Patrick decided to let it slide for now. Maybe the bloke was just worried his age would show him up? "No problem," he said, leaving it open.

"Have you always worked in the charity sector?" Mark asked after a pause.

"Well, I did other jobs when I was younger—usual weekend stuff just to get a bit of cash—but this has been my only proper job."

"Oh? You must have interviewed very well to get the job with no experience whatsoever."

Patrick would've been more flattered by the admiration in Mark's tone if it hadn't been mixed with a healthy dose of surprise.

"Well . . . one of the jobs I did when I was starting out was charity fundraising. As a chugger—you know, the ones who mug you when you come out of Marks & Spencer and try and sign you up for a standing order to whatever charity they're plugging that week?"

"Oh God, yes. What's it like, being on that end of it?"

"Says the bloke who clearly doesn't like being on the other end of it."

"Not much, no. I'd rather choose which charity I donate to based on its merits, not on the persuasive abilities of some young person who's just accosted me on the street."

"Yeah, but do you? Donate, I mean. A lot of people never get around to it without a bit of a push."

"Well, my employer—my old employer—had a scheme where you could have part of your salary paid into a charity account, and they'd match it. So yes, I do."

"Glad to hear it. But you know, chugging gets a bad press, but for charities, it's a major source of income. Even after the chugger gets paid. See, people give to people, not to charities. And the standing orders they collect last an average of six years, so it's good for budgeting." Patrick laughed, feeling a bit self-conscious. "And I'll be getting off my soapbox now, all right?"

"No, no, it's okay." Mark smiled, and suddenly Patrick felt a bit short of breath. Hard work, this three-legged walking. Even though they'd been standing still for the last ten minutes. "It's great you're doing something you really believe in."

Patrick was still trying to work out whether he should ask Mark about his work situation—he'd said former employer, so maybe he'd been made redundant? He might be a bit touchy about it—when Mark spoke again. "Look, about earlier—I mean, what Rory said. I don't want you to feel I'm uncomfortable about you being, well, however you'd describe yourself."

Patrick gave a one-shouldered shrug. "I've never really bothered much with labels."

"No?" Mark's smile was weird, sort of wistful but not quite. "If it wasn't for labels, I'm not sure I'd know who I was half the time."

"Well, if I had to pick one, I guess I'd say bi. Or gay, maybe. Somewhere in the middle, really. I've been out with more girls than blokes, but I think maybe I was trying too hard, you know?"

"You didn't want to be gay?"

"Didn't wanna be with a bloke."

"There's a difference?"

"Oh yeah." Patrick forced a smile. "Nothing you wanna hear about, though. So what about you? Bi?" It was a bit mean, maybe, pushing the bloke—but sod it, he'd been the one to bring up the subject, hadn't he?

Mark's Adam's apple bobbed as he swallowed. "Gay."

"But you were married to Fen's mum? What was it—you trying too hard, and all?"

"More like too successfully." Mark made a face. "She got pregnant, Ellen I mean. We went on holiday to Italy, and that was when I knew for sure. We had a great time, got on really well—and all I could think of was how much I'd rather be with one of the waiters."

"Lemme guess—snake-hipped, dark-eyed, curly haired and as macho as hell?"

Mark nodded. "It wasn't any one in particular. They were *all* like that. So when we got back, I told her I was sorry, but I didn't think it'd work between us. I mean, I didn't tell her *why*. And she was upset, obviously, but she accepted it." He grimaced again. "Maybe *she'd* rather have been with one of the waiters too. But three weeks later, she told me she was pregnant."

Patrick hesitated, but for Christ's sake, the bloke had to have thought of this. "Look, not being funny or anything, but are you absolutely sure you're Fen's dad?"

Mark gave him a look like Patrick had asked if he was sure bears shat in the woods. "Well, of course. Ellen wouldn't *lie* about it."

Right. Not going *there* again.

"So you got married." Patrick's smile felt a bit twisted. "You do know most blokes wouldn't bother these days?"

"She's my *child*," Mark said like that explained everything. And Christ, way to make Patrick fall in love with him, the bastard. "She doesn't know any of this, of course," Mark went on. "We told her we were married in May, not September. Before the holiday."

"Uh-huh. And what about when she finds out?"

"Why would she ever find out?" Mark's tone was sharp.

"Hey, I'm not gonna grass you up. Just, it's a matter of public record, innit? What if one day she, I dunno, gets the urge to draw up a family tree or something? Births and marriages, that's how you start all that. Or what if your mum has a few too many glasses of sherry one Christmas and lets it slip?"

"My parents are both dead, so it's unlikely, I'm afraid."

"Sorry." Patrick found himself giving Mark another squeeze.

"Well, I never really got on with my father in any case."

Patrick huffed in sympathy. "Tell me about it."

"But you live with your mum, don't you? At least, I think that's what Barry said."

So Mark had been asking about him, had he? "Yeah. Her and my dad have been split up since I was a kid, so it's always been just us two. She's a radiographer up at the hospital."

"You're proud of her, aren't you?"

"Yeah. Yeah, I am." Patrick hesitated, but sod it, Mark had been open enough with him. Least he could do was pay him back with the same coin. "See, my dad's a bit of a shit. As in, in-and-out-of-jail, knocked-her-around type of total shit. She was in a right state when I was little, but she pulled herself up, kicked him out, went back to college and stuff. Got a decent job and made us a home. So yeah, I'm proud of her." He looked at Mark closely. Was that too much for the bloke to handle? Finding out Patrick came from a family of violent criminals? Well, *a* violent criminal. "You all right, mate?"

Mark was breathing hard. And blinking a bit fast. "Fine," he said, and pulled up a wobbly smile. "But I think this calls for another drink." He downed the rest of his pint in one, then seemed to remember there was no way he was getting to the bar for another without Patrick, not tied together as they were. "Um. If you're ready?"

"Yeah, no problems." Patrick tossed back the rest of his beer, even though he'd had a bit more left in his glass than Mark had. "C'mon, then. Although you know we're only supposed to be having one drink per pub, right?"

"That's official Spartans rules, is it?"

"Nah, it's official pub crawl rules, innit?" Patrick grinned. "We've got to get you out more."

They sidled in the door and made their way to the bar, not without a bit of awkward threading their way through tables and around carelessly scattered barstools.

"Two pints of Tea Kettle," Mark said, getting out his wallet.

The barmaid seemed to be fighting a laugh. "All right, but you do know the rest of 'em left ten minutes ago, don't you? Your lot, I mean, with the three-legged bit and the collecting buckets."

"What? The wankers. What do you reckon, Mark? Stay here, or try and catch 'em up?"

"What's the route from here?"

"Up to the Sticky Wicket—it's a fair old walk, mind—then back over the fields to the Pig & Poke. You know it?"

Mark shook his head.

"It's a bit spit-and-sawdust, but they do good pub grub there. And the beer garden's nice in the summer."

"How about," Mark said thoughtfully, "we have our pints here, maybe take our time a bit, and then catch up with the others at the Pig & Poke?"

"Good plan. *Very* good plan. That'll teach 'em to ditch us."

"You tell 'em," the barmaid said, already pulling their pints.

"Wanna go back outside?" Patrick asked when they had their drinks in their hands.

Mark took a slow swallow. "Maybe warm up a bit in here first?"

As they pulled two stools together and sat down, Patrick wasn't sure if he was relieved or sorry. On the one hand, it had been a lot more, well, intimate out there in the dark, just the two of them, huddling together for warmth. Or something. On the *other* hand . . .

On the other hand, he wasn't sure if he was ready for any more of that just yet. And he was pretty sure Mark wasn't, seeing as he opened the conversation with a discussion of how City pubs were different from country pubs, and whether it was a good thing or not that the restaurant trade was saving so many of them from closing down.

Mark maybe noticed it wasn't a subject Patrick was all that fired up about—after all, if all you had to worry about was whether your local was losing its character, Patrick reckoned you were doing all right—as he trailed off after a bit. "You're the first person I've ever told all that to," he said.

Patrick gave him a searching look. "Okay, we're not talking about pubs now, are we?" he said after a pause.

"No. The . . . other stuff. About Fen. And me."

"You're not out to *anyone*?" Patrick kept his voice low, even though this part of the pub was empty.

"No—well, not anyone who knows me. Apart from Ellen, of course. I mean, I went to a few bars, back in London." He swallowed. "Tried out a couple of dating sites. Didn't really seem my sort of thing."

"Yeah? Lot of blokes in your position, they'd be off playing musical beds every night. S'pose it's a bit harder with a teenager at home."

"God, no, I don't do any of that now. No, this was before, when Fen was still living with Ellen."

"Oh—so you didn't get custody right away?"

"We have joint custody, but she's always lived with Ellen. We both thought it was best."

"So what changed?"

Mark pulled a face. "She became a teenager. Worse, she got in with the wrong crowd and managed to get herself expelled from school. Ellen was finding it all a bit difficult. That's why I'm here—in the village, I mean. I wanted Fen to have a fresh start, away from all the bad influences."

"Dodgy boyfriend?"

Mark's eyes went wide. "God, I hope not. Ellen never said . . . I mean, she's only fourteen. Far too young to be going out with boys."

Patrick laughed. "Think you'll find she's got a very different opinion on that, mate."

Mark gave an exaggerated shudder. "You've seen how she dresses. No, wait, I don't suppose you have, have you? Just take it from me, I hate to think what sort of boy she'd attract."

"Nah, you can't go judging a book by its cover." Patrick amused himself trying to imagine what got Mark so wound up about the way his daughter dressed. Skirts more than an inch above the ankle? Tops that didn't button up to the neck? Mark seemed like he'd reckon anything short of a full burqa was dangerously revealing, where his little girl was concerned. Seriously, the bloke needed to lighten up.

"Can't I? That's all people seem to do these days. Like on all these dating sites. It's just all so . . . shallow. All about how much they want to jump into bed with you. I mean, Ellen and I were friends before we were anything else. That just doesn't seem to be the way people do things nowadays." His shoulders slumped. "God, I sound about a hundred years old, don't I?"

"Never mind, mate. You don't look it. Not a day over seventy-five."

Mark laughed. "Don't *you* start." He picked up his pint and drained the dregs. Patrick had finished his a while ago. "Right. Are we heading off?"

"Yeah, but I'm gonna need to take a pit stop first." Patrick looked down at their still-bound ankles. Now he *could* offer to release Mark . . . Nah. It'd be more fun this way. "Coming?"

CHAPTER TEN

Patrick could see the indecision on Mark's face. He was pretty sure he could see the temptation too.

"Oh, right. Yes," Mark said at last, and they got up and made for the gents', where the double swing doors proved a bit awkward. There was no one else in there as they stood side by side at the urinals and unzipped. Patrick cast a glance over towards Mark's face and nearly cracked up at the way he was resolutely staring dead ahead at the plain white tiles on the wall. "You can look if you want," he said. "I won't tell anyone."

Mark's face went as red as his shirt. "I wasn't looking!"

"I know you weren't. That's why I'm telling you, you can." Patrick grinned as Mark's gaze darted over for about a millisecond, then nailed itself back to the wall.

Okay, maybe it was the beer—and Jesus, after three pints he really *had* needed to piss—but he wasn't going to let that one go. "So is it all right if I take a look too? Only fair, innit?"

"It's a free country." Mark's voice sounded a bit strained.

And yeah, it was definitely the beer, but if Patrick hadn't already been pissing, he'd have been pissing himself laughing. He took a quick peek—and, oh, wow, that was definitely worth his undivided attention. Patrick took another, longer look.

Just in time, as Mark shook himself off and did up his jeans. "When you're *quite* ready," he said pointedly.

"Yep, I'm done." Grinning, Patrick zipped up, and realised it wouldn't really be polite to put his arm around Mark again before washing his hands. "Okay, this is gonna be a bit more difficult. Go on three?"

Somehow they made it to the sinks without falling over, although their shoulders seemed a lot more in the way than they had before and they were both walking like they'd just got off a horse to compensate. By silent agreement, they didn't bother with the hand dryer over on the other wall, just dried their hands on their trousers.

"*Definitely* easier with a cuddle," Patrick said, slipping his arm back around Mark's waist.

Just as the door swung open and a bloke almost as wide as they were together walked into the gents'. He gave them a good, long look, taking in their arms around each other and Mark's flushed face. "Been having fun in here, have you?"

"Wouldn't you like to know?" Patrick loaded his voice with suggestion. Okay, that beer had a *lot* to answer for.

The bloke took a step back. "Not much, no. I'll come back when you're, um, done." He turned and strode back through to the restaurant like he was aiming for the world speed-walking record.

Patrick and Mark barely made it out of the pub before cracking up.

"Christ, did you see his face?" Mark asked.

"Yeah, I think he was worried he was gonna be next in line for a cuddle."

"I don't think he even noticed the—" Mark gestured towards the band tying their ankles together. Then he sobered. "You don't think he's a local, do you?"

"Nah, never seen him before. Don't worry about it."

Mark shivered, although heat was coming off him in waves where he was pressed against Patrick's right side.

"Getting a bit nippy, innit?" Patrick used the excuse to pull Mark in a bit closer. The breeze blowing down the high street wasn't all that strong, but it was definitely on the chilly side.

"It must be nice," Mark said after a moment. "Not worrying about things like that."

"You mean about people knowing I'm bent?" Patrick shrugged, one shouldered. "Yeah, well, take me down to some dodgy part of London and I doubt I'll be so open about it. But here in the village . . . People might have their opinions about it, but they're too worried what the neighbours'll say to voice 'em, on the whole.

And it's not like I'm the only gay in the village. It's helped, having people like Rob around, and him and Sean getting engaged and stuff. Makes it more just part of village life. See, this is why gay marriage is so important. People say there's other stuff that's more urgent, like campaigning against discrimination, helping homeless LGBT kids, but it's all part of changing attitudes, innit? Making people see we're no different from anyone else, cos we get married, buy houses, raise kids, and all that crap. Just like they do. You get that right, and everything else'll follow." He paused. "I'm up on that bloody soapbox again, aren't I? Sorry about that."

"No . . . No, it's fine." Mark might have been looking at him a bit oddly, although it was hard to be sure what with it being dark and them still being tied side by side. "I agree totally, as it happens. If things had been like they are now when I was growing up . . . God, who knows how things would've ended up. Um. So, this place—not on the pub-crawl route?" Mark waved at Badgers, the wine bar, which was just over the road.

"Nah, we didn't reckon they'd appreciate a bunch of rowdy blokes barging in. Okay, we need to go right here, then up the hill."

"Oh? I thought The Hill was that way?" Mark pointed off at right angles to the way they were now going.

"Yeah, well, that's *The* Hill, with capitals. This is just *a* hill. Come on, keep up. It ain't rocket science." Patrick laughed at Mark's expression. "No, seriously, it's not that hard. My mum's got a cousin who lives in a village called The Lane. Her address is 5 Mill Lane, The Lane. *That's* confusing. This is easy."

"If I get lost on the way home, I'm blaming you. How far up is this place anyway?"

"Just up past the houses and down the lane. That's with small letters. But don't worry. I'll see you get home safe."

"Planning to give it your personal attention, are you?" Mark asked, and there was something in his voice, something warm and yet nervy, that made Patrick feel every inch of where they were pressed up against one another. He couldn't judge right now if he was holding on too tightly, but fuck, no way was he gonna loosen his grip.

The street was deserted, lined with cars parked on the road. The houses were a lot more affordable here than in posher parts of the village, and they looked it. Satellite dishes sprouted from the walls like high-tech fungi, and abandoned tricycles lay drunkenly in the front gardens. Everyone here was either still out at the pub or tucked up indoors for the night. A streetlamp flickered as they passed by the old Methodist church, its steep gables and austere frontage looming over them as if about to pass judgement.

Funny, really. Patrick knew the minister a bit through work, and she was the jolliest God-botherer he'd ever met. Maybe she was trying to make up for the image the building gave out.

"Everything all right?" Mark asked softly.

"Yeah. Yeah, I'm good. Sorry. Just thinking."

Mark huffed a laugh under his breath. "It's that sort of night, isn't it? You've made me think about a lot of things. God, you've made me *talk* about a lot of things. Things I haven't really told anyone before. Christ, it's dark up there. Is that the way we're going?"

They were nearly at the end of the houses, and the lane ahead disappeared into a tunnel of blackness. Patrick frowned. "Think there's a streetlamp burned out up there. But yeah, that's the way."

"I hope we make it without falling into a ditch."

"Nah, there's no ditches up that road. No footpath either, so we'll need to keep an eye out for cars."

"It'd be supremely ironic if we ended the evening being knocked down by the rest of the Spartans on their way back home."

"God help us if any of that lot's driving tonight. Nah, we'll be fine. We'll see cars coming a mile off." Patrick gave Mark a friendly squeeze. "It's just the road we're not gonna be able to see."

"I hope it's not the local farmer's route for driving his cows to the next pasture. I'm rather fond of these shoes."

"Nah, worst I've ever stepped in up here was a dead fox. *Very* dead fox. Took me a whole can of Febreze to get the smell out of my trainers." The face Patrick made at the memory was lost to the darkness, which was probably just as well.

"Wildlife does seem to be flourishing around here," Mark said approvingly. "Judging by the amount of road kill, at any rate."

"Yeah, you might wanna look at your definition of flourishing, there. Just saying."

Mark laughed, and God, it felt good, with their bodies still pressed together at the hip and Patrick's arm warm from its hold around Mark's waist, little vibrations running through them both from Mark's laughter.

They walked on, Patrick trailing his free hand along the hedge because, Christ, it was blacker than his dad's heart out here, with that streetlamp out. Even the moon had stayed in tonight, and the stars weren't making a right lot of effort.

On a dark night like this, you could kiss a bloke right on the street and no one would know. Do other stuff too, long as you kept an eye out for headlamps coming your way. It wasn't what Patrick had planned, but sod it, maybe it'd be easier for Mark to let go like this? Him with all his hang-ups? Patrick could just suggest they stop walking for a mo to catch their breath, and then he could stop feeling up the hedge and start feeling up—

"Is that a light up ahead?" Mark asked.

Patrick would've laughed at himself if he hadn't felt so gutted. He'd missed the boat again. "Yeah, that's the Pig. We were nearer than I thought."

There was a loud cheer when Patrick and Mark walked into the Pig & Poke. And a couple of wolf-whistles too. They'd put this place last on the route for a reason—it was a bit rougher and readier than the other village pubs, more your old-fashioned sort of local where men and dogs went for some serious drinking and unaccompanied women risked being looked at a bit funny, although that was all they risked, the landlord not being the sort to stand any shite. Still, the odd touch of rowdiness was pretty much par for the course on a Friday night.

Patrick had used to come here a fair bit while he was still at school, cos the landlord was a soft touch who'd sell you a pint without asking for proof you were over eighteen just as long as he knew you or you'd come in with a regular. Not so much now, though. He preferred the Three Lions, where he could arrange to meet people like Heather or Lex without worrying they'd feel uncomfortable waiting for him if he got held up.

The lads were all clustered around the bar—no surprise there. Patrick and Mark made their way over to join them, weaving around a table full of young lads without two whiskers to rub together between 'em.

"Thought we'd lost you," Si said, clapping Patrick on the back and giving Mark a good-natured prod in the chest. "Thought this young lad here had led you astray."

Mark coughed, looking a bit embarrassed.

"Give the poor bloke a break. And, oi, where's your other half?" Patrick couldn't see Alasdair anywhere.

Those two tended to stick together, maybe cos they were both non-English. Although, to be honest, Alasdair only looked the part, with his red hair, freckles, and tall, bulky frame that seemed built for tossing the caber. He'd lived way south of the border since he was a nipper, spoke just like the rest of them, and was only Scottish when it suited him, like on Burns Night when the local Caledonian Society hosted a gigantic haggis dinner and general piss-up.

Maybe his and Si's friendship was just down to their mutual love of cultivating big, bushy beards.

"Well, we're at the last pub, aren't we? No need to stay hitched up now." Si gave Mark and Patrick a too-knowing look. "Of course, if you two would rather stay like that . . ."

Mark bent down to untie the band around their ankles a bit quicker than Patrick found totally flattering. Still, it was good to have both legs under his sole control again. The left one had been aching a bit by the time they'd got all the way up here, not that he'd have said anything about it to Mark, of course.

"Right, do I give this back to Barry?" Mark asked, holding up the band as Patrick tried to rotate his ankle without anyone noticing it wasn't the one he'd had tied up.

"Give it here, and I'll put it in the bucket with the rest," Alasdair said over Patrick's shoulder, standing so close his beard tickled Patrick's ear.

Patrick turned. "You looking after the money too?"

"I've got that," Si said. "We thought Barry might not be feeling up to the responsibility right now."

Barry himself stumbled up to join them at that point, dragging Rory with him. *They* were still tied at the ankle, but Patrick would be willing to bet it was more to do with a lack of coordination to untie the knot than to any desire to stay yoked together. Well, on Barry's part, certainly. He was still on the fence about Rory. "All right, lads? Nobody too pished to get home?"

Patrick reckoned Barry was the only one in danger of that. Well, maybe Rory too, now he looked a bit closer. "Yeah, we're good. You wanna sit down for a bit? Maybe get a glass of water down you?"

"I'll get it," Mark said, nipping off to the bar.

Patrick got Barry and Rory uncoupled and then led Barry over to a chair. He hadn't rated his chances of doing it the other way around without someone ending up on their arse. "All right, mate?"

"Coursh I am. You shaying I can't take my drink?" Barry blinked up at him in halfhearted boozy belligerence.

"Perish the thought, mate. Perish the thought."

Mark returned with a pint glass of water. "Here you are. Probably best to drink it slowly." He handed it to Barry, making sure the bloke wasn't going to drop it before he let go.

"Yeah," Patrick encouraged him. "You drink that up, and we'll see about getting you home to the missus."

Barry's face softened. "She's lovely, she is. You seen my missus? She's lovely. Got great . . . great . . ." He couldn't seem to find the word, making vague hand gestures instead. Mark stepped back as the water sloshed in his direction.

"Great big tracts of land?" Patrick suggested, holding back a laugh.

"'Sright. Nosso big, though. Not 'nymore." His soppy smile turned upside down.

"Been on another diet, has she?"

"An' then shome. Dieting, running, gym . . . I just wish she'd ease off a bit," Barry slurred. "'S nuffin' left of her. 'S like bein' married to th'incredible—'scuse me—shrinking woman. Man likes a bit of something to cuddle at night, don't he?" He blinked up at them.

"Er, yes, of course," Mark said. Patrick was still reeling from the alcohol fumes from Barry's god-almighty belch.

"Can't cuddle her anymore. She's all ribs and elbows. Worried if I get on top of her, she'll snap—"

"Okay, mate, we're veering into too much information here." Patrick slapped him on the shoulder. "Come on, let's get you home."

"Y'r a good bloke. But 's all right. Rory'll see me home, won't you, mate? He's my best mate, Rory is. Never let a bloke down. Never get all skinny and make you feel like a lard-arse." Barry looked around blearily. "Where is he?"

Patrick held back a laugh. "He went home. Si and Alasdair took him in their taxi soon as you two untied the knot. Looks like it's just you and me."

"Are you going to be all right with him?" Mark asked.

Barry staggered to his feet. "Course he will be. *Course* he will be. Just cos he's a woofter don't mean I'm gonna . . . gonna . . . What you incinerating?"

Mark was frowning, so Patrick thought he'd better get Barry out of there before it escalated. "You're the one who's gonna get incinerated, mate, if we don't get you home. And it'll be the missus lighting the match. Come on. Leave Mark alone. He knows you're a perfect gentleman."

"Too bloody right. *Too* bloody right. Ask the wife. I always give her—"

"Too much info, remember?" Patrick gave Mark a nod as he steered Barry out of the pub and into the cool night air.

Not exactly how he'd hoped the evening might end.

Even if it *had* ended with him taking a bloke home.

CHAPTER ELEVEN

Mark ended up hitching a lift back down into the village centre with one of the younger Spartans, Kevin, whom he hadn't had a chance to get to know yet. Kevin's tight-lipped wife had come to pick him up in the family people-carrier complete with two tiny children strapped into kiddie seats in their pyjamas, reeking of sour milk and martyrdom. They passed Patrick and Barry on the way, Patrick with his arm around Barry's shoulders to steer him out of harm's way.

Mark told himself it was utterly ridiculous to feel a pang of jealousy.

Mrs. Kevin didn't stop to offer them a lift, which was probably wise. Mark wasn't sure a ride in a moving vehicle was quite what the doctor had ordered for Barry in his current state. He strongly suspected that if he'd had one more pint, he'd have been having a few problems himself.

Fen was in her room when he got back home. Well, unless she'd rigged up some voice-activated sound system to emit an unintelligible grunt in response to his slightly over-loud call of "I'm home, darling." He was eighty-three percent certain that wasn't the case. He'd seen her marks in technology.

Mark debated knocking on her door and insisting upon a few minutes of civilised conversation, but decided in the end that discretion was the better part of slurring his words and/or breathing beery fumes over his impressionable young child. He had a horrible feeling, in any case, that all his conversation would end up being about Patrick.

God. Patrick. He'd been . . . Mark sank heavily onto his sofa, then recollected that a cup of coffee might be advisable and heaved himself back up again. He filled the kettle, emptied out half the water again—Patrick, with his keen social conscience, probably wouldn't approve of wasting energy—and switched it on. Patrick was . . . God, what *wasn't* he? He was funny, kind, focused, energetic . . . and insanely attractive, which really wasn't helping in the current circumstances.

For some inexplicable reason, he actually seemed to like Mark too. Of course, it *could* just be casual friendliness . . . But the things he'd shared about his parents, and the things he'd encouraged Mark to share . . . and God, what about the teasing, and the tighter-than-necessary hold he'd kept of Mark.

Mark wasn't even going to *think* about that little scene in the gents'. Damn it, no, he *wasn't*. The kettle boiled and switched itself off. Mark grabbed the coffee and spooned some into the mug. Then he spooned in a bit more, added milk and hot water, and stirred. The heady aroma that swirled upwards from the mug started to cut through some of the fog in his brain, and he cradled the mug in both hands for a few minutes, just breathing in the fumes.

"Dad?"

Mark looked up. It was, of course, Fen, in her Tatty Teddy pyjamas. They were a bit too short in the arms and legs, and definitely too tight in certain areas. And still her favourite pair, for all her fondness for black, skulls, and general morbidity in her daytime wardrobe.

Mark was glad he'd made his coffee strong. Hopefully its aroma would mask all traces of alcoholic breath. "Oh, hello, darling. Not gone to bed yet?"

Expecting a withering comment about him stating the obvious, Mark was surprised when she just shook her head. "Was it all right, your charity thing?" she asked. "Did you get lots of money?"

"Oh, um . . ." Mark was embarrassed to realise just how little attention he'd given to the official purpose of his evening's outing. "It hasn't been counted yet. But people seemed to be quite generous."

She nodded.

"We're doing a fun run next," Mark went on, desperate to keep the conversation going now she actually seemed to want to talk. "In aid of a local charity for the disabled."

Fen actually looked interested. "Yeah? Can, like, anyone do it?"

"I think so. Why, would you like to?"

She nodded again. "Yeah, okay." There was a pause. "People should do more of that sort of stuff."

"Help the disabled?"

"Yeah." She paused, and then came out with "Do you want to watch something on telly?"

Mark frowned. "Is everything all right?"

"Yeah. 'S fine."

It was a bit late—in fact it was *very* late, at least for a fourteen-year-old—but Mark ended up making her a cup of hot chocolate with the tiny marshmallows she'd insisted on him adding to the weekly shopping list, and settling down on the sofa to watch *Twilight* with her.

Blood-sucking creatures of the night wouldn't have been Mark's first choice of relaxing bedtime viewing, and he had strong objections to some of the messages the film put out—any young man who tried to get into a borderline abusive relationship with *his* daughter would swiftly be given his marching orders—but it was an old favourite of Fen's.

She didn't say anything more to him, but she looked a lot happier by the time she'd reached the dregs of her by now surely stone-cold chocolate. "Night, Dad," she said, and went off to bed, leaving Mark in that annoying state of bone-tired yet wide-awake he always seemed to reach if he stayed up too long after drinking.

Somehow, though, he couldn't bring himself to regret it. He just made himself a milky cup of tea and took it to bed, where he lay reading E.M. Forster's *Maurice* (a classic, and therefore no need to hide it from Fen as "gay fiction") until the early hours so he wouldn't just brood on Patrick all night.

The next day was Sunday, a day on which Fen took it as her God-given right to sleep in until noon. This was fortunate as Mark somehow managed to remain dead to the world until gone eleven, having finally dropped off to sleep and dreamed not, as he'd expected, of Patrick, but of Fen, who wouldn't listen to reason over her firm desire to become a vampire.

For the first thirty seconds after he'd woken, her argument *"But it'll be perfect, cos, like, they wear black all the time and they never have to grow up"* still ringing in his ears, Mark wasn't sure what was real and what wasn't. He staggered out of bed in a state of some confusion, heading for the kitchen and, more importantly, caffeine.

Having downed his first cup of the life-giving elixir—coffee, that was, and not blood—Mark had just pulled his clothes on and was contemplating a second when the doorbell rang.

Expecting to see Ellen, Mark opened the door and blinked in surprise.

It was Patrick, looking bright and fresh in dark jeans and a lavender shirt that seemed entirely un-ironic and, more to the point, really suited him. Mark suddenly wished he'd worn some of his new clothes, rather than donning the tweedy shirt he'd rescued from David's pile of rejects in a faint attempt to ingratiate himself with Ellen, who'd bought it for him.

Patrick's friendly smile had turned a little uncertain while Mark stared at him, presumably gaping like a not-overly-intelligent guppy. "All right there, mate?"

"Yes! Fine. Sorry. Um." Mark reminded himself feverishly that Ellen wasn't, in fact, due for another half hour, and was almost never early. Well, not *this* early. "Would you like to come in?"

"Cheers."

Mark stood back to let Patrick enter, his heart beating faster. Which was ridiculous, because Fen was upstairs so clearly nothing was going to happen. Not that it would have even if she *hadn't* been upstairs. Obviously.

But Patrick was *here*, in his *house*, and apparently Mark's subconscious wasn't going to listen to reason. At least, he preferred to think of it as his subconscious. Rather than, say, his libido.

Oh God. He was staring again. "Coffee?" he blurted out.

There was time for a cup of coffee before Ellen came round, wasn't there? And even if there wasn't, there was no reason for her to jump to conclusions if she found Patrick here.

Except, of course, that there was *every* reason for her to jump to conclusions.

Maybe Patrick would decline?

Patrick smiled. "Thanks, coffee would be great. I just came round to drop this lot off." He raised a large, sturdy carrier bag emblazoned with the name *Waitrose* above pictures of organic vegetables and sustainably fished seafood.

Mark raised an eyebrow. "Your shopping?"

That earned him a chuckle, which absolutely did not make things any easier for his lib—his *subconscious*, damn it.

"Nah, this is for your induction on Friday. Barry asked me to bring it round, seeing as he's feeling a bit *under the weather* today, can't think why. Oh, and he's gonna look for the spear. Don't ask me how you can lose a seven-foot spear, but somehow he's managed it."

"My induction?" Apparently Mark had lost the ability to form complete sentences. He headed for the kitchen in the vague hope that performing a mundane task like boiling the kettle might prove sufficient distraction for it to return. If not, well, at least Patrick would get his promised cup of coffee.

Wait. A spear?

"Yeah . . ." Patrick ran a hand over his hair. It sprang straight back into position afterwards, like a carefully coiffed field of corn. Mark's fingers itched to run through it. "I was s'posed to talk to you about it last night, but I got a bit off track. Sorry about that."

"No problem." Mark successfully freed a couple of mugs from the mug tree without dislodging the others. It had been a wedding present from one of Ellen's colleagues. Mark had never liked the woman, and he strongly suspected the feeling to have been mutual, as she'd managed to gift them with the only tree in the world that dropped its fruit not merely at the end of summer, but at the slightest provocation. "Um. Coffee all right? Or tea?"

"Coffee's great, cheers. Milk, no sugar. Ta."

Mark stirred the drinks and handed one over, hoping his reaction wasn't too obvious when their fingers accidentally brushed. "So . . . A spear?"

"Yeah . . . See, it's just a bit of a laugh, really. And they're used to it in the Three Lions. Nobody takes that much notice anymore." Patrick sounded apologetic.

Apparently, raised suspicions worked just fine for sorting out one's sentence-forming ability. "Why do I get the feeling I'm not going to like what's in that bag?"

"Well . . . it's a tradition. You join the Spartans, you get to dress up as a, well, a Spartan."

"As a Spartan. You mean, like the film? In sandals, a leather nappy, and nothing else?" Mark was aware his voice was rising to hysteria pitch and took a gulp of coffee to calm himself.

It could possibly be said to have worked, in that the burning sensation down his oesophagus was definitely distracting him from less immediate woes.

"It's not a nappy," Patrick said reassuringly. "More of a skirt."

"That's supposed to be an *improvement*?"

"And you get a cloak to cover up with as well. And a helmet."

Mark was torn. Half of him was lusting over the mental image of Patrick dressed up—or rather down—in that outfit, and sincerely regretting that he'd never got to see it in the flesh. The other, rather larger half of him was having a panic attack over the image of *himself* in that outfit. "Is this . . . compulsory?"

"Well, no one's gonna force you, but some of the lads might feel you're letting the side down if you don't. We've all done it. Even Barry, and you do *not* wanna see the photos of that."

The panic attack threatened to become full-on hysterics. "There'll be photos?" Mark squawked. He cleared his throat.

"Yeah, but seriously, you got nothing to worry about. You'll look well fit." Patrick hesitated, then stepped a bit closer. His tone dropped, becoming lower and huskier. "Been looking forward to seeing a bit more of you, personally."

Oh God. This was killing him. It was akin to one of those cautionary tales of the supernatural, where the protagonist got the devil to grant his wish—but only in a way that was utterly useless to him. There was no mistaking it: Patrick, for reasons both unknown and inexplicable, wanted him.

And Mark was going to have to turn him down. Even if it killed him. He gulped as Patrick took another step. They were almost touching now, and with his back against the kitchen counter, there was nowhere for Mark to go.

A large part of him—growing larger by the minute—didn't want to go anywhere. But damn it, Fen was more important. And, God, Ellen could be here at any moment. "We can't," he said weakly, his voice matching Patrick's for huskiness and tending to give the lie to his words.

"Why not?"

"Fen. She's upstairs."

"And?"

"She doesn't know I'm, well, gay." Mark winced at Patrick's frown.

"Seriously? I mean, I know you said you weren't out to anyone, but she's your daughter. What did you tell her about you and her mum splitting up, for God's sake?"

"Just that we'd grown apart. She's a child. She shouldn't have to know about . . . that sort of thing."

Patrick's eyebrows were fast approaching his hairline. "She's a teenager, not a toddler. You do know they start learning about sex in primary school, right?"

"Yes, but that's . . . abstract. Clinical."

Patrick gave a scornful laugh. "You reckon? So where were you when they had a meeting for parents and showed that video of a cartoon woman chasing her bloke around the bedroom with a feather?"

"At work, probably— Wait, *what*? A *feather*? What the hell are they teaching kids these days? And how do you know all this, anyway?" Mark frowned. Even allowing for the age difference, Patrick surely couldn't have been in primary school *that* recently.

"Lads at the Spartans. Barry couldn't stop going on about it for weeks, when his eldest was in year six."

Mark shuddered. Sex education in his day hadn't happened until he was fourteen. It'd largely consisted of tracing a diagram of the reproductive organs of a rabbit, followed by their biology teacher handing around a photocopied sheet comparing the effectiveness of methods of contraception, with a shame-faced mutter of *"For your own use."*

"You've got to tell her," Patrick was saying. "How's she going to feel if she finds out and you haven't told her anything about it?"

"She's not going to find out. That's what I'm trying to tell you." Mark took a deep breath. "There's not going to be anything to find out. That's why we can't do this."

Patrick's expression, which had been friendly, if argumentative, hardened. "What? Bollocks. You're going to let some old-fashioned ideas about girls having to be kept innocent run your whole life? This isn't the bloody Dark Ages."

Mark's blood boiled. Just who did Patrick think he was to be telling him how to raise his daughter? "*If* you had children of your own—"

"Then I bloody well hope I wouldn't try and keep them wrapped in cotton wool. You can't keep the whole world away from her. What's going to happen when she leaves home and finds life *isn't* a sodding picture book? You think she'll thank you for that?"

"For God's sake, keep your voice down!" Mark snapped. "The foundation for a happy adulthood is a secure childhood. There's plenty of time for her to learn about the bad things in life—"

"You mean, like her dad wanting to shag blokes? Ever think maybe you might have one or two issues about being gay?" Patrick might have lowered his tone, but he was right up in Mark's face now.

"Oh, for—" Mark threw up his hands. "It's all right for you, isn't it? When were you born? 1990? 1991? Section 28, 'Glad to Be Gay,' it's all ancient history to you, isn't it? You've never even *known* a time when you had to worry about your boyfriend getting arrested because you were under twenty-one—"

"Bollocks. 'Glad to Be Gay'? You must have still been in nappies when that song came out. You're thirty-nine, not ninety-nine. And how many boyfriends did you have before you were twenty-one anyway? Let me guess. A big, fat zero." Patrick slammed his coffee mug down on the kitchen counter. The contents sloshed over the edge and left a muddy stain on the white countertop. "Right. Well, you won't want me hanging around here. Might corrupt your daughter, having a bloke like me in the house. And people might talk, and you wouldn't want that, would you? I'll see you around."

He stormed out, which was just as well. Any more of that and Mark might have been tempted to throw him bodily out of the house. Where the hell did he get off, speaking to Mark like that? In his own home, for Christ's sake? Patrick quite clearly didn't have a bloody *clue* what the world was like, growing up in his gay-friendly bubble.

Mark was still fuming when the doorbell rang once more. Patrick? Already regretting his words? And so he bloody well should. Trying to ignore the jolt of hope that shot through him—because he'd be damned if he was going to forgive and forget *that* easily—Mark ran to open the door.

It was Ellen, her pale eyes narrowed above a nose that seemed a lot more sharply pointed than Mark remembered. "Who was that?" she demanded in lieu of a greeting. "I saw someone leaving when I was parking the car. Who was it?"

Mark swallowed, disappointment settling on his shoulders like a shroud. "No one. A friend. That's all. Just a friend."

CHAPTER TWELVE

Patrick wanted to punch something as he marched out of Mark's house and out of his fucking life. He'd felt on top of the world, going round to see the bloke. That was *why* he'd gone round there— he hadn't *had* to volunteer to take that kit round after popping in on Barry to check he hadn't died of alcohol poisoning. He'd thought him and Mark could have something. Especially after last night.

See, this, *this* was why he looked before he fucking leaped when it came to blokes. In case it turned out they were closet cases with attitudes so bloody medieval the Knights of the sodding Round Table would've thought they were a bit quaint and old-fashioned. What the hell was Mark's problem?

Didn't he realise how it sounded, him lumping in nonstraight people with all the bad crap he wanted to keep away from his daughter until she was thirty or something? Patrick jammed his hands in his jacket pockets as he passed the church and went to cross the road, squinting a bit in the bright spring sunshine. It was almost blinding, reflected off the yellow daffodils that sprouted in the village like little baby suns, anywhere and everywhere there was room to bung a bulb. The sky was the sort of blue you saw on postcards from Ibiza, and the breeze was mild with the promise of summer, just a whiff of winter left in to freshen it up.

Even the weather was sodding mocking him. Patrick's anger burned brighter than the daffs for a mo, then fizzled out in a puff of self-knowledge. *Get over yourself, Owen.* He was acting like a kid who'd been promised sweeties and had 'em snatched away at the last minute—and cheers, Dad, for that little memory.

Christ, though. Of all the reasons to be turned down . . . Mark had to see he was wrong, didn't he? Patrick might not know Fen well, but there was no teenager on earth who liked their parents treating them like a little kid. Or lying to them, for that matter.

Patrick was glad he'd walked down to Mark's. The walk back up The Hill was clearing his head. It still pissed him off, but yeah, he was prepared to admit there might be a bit of bruised ego going on there. If he was brutally honest, he'd probably had less than his fair share of rejection in the past. He scrubbed up all right and made an effort with his appearance, and blokes seemed to appreciate it. Girls too.

Course, that'd been when he'd still been going clubbing. He couldn't be arsed with it much these days—what was the point of making all the effort to pull someone for a night when you already knew they wouldn't want you around next morning? Might as well just save time and go on Grindr. Yeah, there was plenty of rejection to be had there, if someone else came along who was better looking, better hung, or whatever, but it didn't mean anything apart from, Christ, some of these blokes were shallow.

Mark turning him down, though . . . That hurt. And it was just so bloody stupid, because Mark *liked* him. Patrick knew he did. He just didn't think Patrick was worth the bother of getting over his stupid issues.

It couldn't have been *that* different when he was growing up. Could it?

Reaching home, Patrick opened the door and kicked off his shoes on the mat. Mum was upstairs—he could hear her singing along to the CD player. Ironing, then. She'd tried doing it in front of the telly but had kept scorching the clothes every time *EastEnders* got really gripping, so she just played music these days. He stood at the foot of the stairs listening for a mo, trying to work out what she was listening to. It wasn't easy. Mum's voice was way louder than the music, but she only hit about one note in three, and the words weren't always in the right order either.

Patrick gave up with a smile. He liked hearing Mum sing. She'd never really done it when he'd been little. He padded into the kitchen and put the kettle on.

By the time it was about to boil, Mum had come downstairs.

"Cup of tea?" Patrick asked her, already getting out the mugs.

"Ooh, cheers, love. Could murder one."

He stirred in milk and handed over one of the mugs, then leaned back against the counter, cradling his own mug in his hands. "Mum, you busy?"

"Nothing I wouldn't rather put off anyhow. What is it, love?" She gave him a piercing look over the rim of her mug.

Patrick sighed. "When you were growing up, what was it like for gay kids?"

"Oh Lord. If it's that kind of thing, I want to sit down. I've been on my feet all morning with that ironing."

Patrick wasn't moved by her look of martyrdom. "Mum, I did most of it before I went out. There were about three of your tops left and a couple of hankies."

"So? Those tops can be fiddly." She led the way through to the living room and sank down on the sofa with an *oof*.

Patrick sat down on the other end and stretched out his legs, trying to make himself relax. "Yeah, right. So anyway—gay kids when you were a teenager?"

Mum wrinkled her nose. "Didn't really know any. Least, I didn't *know* I knew them. No one was out back then. Not in Brentwood, anyway. Even George Michael wasn't out back then. I used to really fancy him too. Had his poster up on my bedroom wall." Her eyes turned scarily dreamy.

"Mum, focus?"

"Well, what do you want to know?"

"Just—look, say you were a lesbian, all right? Back then I mean. What do you reckon it'd have been like?"

"Well, I dunno, do I?" Mum pursed her lips. "I'd have got more O Levels, maybe? Wouldn't have spent all my time mooning around after boys."

"Yeah, but Mum, you'd have been mooning around after girls."

"God, I hope not. They were a right load of tarts at my school. Why d'you think I haven't kept in touch?" She looked at Patrick and sighed. "Look, it just wasn't talked about then. Not like it is these days. I mean, it wasn't like it is now, with gay people on the telly and that. Well, all right, they *were*, but it was only camp comedians and that sort of thing. And nobody talked about them actually *being* gay. Not to kids, anyway."

"Yeah, but there were films and stuff, weren't there? Hang on." Patrick got up and rummaged through their DVD collection, which had got too big for the shelf unit and spilled over into a pile on the floor. "Here you go. *My Beautiful Laundrette*, 1985. You were still at school then, weren't you?"

"Well, yeah, but that was a film. It wasn't real life. Not like *EastEnders* or something. You've got to remember, love, in those days it was two steps forward and one step back. I mean, Section 28 must have been around that time. You know—that law where schools weren't allowed to say being gay was all right."

"Yeah. I know." Patrick stared at the cover of the DVD in his hands. Gordon Warnecke and Daniel Day-Lewis with a bad bleach job stared back at him, the Asian guy defiant but the white guy with a sardonic twist to his mouth. Patrick hadn't watched the film in years, but now it was coming back to him. Thatcher's Britain, AIDS hysteria, everyone out to make as much money as they could and sod everybody else. The fashions and the attitudes. It'd seemed like a history lesson when Mum had sat him down to watch it.

But Mark . . . Christ, Mark had lived through this.

Shit. Age wasn't just a number, was it?

Mum's voice broke into his thoughts. "Am I not supposed to guess this is about your mature bloke?"

Patrick looked round at her, startled. "No?"

"Dream on, love. I may be old, but I'm not daft. So are you seeing him?"

"Turned me down, didn't he?" Patrick stared at the telly. It'd have been a lot more interesting if they'd switched it on.

"Turned you down? Turned you *down*? Who the bloody hell does he think he is, then? God's gift to gay men?"

"Nah. He's not out. Doesn't wanna be. Not even sure he wants to be gay, for that matter."

"That's just . . . *Oh*."

Patrick looked round. "Oh, what?"

Mum's eyes had gone wide, and she was looking serious. "Do you reckon he had something bad happen to him when he was young? Is that what this is all about?"

Okay, that hit with an unpleasant jolt to the chest. Patrick hadn't even thought of that. Christ, how bloody oblivious could he be? People still got gay-bashed these days—how much worse must it have been back when pretty much everyone seemed to have been on the side of the gay-bashers?

"Love?" Mum sounded concerned. How long had he been silent?

"Uh, yeah. Sorry. Nah, it was just some stuff he said." Christ, now he was feeling guilty for getting so pissed off at Mark. "You know. About things being different when he was young."

"Well, that's it, innit?" Mum took a slurp of tea. "That's why these age gap things don't always work out. It's nothing to do with 'em getting all wrinkled and saggy—"

"Cheers for the image, Mum."

"—it's more about having different outlooks on stuff. If you love 'em, you don't care about the looks, but it's a bit harder if you can't see eye to eye on things."

"Yeah, but fourteen years . . . Can it really make that much of a difference?"

Mum shrugged. "'S up to you, innit? You and him. You've just got to work it out between you."

Patrick still hadn't worked out what to do about Mark come Monday morning. He'd thought about talking to someone else about it, Heather maybe, but honestly, what did she know? Her bloke, Chris, was the same age she was and not exactly the most grown-up bloke on the planet.

It made it hard to concentrate on work. Not that the correspondence was exactly riveting. Most people seemed to think organising a fun run was just a matter of putting up a poster and getting people to sign up for it, but in fact there were a shed-load of rules and regulations to deal with. Course, he'd dealt with most of the big stuff already—like walking out the route, getting permission from landowners and the council, organising first-aiders, doing a risk analysis and sorting out insurance—but there was still a fair bit to do. Like getting the sponsors to actually hand over the money they'd promised, hiring a bouncy slide for the kiddies, and organising delivery of donated drinks. Plus the walkie-talkies had gone walkies since last time, which meant nearly a dozen phone calls until he tracked down who'd borrowed them and forgotten to return them.

Patrick said his good-byes to a very apologetic vicar, put the phone down, and sat back, rolling his shoulders. Christ, it'd got late. No wonder his stomach was rumbling. He turned to Lex, who was knee-deep in the finishers' medals they'd be handing out to the kiddies.

"Sod it. Fancy lunch at the caff? I'm paying."

Lex looked doubtful. "I brung a salad."

"So? You can leave it in the fridge for tomorrow's lunch."

"Nah, won't keep till tomorrow. 'S organic. That stuff goes off if you look at it funny. But I s'pose I could take it home and have it for my tea. Just for you."

Patrick grinned. "And here was me thinking I was doing you a favour. Come on, then, before all the tables fill up." They grabbed their jackets and headed out, Patrick making sure to lock the door behind them cos some shites would rob anyone. The village shops all had to have their charity boxes on chains now, which pissed him off something chronic.

It was only a short walk to the café. Patrick was just about to follow Lex inside when Mark came round the corner.

And it was just daft, cos if he'd only kept going, he'd have been fine, safe in the café and reading the menu before Mark even noticed he'd been there, but Patrick just had to stop dead on the doorstep and stare long enough for Mark to look up, didn't he?

It was well awkward. Patrick nodded to him.

Mark nodded back. His smile flickered but ultimately failed to launch. Facial expressions aside, he was looking good. Way too good for Patrick's peace of mind. Christ, he wished the pain in his chest would go away. Or, at least, this weird paralysis would lift and he'd be able to get out of here.

Mark opened his mouth, closed it again, and looked at his shoes.

Then, thank God, someone came out of the café, pushed past Patrick, and broke the spell. Feeling like an idiot, Patrick stomped inside where Lex was waiting, eyes wide.

"That your bloke?"

"No, and he's not likely to be." Patrick tried to keep it light, keep the hurt out of his voice. Maybe he overdid it. "But yeah, that was Mark Nugent."

He pulled out a chair from the nearest empty table—make that the only empty table; good job he hadn't pratted around on the doorstep any longer, or they'd have been out of luck—and they both sat down.

Lex grabbed the menu from between the ketchup bottle and the brown sauce, and frowned. "But he looks all right. I thought he'd be older. Looks sad, though. Oi, what happened? He try it on and you turned him down?"

"No. Try the other way around." Patrick made grabby hands at the menu. "Come on, hand that over. You know you always get the same thing."

"So? I like to check if they've changed anything." Lex gave the clearly not brand-new card a glance and passed it over. "What, *he* turned *you* down? You sure you heard him right? Is he straight? Or, like, ace or something?"

"Nah, just . . ." Patrick ran his hand over his hair. "Closeted. Doesn't want his daughter to know he's queer."

"That's shitty."

The waitress came over to take their order at that point, so Patrick had to bite his tongue on his angry gut reaction. He snapped out an order for a chicken wrap and a cup of tea and waited impatiently while Lex faffed around over drinks, thrown by them having run out of ginger beer.

"Mark's just trying to give his daughter a stable home," he said firmly when they'd finally been left in peace. "She's been going through a rough patch, getting into trouble. He doesn't wanna risk her going off the rails again if she takes it wrong. And it's not so easy for older blokes, all right?"

Lex leaned back. "Sor-*ry*. Jeez."

Patrick grimaced. "Sorry. Didn't mean to go on at you. Just . . . Ah, I dunno. S'pose I'm feeling guilty for going off on him about it. Been thinking about it, and I s'pose I see his point. He lived through some rough times for gay people. Well, tougher than now, anyhow. You know, back in the eighties."

"Yeah, but he's not living in them now." Lex's face was a lot harder than Patrick would've expected if their tone hadn't clued him in.

"Meaning?" he asked neutrally.

"Meaning yeah, he's gay, but he's also a cis white male, and I bet he's got good health and plenty of money. Just feels a bit first-world problem to me, all this bloody angsting over whether his daughter's gonna get the sulks if he tells her he's gay."

Patrick could see Lex's point. He'd met Lex's dad, one time Lex had been trying to drag the bloke home from the pub before he passed out, and within five bloody minutes, the bastard had made some stupid crack about having "three kids—one of each" with Lex standing *right there.*

"Look, I get what you're saying. Just . . . everyone's different, you know? It might not seem like a big deal to you, but it does to him, all right?" He gave a rueful smile. "Thought you liked him, anyway?"

"Yeah, I *did.* Gone off him a bit now I know he's a whiner." Lex smiled back, which took the sting out of it.

"He's not a whiner," Patrick protested.

"Is."

"Isn't."

"Is."

"Is—" Patrick broke off as their food arrived. "Uh, cheers."

The waitress, who, fair dues, was old enough to be Patrick's mum and had probably seen it all before, smirked. "We've got some colouring sheets and crayons if you'd like 'em. Just saying." She swished away.

Lex cracked up.

A bit hot under the collar, Patrick gave Lex a stern look. "Do you want me to walk out and leave you with the bill?"

"You'd never. Not in, like, a zillion trillion years."

"Oh, yeah? Try me."

"Go on, then. Walk out. See if I care." Lex sat back in their chair and made shooing gestures. "Go on. Bye. See ya."

Patrick had to laugh. "God, I hate you sometimes."

"Nah, you don't. You *lurve* me. You wanna *marry* me."

"What, and have your hairy biker bloke coming after me with a monkey wrench? How's that going, anyway?"

"'S good," Lex said around a mouthful of bean burger.

"Yeah? You met his mates yet?"

"Nah. He says he wants to keep me all for himself."

Lex grinned, but Patrick wasn't bloody smiling. It sounded well dodgy to him. "So when do I get to meet him?"

"Dunno. Not sure what we're doing next weekend."

"What, does his mum not let him out on a school night?"

"Nah, he's on call out this week, so if I see him, I'll be going round to his." Lex put down the bean burger, exactly half eaten, and started on the chips. "You want some of these?"

"Go on, then," Patrick said, and scooped around half of them off the proffered plate, then dumped a shed-load of ketchup on top.

"You know that stuff's, like, three hundred percent sugar?"

"Yep, and that's why it tastes so nice. So what's he do for a living, your bloke?"

"Locksmith. He's teaching me how to crack a safe. It's way harder than it looks on the telly."

Patrick laughed. "I guess that could be a useful life skill. So he does emergency stuff, does he? Better get me one of his cards for the next time Mum breaks her key in the lock."

Lex gave him a sly look. "Or the next time you lock up the office and lose the keys."

"Hey, that was one time, all right? And I found 'em again, didn't I?"

"Eventually."

"I get no respect. None at all."

CHAPTER THIRTEEN

E llen's visit on Sunday had turned out both better and worse than Mark had feared. She quite clearly hadn't believed him about Patrick being just a friend—all the more painful when he was quietly panicking that they wouldn't even be that anymore.

"We agreed you weren't going to *do* this," she ground out sotto voce. She'd had her light-brown hair cropped even shorter since the last time he'd seen her, and the spikiness of it certainly added to the impression of tightly wound anger. She looked like a hedgehog that had just got home from a hard day's rooting for slugs to find its favourite hedge had been replaced with a barbed wire fence. "Florence needs stability, not even more upheaval."

"This? There is no *this*," Mark hissed in reply, his eyes on the stairs in case Fen had heard her mother arrive and was even now hurtling down to have her ears sullied by her parents arguing. Again. "Patrick is a *friend*. From a charity organisation."

"And in any case, he's *far* too young for you. Almost as bad as that PA who was slobbering all over you at the last Christmas party. You're making yourself look ridiculous, chasing after boys young enough to be your son."

"Chasing after? *Chasing after*? There has been *no* chasing on my part. And what do you mean, young enough to be my son? I'm thirty-nine, not fifty-nine. There are only fourteen years between me and Patrick."

"Oh? Remind me, just *how* old is your daughter?"

"That's . . . that's completely irrelevant, mathematically speaking. You know that."

"All *I* know is for someone who's supposed to be providing a stable home environment for our daughter, there seem to be an awful lot of young men sniffing around—"

"Mum?"

They both turned—damn it, when had Mark stopped watching the stairs? Fen was standing on the bottom step, looking strangely young.

Oh God, had she heard?

"Darling!" Ellen's face softened, and she ran to her daughter, wrapping her arms around her in a, from Fen's expression and muttered "*Muuu*-uuum," not entirely welcome hug.

Mark's alarm grew as Ellen sniffed for real this time. "It's been so quiet without you in the house," she said. "Is everything all right? Are you getting on okay at school?"

"I told you on the phone. Everything's fine. Are we going out? Like, for lunch?" Fen darted a defiant glance over at Mark.

What the hell had *he* done?

"What would *you* like to do, darling?"

"There's this pizza place in Bishops Langley."

Mark managed not to roll his eyes. She meant the one Mark had refused to take her to on the grounds that it was ludicrously overpriced and perfectly decent pizzas could be bought at any supermarket.

"We'll go there, then." Ellen darted an almost identical glance at Mark. "Do you want your father to come? Or would you like it to be just us girls?"

Fen looked at him. "You can come if you *want*."

Mark knew how to take a hint. "Thanks, but I'm sure your mum would like you to herself for a bit. I've got things I need to be doing anyway."

Ellen muttered something that sounded a lot like "So what's new?"

"You can—" Fen glanced at Ellen this time, and stopped mid-sentence.

Ellen and Mark turned enquiring looks at their daughter. It was, Mark reflected, probably the first time in years they'd acted as one.

"Nothing," Fen muttered. "I'll go get changed."

She scampered upstairs, leaving Mark once more facing Ellen's unfair suspicion. "What was she about to say?"

"How should I know?" Mark protested. "I'm not a mind reader. Why don't you ask her?"

"Because I'd be wasting my breath, and you know it." Ellen sighed. "*Is* she all right? She's not been getting into bad company again, has she?"

"As far as I know, she hasn't been getting into *any* company. Ells, she's only been at her new school a couple of days. She hasn't had a chance to make friends, good or bad. And I know she needs to make friends," he added hastily. "I'm keeping an eye on it."

Ellen didn't look happy. "Are you sure this is really—Florence Esther Nugent, just *what* do you think you're wearing?"

Fen stood on the bottom stair dressed in fifty shades of black, her eyes so heavily kohled, her face was a mirror of the death's-head on her T-shirt. "Dad bought me this," she said smugly.

Ellen's lips had all but disappeared. "*Did* he now?"

Oh, what the hell. "Ells," Mark said sweetly. "I know it's hard, but I'm afraid you've got to accept it. Our little girl's growing up."

Mark paid for his moment of smugness when Fen and Ellen returned. He had to endure a stern lecture on age-appropriate clothing, most of which he actually agreed with, but couldn't admit to doing so without relinquishing his self-imposed position as devil's advocate. *Then* he had to turn comforter when Ellen's anger, always a brittle thing, inevitably shattered into tears.

All in all, it wasn't the most relaxing Sunday he'd ever spent.

The week that followed did little to reduce his blood pressure. True, Fen's new school somehow managed to stay open the full five days, and if Fen broke any more school rules, her infractions weren't of sufficient gravity to warrant informing Mark and/or sending her home.

Seeing Patrick by chance on Monday had shaken him, though. Patrick had looked so . . . vulnerable, standing there alone on the doorstep of the café.

It had been a lot easier to stick to his resolve when confronted with angry words. Mark wasn't at all equipped to deal with hurt looks.

And he'd be seeing him again on Friday. April first. Mark's apprehension over his coming induction into the Spartans was not lessened by the realisation it was to take place on April Fool's Day. By determined internet searching, he managed to track down some photos of previous Spartans being inducted—Patrick had been quite right; those photographs of Barry, bare-chested and hairy-shinned in a leather kilt, should have been censored for the sake of humanity— so it *probably* wasn't some horrible practical joke they were playing on him.

He tried on the outfit, after making sure the blinds were closed and Fen was safely at school. He looked *ridiculous*. The only saving grace was the cloak, which was long and voluminous, and turned out on closer inspection to have started out life as somebody's living-room curtains. The skirt—kilt—whatever—barely reached mid-thigh on his long frame, leaving a horrifying expanse of winter-pale, hirsute legs underneath. And the less said about what was visible above the belt, the better. The same internet search had turned up a multitude of images from the *300* film, all of which showed the firm, bronzed bodies of actors who appeared to think if you only had a six-pack, you weren't trying hard enough.

Coincidentally, he finally got around to making some efforts to improve his fitness during the week—he went running three times and did sit-ups and crunches every morning. They didn't make him look noticeably more like the actors in *300*, with their improbably sculpted bodies and impossibly defined abdominals, but at least he wasn't getting any worse. Probably.

And the exercise took his mind off Patrick. Well, some of the time it did. *Some* of the time, the mindless one-foot-in-front-of-the-other slogging through the village, across the fields, and down by the river just gave him more time to brood on the object of his hopeless affections. The second time he went out, he passed a couple of young men running together who caused his thoughts to drift in a wistful direction—they looked so happy together, the redheaded, more solidly built one turning to laugh at something his slender, dark-haired companion had said. Of course, they wouldn't actually *be* a couple— they were undoubtedly just friends. But for a moment, Mark's heart ached for that sort of easy companionship.

He'd had it in his grasp, too—before he'd thrown it all away. Was Patrick right? Would Fen really take the news of him having a boyfriend with equanimity? She seemed to like David well enough. Perhaps she'd cope perfectly well with her father being gay.

Could he take the chance she wouldn't? And in any case, would Patrick still want him after all that had passed between them?

At least Fen was starting to develop some healthy outside interests. She'd decided, entirely of her own volition, to go along to a children's and young people's theatre group that met in the village hall at four o'clock every Wednesday. Mark was rather proud of his strategy for encouraging her to go, which had consisted of mentioning it once and once only, and then just leaving the flyer he'd picked up in the chemist's shop lying around next to the biscuit tin.

He'd read an online article recently that bemoaned the "poshness" of acting as a profession—apparently there was barely a young actor in the country who could convincingly portray a working-class man. So it ought to be safe enough for Fen, from the point of view of not falling into bad company again. And she'd loved acting when she'd been tiny. Mark hadn't been able to take the time off work to go to see her school plays, of course—at least, it hadn't seemed possible at the time, although he was hard-pressed now to recall exactly what had been so urgent—but he'd seen videos. This time, he told himself, he'd be there in person, applauding the loudest.

Assuming she stuck it out for more than one session, of course.

There wasn't a lot of leeway between Fen getting home on the bus from school and it being time to leave for the drama class, so Mark greeted her arrival Wednesday afternoon with, "Right, still up for drama? If you're getting changed you'll have to be quick."

"Well, *duh*. I'm not going like *this*," she muttered, dumping her bag in the middle of the hall. Mark sighed and moved it somewhere less hazardous as she stomped up to her room.

He counted it as a win that he'd only looked at his watch three times before she came back down, in black leggings, black skirt, and a black jumper. While not necessarily approving of such a funereal ensemble—hadn't she been the one to tell him to wear brighter colours? Why didn't the same hold true for her?—Mark would have had to admit it suited her a lot better than maroon. "Ready? Let's go, then."

"Why are you coming?"

"To take you there?"

"I don't need you to hold my hand, Dad. I'm old enough to go walking through the village on my own. It's not even *dark*."

"Humour me," he said firmly. "Won't it be nicer to walk there together?"

"S'pose they might ask for some money," she said grudgingly, which was all the agreement Mark was likely to get.

"Did you have a good day at school?" he asked, as they left the house.

"'S all right."

"Made any friends?"

"*Daaa*-aaad."

"What?"

"You can't just ask that stuff."

He couldn't? "Why not?"

"Cos it's *private*, all right? Have you sorted anything with David?"

"Oh—yes, actually. He emailed me today about going to see *Wicked*. Interested?"

"Well, *duh*."

Mark tsked audibly. "*I think you meant,* 'Yes, please, so kind of you to offer to pay extortionate sums for theatre and train tickets, you're a wonderful father, how can I ever repay you?'"

"Whatever. So we're going? Dad, we're going, aren't we?" She looked so much prettier when she smiled. Prettier, and younger too.

Mark smiled back. "Yes, we're going. I'll ask him to get tickets for half-term."

"And we can meet him early, and have a meal out in London, yeah? It's gonna be *sick*. But we're seeing David again before that, aren't we?"

"Are we?"

"Well, yeah. Or . . . or he'll think you don't like him except for theatre trips."

Mark bowed to the inevitable. "I'll give him a ring while you're at the group, how about that?"

"Tell him to come over this weekend."

"Darling, he might actually have a life, you know."

"He doesn't have to come for the whole weekend. He could just come one night for tea, couldn't he? Dad, let's get pizza. I haven't had pizza for *ages*."

It had been three days, as Mark recalled. "We'll see, all right? He might have plans."

They'd reached the village hall by now, a surprisingly spacious building which, on closer inspection, proved to encompass a small library as well as the main hall. Large notice boards were emblazoned with posters exhorting villagers to make use of various local support groups set up for those affected by diabetes, Down's syndrome, and dementia, to name but a few. There was also a poster advertising the Thursday food bank, which caught Mark up short.

Somehow he hadn't expected evidence of actual need in such a pretty, outwardly affluent village.

"It's in here, Dad," Fen huffed impatiently. "Are you coming or what?"

"Just looking at the notices. You know, we should join the library—"

"*Daaa*-aaad." Fen tutted.

Mark took that to be shorthand for *You're so old and boring, why aren't you dead yet?* He suppressed a sigh and followed her into the main hall.

Once inside, they were greeted by a . . . person. Mark blinked. He? She? They were definitely young, with pale skin and dark hair, and a face so multiply pierced it probably constituted a serious risk in a thunderstorm.

Mark was struck by a vague sense of familiarity, but was fairly sure they hadn't actually met. He must have seen . . . them . . . around the village at some point, that was all.

The person smiled at Fen. Mark could swear the piercings jangled. Or possibly it was just their frankly alarming boots, which, with all the buckles, studs, and chains adorning them, appeared to be made out of more metal than leather. Mark caught Fen eyeing the boots and hoped she wasn't picking up fashion tips.

"'Ullo, you new here? Come on in and meet Hev." The voice, with its rough edges yet light tone, gave no clue to the speaker's gender.

What with the grungy, shapeless clothing, Mark was still wondering when they were handed off to the promised Hev, who'd been over by the rather impressive stage talking to a group of around a dozen children who appeared to be aged from around ten upwards. Beginning to think he and the online article must have got theatre people drastically wrong, Mark was almost relieved to find Hev was the pretty—and relatively conservatively clad—mixed-race girl who'd been at the Three Lions the night Mark had met Patrick. *Almost*, because the memory was accompanied by a stab of regret which he ruthlessly quashed. "Oh, hello. Are you the group leader?"

"Yeah. Heather Matthews." She held out a slender arm, and he discovered she had a firm handshake. "I work for Masons, who sponsor the group. And this is?"

"Fen," Fen said quickly, presumably worried he might introduce her as Florence.

"My daughter," Mark clarified. "Is it all right for her to join partway through the year? We've recently moved into the village."

Heather turned her sharp gaze on Fen. "As long as you're okay with only getting a small role in the end-of-year production, yeah? We started working on it back in January, so it's all cast already, but there's always room for more in the chorus. And it'll be a good way to ease you into the group, see if you like the way we do things here, yeah?"

Fen nodded.

"Right." Heather turned back to Mark and went on briskly. "We just need full name and emergency contact details, then it's twenty quid for the term."

"Really?" Mark blurted out. Then he realised it could be taken in two ways. "I mean, that seems very cheap."

Heather smiled. "We get a grant as well as the sponsorship, so yeah, really. And we're all volunteers, so it's just the hall hire that needs paying for." She glanced at the clock, now showing five past four.

Mark took the hint and paid up quickly after scribbling down his mobile number on the photocopied form she'd handed him.

"You can go now," Fen said firmly. "I'll see you later."

Mark cast a final eye around the hall. Group numbers had swelled to around a couple of dozen, most of them girls but with a few boys who were punching above their weight in the volume department.

With their hoodies from Marks & Spencer and their sensible plimsolls—Mark hoped Fen's Doc Martens would be forgiven for one week—they all seemed reassuringly middle class.

"Don't worry," the person with the piercings said from behind him, leading Mark to jump a little and wonder how on earth stealth was managed while carrying around so much metal. "She'll be fine. They're good kids here. We 'ad a couple of louts last year, but Hev don't stand for no nonsense, so they din't stay more'n a couple of weeks."

"Um, thanks," Mark said. Telling himself firmly he was doing the right thing, he left.

When he got home, there was a seven-foot spear propped up on the doorstep. It had a Post-it note stuck to the blade that simply said, *See you Friday*.

Oh God. The induction was really going to happen.

Two hours later, Mark was halfway back to the hall to meet his daughter when a text pinged through on his phone.

It was Fen: Dont pick me up. Goin to cafe w Lex.

Lex? Short for Alexia, presumably. Or perhaps Alexandra. There had been a few girls of similar age to Fen at the group, and it was good she'd made a friend. Even though it would have been rather more considerate to tell him of the change of plan *before* he'd set off to meet her. Still, perhaps she hadn't had the chance, or had only just received the invitation from the mysterious Lex. Mark wondered if it was someone who went to her school.

Will you be back for tea? he texted back.

NO IM GOIN TO CAFE. Mark swore he could hear a silent *DUH* at the end of that text message.

Be back by seven, he sent, and wondered if he was being too lenient.

There was no reply. Mark waited five minutes, then re-sent the text.

Ten minutes later, his phone pinged back at him: *K.*

That, he supposed, would have to do, although he'd have preferred a wordier answer. And since when had *K* become a thing, anyway? It made Mark's fingers itch to add a prosthetic *O*.

He sighed. The phone call to David regarding the planned theatre trip had turned into an exchange of woes—David complaining loudly of how unreasonable Charles was being, and how the office just wasn't the same without Mark, and Mark bemoaning his lack of connection with his daughter. Which was fine, really; in fact, Mark felt significantly better having vented somewhat and hoped David did too.

The trouble was, Mark had somehow managed to slip in a bit of venting about his upcoming induction to the Spartans, or rather the ridiculous costume they'd be forcing him to wear. At which point David had been all over that like glitter on a pride parade, and insisted on coming round Friday night *to help Mark with his makeup*.

Which meant that not only did Mark have to face the prospect of humiliating himself in front of everyone in his new life, but given David's talent for spreading gossip, everyone in his *old* life was bound to hear about it by Saturday as well. And would probably have seen the pictures to boot.

Mark decided to do a few more sit-ups while he thought about it.

CHAPTER FOURTEEN

"Oi, you're never gonna guess who I was talking to last night," Lex said on getting into the office Thursday morning.

Patrick looked up from his paperwork. "Simon Cowell. He wants to turn you into the next Britney Spears."

Lex stuck a finger up and swivelled it gently. "Nope. Your bloke's daughter. She went along to theatre group last night, and we got talking." Lex hopped onto Patrick's desk and sat there, New Rock boots swinging. Not the sort of thing Patrick would be caught dead in, but they looked wicked cool on Lex. "And you're not gonna believe what we was talking about."

"Go on then, try me."

"Well, see, Fen—she's really sweet, ain't she?—she's not s'posed to know her dad's queer, right? 'Cept she was telling me all about how there's this bloke he likes. This *younger* bloke he likes." Patrick tried not to let the jolt that had just run through him show as Lex paused to give him a significant look. "And she dun't know whether to tell him she knows, that's her dad I mean, cos *she* reckons *he's* trying to keep it all a big secret, cos he thinks she's like five years old or something."

"You talked about all this at theatre group?" he managed. It was daft—he *knew* Mark liked him. Hearing it confirmed shouldn't affect him like this. Not at all.

"Nah, we went to the caff for bean burgers after. She ain't even veggie, but she din't wanna eat meat in front of me—din't I tell you she's sweet? But anyway, point *is*, she's not gonna have a strop about him being gay cos she already knows and she's cool with it."

"So did you tell her to tell him?"

Lex shrugged. "Din't know what to say, did I? I mean, usually it's the other way round, innit? Parents what know their kid's gay and don't know whether to say nothing. And then, they always say, like on the internet and stuff, that the parents oughta wait for the kids to say something first. But I din't know whether that's a rule, like, it's the kids who get to bring it up whatever, or if it's the gay person who gets to. Plus, I dunno, you reckoned he was right in the closet, yeah? So what if *he's* the one having the strop if she goes and says she's all right with him being gay? So anyway, I thought it'd be safest if you said it."

Patrick rolled his eyes. "Right, cos that couldn't possibly go wrong."

"What? Why would it go wrong?"

"You never heard of shooting the messenger? That's even if he *doesn't* jump to the conclusion I'm the one who's outed him." His eyes narrowed. "So what exactly did you tell her about me?"

Lex looked hurt. "Nuffing! Din't even tell her I knew who she was talking about. It was all hyper-fetticals. No names mentioned on either side. I mean, when she first brung it up, I thought maybe it was cos she knew I knew you, but I reckon it's just cos I'm, well . . ." Lex waved a hand at their androgynous, alternatively styled self.

Yeah, Patrick couldn't blame Fen for assuming Lex would be pretty open-minded about people being gay, and might even have some useful advice to give. Trouble was, Mark probably wouldn't be so happy about it. Shit. "She shouldn't have been talking about it to you anyway. Mark's gonna be well pissed off if he finds out his daughter's outed him to someone she's only just met."

"Yeah . . ." Lex stared at the New Rocks' toe-caps. They weren't swinging quite so breezily now. "Din't think of that. I mean, she just said she had this problem and could I give her some advice, and I sorta forgot it wasn't all about her. 'Specially when I realised it was you she was talking about. Sorry."

"Nah, it's no skin off my nose. Next time you see her, though, maybe tell her there's stuff she oughta keep quiet about unless her dad says it's okay?"

Lex looked a bit happier. "Yeah. S'posed to be seeing her at the weekend."

"Yeah? Not busy with the metalhead?"

"Nah, he's got a family thing." Lex didn't look worried about it, so Patrick let it go because, yeah, it *was* too soon for introductions to the family and all that. It didn't have to mean the bloke didn't want the family to meet Lex *ever*.

Not that he wasn't gonna be watching that space.

"So what are you gonna do?" Lex asked.

"What, at the weekend? Thought I'd go down the pub with the lads, maybe do a bit of shopping and a couple of odd jobs for Mum—"

"No, you prick. About Fen's dad."

"Mark. He's got a name of his own."

"Yeah. *Mister* Nugent. Nugent *Senior*." Lex laughed at Patrick's raised finger. "All right. *Mark*, who is in no way old, wrinkled, and totally past getting it up without a crate full of Viagra and a forklift. What you gonna do about him?"

Patrick thought about it. "Dunno. *Not* tell him Fen knows he's gay. And . . . well, we kind of parted on bad terms."

"So? You can go round and apologise."

"Who says it was my fault?"

"Oh, I dunno. Maybe the fact you still fancy the thermal undies off him? You're the tenth Doctor, you are."

Patrick blinked. "You what?"

"Remember? David Tennant onna spaceship at Christmas, his first one as the Doctor, the aliens try to stab him in the back and he fights 'em off with a satsuma? 'No second chances,' that's what he says. That's you all over. If this Mark was the one in the wrong, you'd've deleted his number and forgotten his name already. *And* you was apologising for him the other day when we went to lunch. Might as well apologise *to* him and all."

"Yeah, all right. I'm not saying it was totally my fault, but all right. But it still leaves him with his reason for us not going out together— unless I tell him what you told me. Which I'm not gonna."

Lex screwed up their face. "Well . . . maybe you could just sort of bring it up in conversation? Or I know what, you wait till he goes for a pee and then you and Fen have a confab? Cos we know she's on your side already."

"Yeah, and do what? Hold a bloody intervention?"

"Well, I dunno, do I? Can't solve all your problems. And I ain't got time neither. Some of us got work to do."

Patrick rolled his eyes at Lex's hunched back and got back to his own work.

It made him think, though. Cos, basically, what this meant was there was *no reason* him and Mark couldn't be together. There had to be some way of getting Mark to see that without totally cocking things up, right?

CHAPTER FIFTEEN

Friday night, David turned up at Mark's house at six o'clock prompt, bearing carrier bags. "Now, you've got the basic costume, haven't you? I've brought the fake tan and the eye shadow."

Fen giggled. "This is gonna be *sick*."

Mark was privately inclined to agree. He struggled to recover his powers of speech. "Wait—spray tan? Eye shadow? I am *not* wearing eye makeup."

"It's not for your eyes, silly. It's for your abs. You want a bit of definition, don't you? I know *I* would." David pouted. "I was so nearly going to dress up with you, you know. I had *such* a fantastic idea for a Xerxes costume: gold lamé shorts, sparkly black cape and more bling than you could shake your booty at. But Fen thought I'd be stealing your thunder, and anyway, it wouldn't really work unless I shaved my head, which we both agreed would have been an absolute tragesty."

Mark blinked. "A what?"

"It's a tragedy *and* a travesty," Fen said in what Mark had come to think of as her *duh*-voice.

"*Totally*," David agreed. "So anyway, we came up with a compromise." He rummaged in his backpack. "Ta-dah!"

Mark stared in horrified fascination at the teddy bear that had been thrust under his nose. Gone were the trench coat, dark glasses, and miniature fedora, and in their place were, well, pretty much the costume David had described. "Gregory?"

"Isn't he *fabulous*? I made it all myself. And if I get him to do a little shimmy, he jingles." David proceeded to demonstrate.

Fantastic. Absolutely marvellous. So now Mark was expected to not only go out in public in a ridiculous state of undress, but also to do so cuddling a teddy bear that looked like a refugee from a sex shop?

Say nothing, he told himself desperately. Say nothing, and just "forget" to pick it up on the way out.

"So come on, let's see you in full regalia." Rolling his *r*'s, David somehow managed to make the word *regalia* sound obscene.

"What, now? No," Mark said firmly. "We're eating first."

Any objections David might have made were drowned out by Fen's enthusiastic cry of "Pizza time!" as she ran to switch on the oven.

Mark followed at a more leisurely pace to open a bottle of merlot. It probably wouldn't mix well with all the beer he'd be drinking later, but there was no way on this earth he'd be going out in costume without a bit of Dutch courage inside him. Or more accurately—he glanced at the label—South African courage.

Fen and David, it transpired, made a perfect team when eating pizza—he merely picked off all the meat and filled up on salad, leaving her to enthusiastically shovel down the rest. Mark wondered where she was putting it all. *He* didn't get to eat anything like as much, getting his wrist slapped—literally—as he reached for his third slice.

David wagged a finger at him. "Ah ah ah. Do we *want* to look like a bloater tonight? There's only *so* much makeup can do."

Mark narrowed his eyes and chomped aggressively on a lettuce leaf.

After dinner came the excruciating task of transforming himself into an object of ridicule in front of his ex-subordinate and his only child.

Actually, Mark was almost glad they were there. At least their presence (and oh-so-helpful comments) distracted him from the growing paranoia that this would all turn out to be some terrible April Fool's joke. He could see it now: the whole of the Spartans—no, the whole of the *village*—turning up at the Three Lions to point at him and laugh. After all, what did those pictures of Barry on the internet prove? Just that they were working the long con, that was all—

"*Daaa-aad.* Are you even listening? I *said*, what are you going to wear for shoes?"

Mark blinked down at Fen, her pretty face flushed with excitement and, perhaps, overeating. "Trainers."

"*Trainers*?" Fen gave him a look that clearly doubted his intellect, if not his sanity.

David just frowned. "That's not very authentic."

"And the rest of the getup *is*? Anyway, in the absence of anything resembling gladiator sandals, they'll have to do."

"I could lend you my flip-flops," Fen suggested. "I don't like them anymore anyway."

"That's because they're pink with flowers on. Thank you, but no."

"Oh, well. I don't suppose anyone's going to be looking at your feet anyway. Now, off you hop and get changed, and then we can start putting your face on." David visibly caught Mark's glare. "Figuratively speaking, of *course*," he added hastily.

Twenty minutes later, Mark found himself standing in the kitchen dressed only in a leather kilt and what had seemed like a whole bottle of fake tan when Fen, giggling, had applied it. God alone knew what he looked like. Well, David and Fen did too, but Mark hadn't dared glance in a mirror, and he wasn't even finished yet. David was on his knees in front of him, painting muscles on with makeup. "Can you do that a bit harder?" he asked without thinking.

David looked up at him, eyebrows making a concerted bid for the ceiling, and opened his mouth to say something Mark was instinctively aware needed to be headed off at all costs. Particularly as Fen was only three feet away.

"I mean," he said quickly, "so it's not so ticklish?"

"Oh, is that *all*?" David pouted. "You'll just have to man up and deal with it."

Fen giggled, just as a sharp, confident rapping reverberated down the hallway. "Oh, there's someone at the door," she said helpfully.

"Well, aren't you going to answer it, then?" Mark said after a lengthy pause. "Or did you think I was going to go like this?"

"Oh. Yeah. Okay," she said, and scurried for the door.

"But for God's sake, don't bring them in here," Mark called after her, half turning.

"Stay still," David ordered, grabbing Mark's hips and yanking them back into position. "Do you *want* wonky abs?"

"Surely they're all right now?"

"Oh no. I haven't *nearly* finished with you yet," David purred in his flirtiest tone, looking up at Mark from his kneeling position through suspiciously lustrous lashes. He was still hanging on to Mark's buttocks with both hands, and his face was *far* too close to Mark's groin for comfort.

Especially seeing as Patrick was now standing in the kitchen doorway. Glaring at them both.

Oh God.

Patrick barked out an incredulous, mirthless laugh. "What the hell's going on here?" he asked, his tone rough.

David's grip on Mark's arse tightened. "And this is any of your business *because*?"

Mark's face grew hot, but hopefully the blush wouldn't show through the fake tan. "Patrick? Um, this is David. My PA. Ex-PA."

"*Enchanté*," David said flatly.

"He's helping me get ready for tonight," Mark babbled on. "Um. David, I think you could let go of me now."

"Just a bit," Patrick said, stony-faced. "Thought this was your induction, not a bloody coming-out party."

"It's not a— There's nothing going on!" Mark looked around in a panic, but Fen was nowhere in sight, thank God, and the faint sounds of some music channel could be heard from the living room.

"Not *now* there isn't," David muttered sulkily.

Patrick's expression went from granite to tungsten carbide.

Mark threw up his fake-tanned hands in exasperation. "Oh, for— Do you honestly think I'd, well . . . what *you* were thinking . . . with my daughter in the house?"

"Whatever," Patrick said. "I'll see you up at the pub."

He turned on his heel and stalked back the way he'd come. After a moment, the front door slammed.

"Well, *that* was rude." David *tsk*ed.

Mark sighed. "Brilliant. Absolutely bloody *brilliant*. Look, for God's sake, stop faffing around with that bloody brush. It's not going to get any more convincing."

David got slowly to his feet, a hurt expression on his face. "Well, if you didn't *want* my help, you only had to say."

"It's not . . ." Mark struggled for a few moments for a way to explain without outing himself to David, who must have assumed Mark was simply horrified by someone catching him in an apparently compromising position with a gay man. He hoped. None, alas, presented itself. "I'm sorry. I'm grateful, honestly. Just a bit . . ."

"Stressed?" David asked, perking up. "I do a *wonderful* sensual massage. It's just the thing for stress."

"No," Mark said firmly. "I mean, thanks, but I haven't got time. I need to get up to the pub before the others decide I've wimped out." Or Patrick told them all he'd cried off in favour of a party for two in the kitchen. "But, really, thanks for all your help. Are you coming up for a drink before you head off home?" *Please,* please *say no*, he thought desperately.

The evening was unlikely to improve with Patrick and David spending any *more* time in each other's company.

"Mm, no. I thought I'd stay and look after the little moppet. Save you worrying about her while you're out."

Mark blinked. "Thanks. That's very kind of you—and, well, Fen adores you, you know that." He mustered a smile. "You've certainly made life more interesting for both of us since we moved here," he added with absolute sincerity as he threw his cloak around his shoulders. David fetched the replica helmet from the kitchen counter and handed it to him with a flourish.

Mark jammed it on his head. The more disguised he was, the better. "Fen? I'm off now."

"Hang on a mo," came from upstairs, swiftly followed by the sound of Fen scampering down, phone in hand. "Wow, you almost look fit, Dad. For an old bloke. Try and look fierce."

Mark sighed and put on a snarl for the inevitable photos. "Can I go now?"

Fen handed him his spear and took another photo. "There you go, Dad. Come back with your shield or on it." She giggled. "David told me to say that."

"Actually, now we come to mention it, why haven't you got a shield?" David asked, cocking his head.

"Probably to stop me hiding behind it," Mark answered gloomily and patted the pockets of the shorts he was wearing under his kilt in the forlorn hope they'd make him feel a bit less naked. He turned to David. "Right. I've got my money and my car keys—"

"You're driving?"

"Look at me. Did you really think I was planning on *walking*?"

"Hm, fair point."

"*Anyway*, as I was about to say, I haven't got room to carry my phone. But I'll only be up at the Three Lions, so in case of emergency—"

"*Daaa*-aaad."

"—you can either ring the pub or just run up there."

"We'll be fine," David said firmly. "You just take your spear and knock 'em dead. Although not literally. Well, not unless they get *really* frisky with you."

Mark managed a weak smile in farewell, then gathered his curtain cloak around him and set off to dine in hell.

CHAPTER SIXTEEN

The evening was a *disaster*. The best that could be said about it was that he was greeted by neither a jeering crowd shouting *April Fool* nor a hail of arrows from the massed Persian army. Of the two, Mark thought he'd probably have preferred the latter.

What actually greeted him was a rousing cheer and an offer from Barry to buy him a half. This turned out to be a half *yard*, not a half pint, and Mark was challenged to down it in one, which he did to loud catcalls and a couple of wolf whistles.

The evening went downhill from there. Patrick didn't speak to him all evening. Didn't even *look* at him. The Three Lions, often a relatively oestrogen-free zone, was tonight packed to the rafters with women of all ages. Mark began to wonder if Barry had been selling tickets. They kept coming up to him, asking to feel his abs and making suggestive remarks about his weapon.

The collecting buckets were out again, and at the end of the evening, Si cheerfully informed him they'd raised more money for charity than any other induction night on record. Probably because Barry had made Mark charge for photos.

Mark just knew those photos were going to haunt him for the rest of his life. Who the bloody hell had ever thought something like the internet would be a good idea?

Darkness having now fallen, he'd been planning to leave the car at the pub and walk the short distance home, but in the end caught a lift from Mrs. Kevin again. She seemed in a slightly better mood this evening, if you could count suppressed laughter every time she sneaked a look at Mark. The youngest child, awake this time, stared at Mark goggle-eyed for the entirety of the short ride while his worse-for-wear father snored beside him.

When Mark finally got home after the longest night of his life, he found Fen and David in the living room watching *Beauty and the Beast*. At first glance, he thought Fen was wearing her dressing gown on backwards, but on closer inspection, it appeared to be a blanket with sleeves. There was a large bowl of popcorn on her lap. Mark was seventy-five percent certain he'd have remembered buying popcorn, so where the hell had that come from?

David looked up and beamed. "Hail the conquering hero! Did they all kneel at your feet?"

Fen giggled. "Your abs are all smudged."

Not only that, he'd got fake tan all over the cloak. Mark hoped it was machine washable, or he'd be scouring the internet for replacement red curtains. "I'm going to have a shower," he said. "David, if you want to head off…"

"Dad, he can stay. Can't he? It's really late now."

It wasn't *that* late. Then again, Mark was far too worn out to argue. "Fine. If that's what you'd like, David? I'm sure Fen can make up the spare bed for you," he added with a last-minute surge of assertiveness.

"Yeah, no probs," Fen said, and giggled again.

Suspicions aroused, Mark poked his head in the spare bedroom on his way to his desperately needed shower. The spare bed was already made up, with Gregory perched on the pillow, changed out of his Xerxes costume and into a pair of paisley pyjamas.

Mark sighed and carried on to the bathroom.

Vast quantities of hot water and shower gel later, Mark was feeling a lot better about things. So what if his daughter and ex-colleague were conspiring to take over control of his life? At least Fen seemed a lot happier these days. He pulled on a pair of jogging bottoms—ye gods, he'd never appreciated trousers so much in his *life*—and a T-shirt—ditto—and went downstairs to gently encourage his daughter to go to bed.

Predictably, *gently* clearly wasn't going to cut it. "*Daaa*-aaad. We're watching a *film*. And it's not like I've got school tomorrow."

"What about homework?"

"Like I was gonna do that on Saturday morning even if I *did* get up."

It was a fair point, Mark supposed. "All right. But just until the end of the film, all right?" He dropped down into an armchair and stretched out his legs.

David, pouting, patted the sofa cushion next to him. "If you sit over there, you won't be getting any popcorn."

"You could throw it at him," Fen suggested.

Mark raised an eyebrow. "Is that you volunteering to hoover up the mess?"

Fen glared. "Dad, come and sit on the sofa."

Smiling, Mark did as he was bid. He'd get a better view of the telly from there in any case. Belle, in a meringue-shaped yellow dress, was being whirled around a dance floor by a well-groomed Beast. "I thought you'd grown out of Disney films?"

"Bite your tongue," David said sternly. "Disney films are *ageless*."

"We've got to get *The Little Mermaid*, Dad. David says it's brilliant."

"You've never seen it?"

"No. Mum doesn't like it cos Ariel gives up everything for a *man*."

Mark winced. The derision in Fen's tone at the last word could only have come from her mother. "Well, I can understand her point of view," he began cautiously.

"*Totally*," David put in. "Men are pigs. Present company excepted, obviously. Ooh, I just need to get Gregory for this bit. It's his favourite."

Mark stared at the screen. The villagers had begun to assemble into a lynch mob. "He likes violence?"

Then he wondered why he was questioning the tastes of a teddy bear.

"No, silly. The bit at the end, where the Beast goes all sparkly and gets transformed into a fabulous prince. Back in a jiffy."

"We'll pause it," Fen said, doing so. "I want some hot chocolate anyway. David, do you want some?"

"Are there marshmallows?"

"*Duh.*"

"Then do bears spit in the woods?"

Fen giggled. "*No.* But that's a yeah, right?"

"*Oui, ma petite crevette.*"

"I'll make them," Mark said, slightly alarmed by the way they seemed to have developed their own language in the few hours he'd been out.

He escaped to the kitchen and got out three mugs, humming a tune from the film under his breath. God, he'd missed this. Missed family life being *fun*. The last few years of marriage had seemed like a prison, the walls closing in on him and the office his only refuge, and he'd forgotten, for a while, that it hadn't been all bad with Ellen. They'd had fun, in the early years, when Fen had been tiny and before Ellen had got bitter.

He should call Ellen, Mark thought. Call her and tell her he was sorry about the way things had gone. He'd said it before, of course. But this time he really meant it.

The kettle had boiled, so Mark stirred in the hot chocolate powder and got out the half-empty packet of marshmallows.

"Dad?"

Mark looked up to see Fen standing in the doorway. "Got impatient, did you? You can't rush perfection." He smiled at her.

She bit her lip. "No. I just wanted to say . . . Look, I know you're gay, Dad. I *know*, all right? So it's cool if you and David want to, like, hold hands and stuff in front of me."

The marshmallows fell from his grasp and onto the kitchen counter. Mark stared at her as tiny pink and white puffs scattered soundlessly over the surface, then leapt, lemming-like, for the lino.

A hollow seemed to have opened up inside him, and it was echoing with her words. *You're gay, you're gay.* "What?" It came out a bit croaky. God knew he'd been thinking about telling her—but in his own time. On his own terms.

Then the rest of what she'd said hit him. "I mean . . . David? David and I aren't . . ."

"I *know. Duh.* I'm just saying, you *can* be. It'll be great." She frowned at the marshmallows. "Are you gonna pick those up? Cos it's been more than five seconds so *I'm* not eating them. Have we got a new packet? You'll have to buy some more, anyway."

Why was she babbling about marshmallows? Didn't she realise what she'd just said? "But what do you mean, you know I'm gay? How?"

"Well, *duh*. I know you and Mum weren't sleeping in the same room for, like, *years* before you split up. And you *never* look at women's boobs, but when a bloke bends over, it's always eyes straight to bum. And David told me, anyway."

"*What*?" David had told Fen Mark was gay? Mark took a step forward. A marshmallow died an unpleasant, squashy death under his bare foot.

Since when did David even *know* Mark was gay? That didn't matter, though. What mattered was that *David* had bloody well *outed* him to his *daughter*.

Mark had heard the phrase "his blood boiled" before. He hadn't realised until this moment just how apt it could be.

"Dad?" Fen said in a small voice, backing off.

"Wait here." With a final glare at her pale, frightened face, Mark turned to stalk back into the living room. David had returned to the sofa, Gregory in his arms.

"Just what the hell do you think you're playing at?"

David's eyes were twin saucers full of innocence. "Eating popcorn?"

"How *dare* you tell my daughter I'm gay?" Mark's fists clenched at his sides, but he resisted the urge to thump something.

Barely.

The saucers turned end-on as David stood up slowly. "Don't you think it's something she should know?"

"No. Yes. Maybe—but not from *you*, for Christ's sake!"

"Then who?" David snapped in a waspish tone Mark had never heard from him before. "It didn't seem as though *you* were going to tell her." His expression softened. "Look, it doesn't matter to her. Does it?" He directed that last part over Mark's shoulder.

Mark realised for the first time that Fen had ignored his instructions to stay put and was hovering nervously three feet behind him.

"No. Why should I care if you want a boyfriend?" Fen tried a wobbly smile. "And it's been great with David. Like we're a family again. So I just wanted you to know you didn't have to, like, hide it and stuff." She hugged herself, the Tatty Teddy pyjamas riding up and showing her midriff.

She looked on the verge of tears.

Mark's anger seemed to spring a sympathetic leak and drained away, leaving only a desperate weariness. "Sweetheart, it's not going to happen. David and I are just . . ." he swallowed, "friends." Even if he didn't *feel* particularly friendly towards him right now.

Her scrunched-up face tore at Mark's heart. "But you *like* him. I know you do. You're happy with him. Like . . . like dads are s'posed to be. All fun."

"That's because we're friends, sweetheart. But there's never going to be anything more." Mark ran a hand through his hair. "I'm sorry I let you build up this big fantasy—but that's all it is. All it'll ever be. He's not going to be your new mum."

Fen stared at him, her face blotchy and her eyes now brimming over. "Why do you have to ruin *everything*?" She turned and ran upstairs.

"Mark?" David broke the silence, his voice uncertain.

Sighing, Mark turned back to him. "I think you'd better go."

David opened his mouth, then closed it again. He picked up Gregory, turned to Mark, then turned away again.

Then he turned back. "It wasn't . . . It wasn't quite how the little moppet made it sound. She asked a lot of *very* leading questions. I swear I wouldn't have just outed you . . . even if I *did* sort of hope that once things were out in the open, you might decide to give us a go." He licked his lower lip. His very plump, red lower lip. "I don't suppose . . ."

"No," Mark said, but it didn't sound as certain as he'd meant it to even in his ears. "I'm sorry, David, I just don't, well, feel it."

"Sure?" David said with a whisper of a smile. "Sure you wouldn't like to *try* feeling it?"

Mark stood rooted to the spot, his sense of surreality growing as David, still clutching Gregory, moved closer. "I . . ."

David's lips met Mark's. They were soft, as lips went—not chapped or dry. The kiss tasted toffee-sweet and slightly spicy, although it could have been David's cologne confusing Mark's senses. They were evenly matched for height, so there was no awkward stooping, and their noses didn't collide. David slipped an arm around Mark's waist and pulled him in closer. The kiss deepened, and David's tongue tickled Mark's lips. It wasn't *unpleasant*.

But it wasn't right either. There was no spark, no tingle. No escalation of passion. No passion at all, in fact.

There was no *Patrick*.

Mark stiffened—and not in the sort of way David might have hoped for. This was all wrong. This wasn't the man he should be kissing. Desperately wanted to be kissing.

At the first sign of Mark pulling away, David released him, stepping back with a look of regret. "You really don't feel it, do you?"

"I'm sorry." Mark meant it, as much for his own sake as for David's.

David frowned. "You *are* gay, aren't you? I mean, I know you always *said* you weren't, but I thought that was just our little game of protesting too much. Is it the age gap? Because that's a silly thing to worry about. If we'd been ancient Greeks, an age gap would have been practically *compulsory*."

"It's not the age gap."

David's face fell still further, and Mark cursed himself for his lack of tact. He could have lied, damn it.

Then again, didn't David deserve honesty?

"It's because I'm not all macho and straight-acting, isn't it? Too *gay*." David said it flatly, as if it was something people had said to him in the past. He picked up his teddy bear and gave Gregory a defiant little cuddle.

Mark opened his mouth to make a hasty denial, to simply say he'd met someone else—then caught himself. Honesty. Even if Patrick hadn't been in the picture, it wouldn't have happened between him and David. "It . . . Maybe. It's not that I think there's anything wrong with it, or you ought to act straight or anything," he added quickly. "It just . . . It just doesn't work for me. I wish it did."

"Makes two of us," David said with a half smile that hurt to look at. "Silly of me, wasn't it? I mean, I *knew*, really. The little head likes what it likes, and I know I'm not the sort of man you go for. I just thought, well, *hoped*, maybe if we spent some time together, if you got to know the real me . . . What do you know? Turns out it just makes it worse. You've met the real me, and you don't want him."

"I'm sorry." *Sorry* didn't even begin to cover it, but what other word was there? "But if there's anything I learned from being married to Ellen, it's that faking it until you make it doesn't work in love. You'll find someone," he said, half wanting to hug David and not knowing if that would make it worse. "Someone much better than a middle-aged tax accountant whose daughter thinks he ruins everything."

"She doesn't think that. I mean, I know she *said* it, but she didn't mean it. Not really."

"Have you asked her?"

"She actually volunteered the information that you're really quite good at making hot chocolate."

"Great. Mark Nugent: his one skill."

"You've got others," David said softly but didn't elaborate. He tried for a smile again but didn't do a great deal better than last time. "She'll get over it. Everything's so important at that age. I remember thinking I'd *die* when Mr. Harris, my geography teacher, told me he wasn't gay, and if he had been, he wouldn't be into jailbait, and *certainly* not into jailbait that thought the Basque Country was a lingerie outlet, but I survived, didn't I, Gregory? So'll she." He paused. "Um. Would you like a hand cleaning up the carpet before I go?"

Mark looked at the floor. Then at the trails of pink-and-white sticky patches leading from the kitchen. He sagged.

"Tell you what, leave it to me," David suggested. "You might want to go talk to the little moppet. I'll just clean up the mess and then leave. You won't even hear me go."

"Stay the night," Mark said roughly. "It's the least I can offer."

David smiled sadly. "No, sweetie, it's the most you can offer. But that's all right."

Mark nodded. He checked his feet for any further vestiges of marshmallow—no, the carpet had taken care of those nicely. Then he climbed the long, long staircase up to Fen's room and knocked on her door.

CHAPTER SEVENTEEN

Patrick couldn't believe he'd been so fucking blind. So *stupid*. Why the hell had he just assumed the younger bloke Mark's daughter had been on about was *him*? Well, tonight had kicked his ego right in the bollocks.

And, Christ, where the hell did Mark get off, telling Patrick all that crap about not wanting a bloke and then letting that guy David slobber all over him in the bloody kitchen? *Not out, and not coming out*, he says, then he gets off with a bloke so bloody camp they could put him on a poster to advertise Butlins.

At least he hadn't had the nerve to bring him up to the pub. That was the only reason Patrick had stuck around for the night. Well, that and Heather. She'd been up there with her bloke, Chris, cheering on Mark while he strutted around the pub looking like a real bloody Spartan, not a fake one like the rest of 'em.

She'd cornered him at the bar, giggling. "Wow, your bloke's a bit of a hit, in't he? Reckon I could get him to join the Sham-Drams? We could do that Oscar Wilde play—oh my God, you could be his Bosie. You'd be all right getting naked on stage with him, wouldn't you? I mean, come on, fair's fair. You can't keep him all to yourself."

"He's not my bloke. And keep it down, all right? He's not out." Although why should Patrick give a toss about Mark's reputation? Going around with that David, the bloke seemed pretty set on outing himself in any case.

"Oops. Soz. But what d'you mean he's not your bloke?"

Patrick wasn't sure how many beers Heather had had by that point, but he was getting drunk just on her breath. "What I said. Not mine, and I don't want him to be either."

"Uh-oh. What's he done?" She looked like she was ready to march up to Mark and demand they take it outside.

"Tell you another time, all right? No Con tonight?" he added to change the subject.

"Nah. Tristan's taking him up the West End." She cackled, then burped, loudly, just as Chris came to join them.

He slung an arm over her shoulder. "See, that's what I love about you. Such a lady."

"Eff off. I can be a lay-dee." She put on a ridiculously posh voice. "*In Hertford, Hereford, and Hampshire, hurricanes hardly ever happen.* See? Trouble is, what's the point when there's no bloody gentlemen around?"

Chris laughed. "Well, she's got us there, ain't she? You all right, mate? You've been looking like someone pissed in your pint. This new bloke stealing your thunder?"

Patrick huffed out an exasperated breath. "Has *nobody* round here got anything to talk about apart from Mark bloody Nugent?"

Chris shrugged. "Man of the hour, in't he? Don't worry, mate, we still think you're the prettiest princess— Oi, what was that for?" Heather had thumped him on the shoulder.

Patrick put down his half-full glass. "Think I'm gonna call it a night. Don't enjoy yourselves too much, all right?"

He left them still bickering like a couple of kids, and headed off home. Time to quit before he said something he'd regret.

Course, it hadn't helped his mood any that he'd been on the Diet Coke all night, cos no way was he gonna drink when he was pissed off. *Angry drunk* was his dad's thing, not Patrick's. So he didn't slam the door when he got home, and he *didn't* kick his boots halfway down the hall when he got them off.

Well. Maybe one of them.

"Everything all right, love?" his mum asked, poking her head out of the living room right at the wrong moment.

"Fine." Patrick stomped to the kitchen in his socks, got out a mug, and put the kettle on.

She followed him. "Are you sure? Cos you're looking at that teabag like boiling water's too good for it."

Patrick leaned on the counter and huffed out a breath. "Sod it. I'm going to bed."

"Love? What happened?"

He whirled. "Nothing. Nothing happened. Nothing's gonna happen, all right? You were right. I waited too long and I missed the boat. 'Cept it turns out he's a lying piece of shit, so that's all right."

Mum made a face. "Well, that's men for you, love. So who was he, anyway, this bastard? Anyone I know? Just so's if I see him in Tesco, I can run over his toes with my trolley."

Patrick had to smile. "Nah, no one you know. You wouldn't have liked him anyway. The older bloke, remember?"

"Ooh, not that new one—you know, the one who moved into the Claridges' house, after she ran off with that vicar from Bishops Langley? The one with the daughter with the hair?" Mum frowned at Patrick's frankly incredulous look. "What? I got talking to Sally in the chemist the other day."

"Mum, you scare me sometimes. Yeah, the one with the daughter with the hair. His name's Mark."

"I never liked that name."

"It was your dad's name," Patrick pointed out.

"Yeah, but he deserved better. So what did he do? What's he lying about?"

"So you can tell Sally in the chemist?"

"Matter of public interest, innit? Well, I mean, I won't tell her anything private. So go on."

"Nah. Don't wanna talk about it." The kettle boiled, and Patrick poured the water into the mug. "You want a hot drink, Mum?"

"Don't be daft," she said, holding up her wineglass. "Coming to watch telly with me?"

Patrick shook his head. "Gonna take this up with me and get an early night."

She made a sad face. "All right, love. You sleep well. And just remember, he's not worth it."

Right. Sleep well.

That was pretty much guaranteed to be a no go.

Lex rang late the next morning. Patrick had already been up for a while—he'd done a load of washing and got started on the ironing mountain. Mum hated ironing, so he usually did hers as well. These days he didn't even make her pay him in chocolate buttons.

Lex sounded a bit breathless on the phone. "I just wanted to ask if anyfing happened last night? Cos I'm seeing Fen this afternoon, so—"

Great. Patrick's new favourite subject. "Nothing happened. Not with me, anyway."

There was a silence, probably because that had come out a bit sharp.

"What d'you mean?" Lex asked finally.

"I mean, it wasn't me, all right? That younger bloke Mark's into. I *met* him, last night at Mark's house." The humiliation still stung.

"Oh shit. Oh fucking shitting crap, I'm sorry. Shit. I'd never of— I thought she meant *you*, right? Shitshitshit."

Patrick's anger melted away. This wasn't Lex's fault. Mark was the one to blame here, the lying prick. "I know you didn't know, all right? It's okay. You were only trying to help."

"Yeah, but . . . God, was it awful? Was they, like, all over each other? Shit, did he go to the Spartans thing? Did you have to watch 'em at it all night?"

"I don't think they'd have been *at it* in the Three Lions, but no, he didn't go. S'pose he must have stayed with Fen." And Christ, that was twisting the knife. Just how long had Mark been with this bloke, to trust him with his daughter? "Look, don't worry about it, okay? How did your evening go?"

"It was great. Really great. You know that restored 1920s cinema they've got over in Berko? With all the gold and the pretty bits round the walls and stuff?"

"Art deco, yeah."

"Whatevs. He took me over there on the bike. It was dead romantic."

"Yeah? What did you see?"

"*Night of the Living Dead*. You know, the original, not the remake."

"Glad to hear it. Cos the remake wouldn't have been romantic at all."

"Shut up. You're well jell."

"Yeah, right. So what's this with you and Fen, anyway? Since when are you two BFFs?"

"I dunno. I always wanted a little sister. And she's got, like, *literally* no one to talk to round here. It's really sad. I mean, her dad keeps telling her it's all for her, them moving out here and that, but he never *asked* her or nothing."

"Yeah … You probably shouldn't be telling me stuff she says about her dad." Not that Patrick was actually talking to Mark at the moment, but it still felt wrong.

"Shit. Sorry. I sort of forgot he was your Mark. Sorry. Not your Mark. Um. I'd better go, yeah? I'll see you Monday."

"Yeah. Take care, all right?"

"Yeah, you too."

Patrick put his phone back in his jeans pocket and stared out of the window at the plum tree in the front garden, which was showing its usual pitiful crop of pale-pink blossom that never seemed to bear any proportion to the avalanche of plums they got every summer. By this time tomorrow, Lex would know all about David the ex-PA. Maybe have met him too—probably, even. After turning up on Friday night, he'd most likely be staying the weekend, wouldn't he?

Playing happy families with Mark and Fen. Sod it.

CHAPTER EIGHTEEN

Fen didn't roll out of bed until around noon on Saturday. Mark's attempts to speak to her the previous evening had been greeted by increasingly shrill cries of "*Go away*," so he'd gone back downstairs to help David with the carpet and to tell him to not be an idiot and stay the night. Then he'd gone to bed.

David had been gone by the time Mark woke up in the morning, leaving his bed neatly made.

It was probably just as well. Fen still seemed upset; she'd crept down to eat breakfast in the kitchen, then sloped off back to her room, her dirty cereal bowl and the dregs of orange juice in the bottom of her favourite mug the only evidence she'd emerged at all.

Mark gave her an hour or so, then went to knock on her door.

There was no reply.

"Darling? I want to talk to you."

Silence.

"I'm coming in," Mark said, and opened the door.

Fen was sitting on her bed, propped up in a nest of pillows, heart-shaped cushions and cuddly toys, tapping angrily at her phone. Her eyes were red and swollen.

Mark's heart melted. "Sweetheart . . . I'm sorry, but you can't force these things. David and I are never going to be together."

"But you *like* him. I *know* you do."

"I still like your mother, you know. It just didn't work out, us being married, and it wouldn't with David either."

"How do you know if you haven't tried it? You're always telling *me* that."

Mark hoped he wasn't going red at the memory of David's kiss. He certainly wasn't planning to tell her he *had* tried it. "That's when you won't eat your vegetables. Love's not like brussels sprouts."

"But why can't it be? It's not *fair*. Why can't we be a family again?"

"There's all kinds of families, you know. Lots of people grow up with only one parent. You've still got two, even if they don't live together anymore. And your mum and I both love you very much."

"But it's not the *same*."

"I know. But that doesn't mean it can't be just as good."

"Yeah, but ... What about when I go to uni? You're just going to be all on your own."

"Well, we could get that cat you were talking about to keep me company," Mark suggested, trying to lighten the mood.

"*Daa*-aad. That's *worse*." Then she seemed to realise exactly what he'd said. "But we ought to get a cat. Totally. Can we go to the shelter this weekend?"

"We'll see."

"That just means no, doesn't it? *Please*?"

"It doesn't mean no. It means I'll have to think about it. There might be things we'll need to sort out in the house—and besides, I don't even know where the shelter *is*."

"I know where it is." Fen sat up and grabbed her phone. "They've got all these pictures of the cats there, with stuff about them and where they come from and everything."

Mark watched in mildly horrified fascination as she scrolled down columns of cats, each with a winsome picture, a name and a cutesy biography.

It was like a feline version of Grindr.

"So what do you do if you see one you like?" he asked. "Send it a message?" *Hi, I read your profile and I too enjoy eating fish, licking myself, and taking long naps in the sunshine. U wanna?*

"Dad, don't be stupid. Cats don't go online. You have to send the shelter an email. Or ring them up. Or we could just go there."

"Okay. I'll think about it."

"*Please*?"

Mark thought about it. "Actually, I suppose there's no reason we couldn't go this afternoon."

Fen didn't look as happy as he'd expected. "Um. We can't. Lex is coming over."

"Oh—your friend from drama class?"

"Theatre group. Yeah."

"Oh. Good." Mark was pleased to hear the friendship was flourishing. "What time?"

"Dunno. We just said after lunch."

That could mean anytime up to around five o'clock. Possibly even later, these days. "You know, if you ever want to ask anyone around for a meal, you only have to say."

"*Daaa*-aaad. Like anyone wants to have lunch with my *dad*."

Mark winced at the waves of scorn.

Everyone warned you when you had kids, you'd find yourself with no sleep, no money, and no social life.

Mark wondered why nobody bothered to mention you'd have no respect either.

In fact, the ring on the doorbell came shortly after two o'clock. Mark went to open the door, eager to meet Fen's first friend in Shamwell.

He just about managed not to do a visible double-take when he saw who was on his doorstep, facial piercings and all.

This was Lex? The theatre group assistant?

At first glance, the clothing didn't appear to have changed, but on closer inspection Mark thought he could spot a marked increase in the skull motif. And the boots . . . Ye gods, were those *spikes*? Yes; yes, they were. Around *two inches* long and subtly curved, interspersed with smaller studs that looked almost dainty in comparison, leaving barely any room for the inevitable silver zips and buckles. These were the sort of boots Boudicca, legendary Queen of the Iceni, might have donned before trotting off to sack London and slaughter the Roman invaders. Was footwear like this even *legal*?

"'Ullo, Mr. Nugent," their owner said.

Mark wrested his gaze back up to eye level. "Oh. Sorry. Just admiring your shoes. Um. You're Lex? Fen's expecting you." And, judging by the sounds of a herd of adolescent elephants rampaging down the stairs, she'd noticed Lex's arrival. "Oh, and please, call me Mark," he added just as Fen appeared, pink-cheeked and beaming.

"Lex! You made it."

"Course I did. Told you, din't I?" Lex pulled off his/her boots and left them standing neatly to one side in the hall, like a post-modern conversation piece. (*Oh, the boots? I picked those up at a metal festival in Derbyshire. Very self-referential, wouldn't you agree?*)

"Those are just *sick*," Mark heard Fen say. "Where'd you get them?"

He had a sinking feeling she wasn't going to be asking for a pony for Christmas.

"Come on, I'll show you my room," Fen said, pulling Lex by the arm.

Mark opened his mouth to object, then closed it again. He had a strong suspicion he shouldn't be letting his teenage daughter take boys up to her room—but *was* Lex a boy? And how on earth could he ask without giving offence?

And what if one or both of them was gay, anyway? Mark was all for progress, obviously, especially when it came to queer issues, but he couldn't help feeling parenting rules had seemed a bit more clear-cut in the Dark Ages. Perhaps he should just avoid the question entirely by encouraging them to stay downstairs with the promise of snacks?

Unfortunately, by the time he'd thought this through, they'd disappeared.

Mark didn't, of course, hang around outside his daughter's bedroom in the hopes of finding out just what was going on in there. It just so happened there were a lot of things that needed doing upstairs. There was the spare bed to strip, of course, and the bathroom sink to clean. That hadn't been done in *days*. And the airing cupboard could really do with being reorganised. What on earth had he been thinking, putting the towels in by size and not by colour?

Unfortunately, Fen's door might as well have been soundproof for all the good it did him. Mark caught the odd burst of excited conversation: Fen saying, "Oh my God, so you thought I meant . . ." Lex's voice: "No, but see, he's really . . ." And giggles. There were a lot of giggles.

After they'd been in there about an hour, he knocked on the door. "What?" Fen called.

Mark opened the door. He was relieved to see Fen and Lex sitting at opposite ends of Fen's bed, showing no signs of having hastily sprung apart or thrown back on articles of clothing. "I wondered if you wanted any drinks or snacks or anything?"

"'S all right, Dad. We'll get stuff if we want it," Fen said.

"Cheers, though," Lex added.

"Yeah, thanks, Dad." Fen gave him a piercing look. "You can go now."

"Right. I'll just be . . . around." Mark closed the door behind him and winced at the fresh outbreak of giggles that filtered through.

He spent the next couple of hours writing. Technically speaking. He'd certainly sat at the computer for the entire time, and he was sixty-three percent certain he'd decided on a radical rethink of the whole concept.

And he'd come up with three clear favourites from Fen's cat dating website: Honey, a shy ginger seven-year-old who claimed to like a quiet life; Greebo, an enormous neutered tom who was far too fat to do anything but enjoy a quiet life; and Mochi, a skinny half-grown Siamese who had no opinions on quiet lives but did have beautiful blue eyes the exact colour of Patrick's.

He got so caught up in the subject, in fact, he didn't even notice when Fen and Lex came down to forage in the kitchen. Much like earlier, if it hadn't been that they'd left the countertops looking like a smaller-than-average dustbin had just been raided by a messier-than-average fox, he wouldn't have known they'd been there at all.

Mark didn't see Fen again until the slam of the front door heralded Lex's departure. He jumped up from his desk and strolled casually into the kitchen, where rustling sounds had indicated Fen was in search of yet more food.

Either that or they had an extremely large rodent problem. Maybe he'd been right about that fox.

Luckily, his first guess turned out to be correct. Fen jumped as he walked in, a violently pink packet in her hand. "Oh. Dad. It's all right if I have some crisps, isn't it?"

"You mean some *more* crisps."

She looked shifty. "You *said* we could have snacks while Lex was here."

"Oh, go on, then. But for God's sake, eat an apple or something next time."

"Whatever." She opened the crisps, and the room filled with the cloying aroma of prawn cocktail flavour. It intensified as Fen waved the packet at Mark. "Want one?"

He shuddered. "Not if they were the last crisps on earth."

"Dad, you're so boring," she said, although at least it sounded fond.

"I do what I can. Lex seems nice," he added casually.

Fen crunched in reply.

Mark cleared his throat. "Is . . . Um. Is Lex a girl or a boy?"

Fen swallowed her mouthful a bit too quickly and started coughing. Mark handed her a glass of water. "*Daaa*-aaad," she said when the fit had passed. "*No.*"

Mark blinked. "Er . . ."

"What does it even matter? Lex is just Lex. A *person*. Why do you have to put everybody in *boxes*?" She gestured angrily with the crisp packet.

"Okay, that's a fair point," Mark allowed, feeling distinctly off-balance. He'd considered how he'd react to the news that Fen had found her first boyfriend. (Dire threats and constant vigilance.) He'd considered how he'd react to the news that she'd found her first *girl*friend. (Veiled threats and discreet chaperonage.)

At no point had it occurred to him he might not have covered all eventualities.

He took a deep breath. "Are you and Lex . . . Is Lex your, um, person-friend?"

Fen rolled her eyes. "*Daa*-aad. *No.* And *please* don't ever say *person-friend* again, 'kay? That's just . . . Just *don't.* Lex has got a bloke, anyway. He sounds totally old. He's even got a beard, which, *ewww*. Imagine kissing him. That's just *gross.*" She shuddered.

What was so bad about beards? On the right man, they could be very attractive. Mark could certainly imagine kissing a man with a beard. Say, if Patrick decided to cultivate facial hair—he'd keep it well groomed, Mark decided, not mountain-man bushy like Si and Alasdair at the Spartans—

"*Daaa*-aaad. Are you even listening?"

Mark blinked. "Sorry, darling. What were you saying?"

"I was just saying, about you and David."

He sighed. "Darling, I'm sorry, but it's not going to—"

"Yeah, I *know*, Dad. Jeez. I just mean, if you want to go out with someone else, then you should, you know? I won't mind. Not if they're nice too." Her cheeks flushed a warmer colour.

Mark's neck twinged with phantom whiplash from the abrupt volte-face. *What?* He'd expected weeks of unsubtle hints about how great David was, alternating with rage against his lack of reasonableness in failing to arrange his love life to suit his daughter. Not mature acceptance.

He stared at Fen. Maybe Lex was good for her.

"So is there?"

Mark startled. "What?"

"*Duh.* Anyone you wanna go out with? At the Spartans, maybe?"

"Why exactly are you asking this *particular* question?" He frowned. "Have you heard something?"

Fen's cheeks were now pinker than the crisp packet. "Sort of. Maybe. 'Cept I promised I wouldn't say anything."

"Sweetheart, if people are talking about me, don't you think I've got the right to know?"

"It's not like that! It's just Lex works with this bloke called Patrick..."

Mark had any uneasy feeling his own face was now a close neighbour to Fen's on the Pantone colour chart. "And?"

"And Lex said he really likes you. And he's really nice, so I was thinking..."

Mark was barely listening to her. Oh God. Patrick. Mark needed to see him. Talk to him. Explain. But would he even be at home, on a fine—all right, only slightly drizzly—Saturday afternoon like this?

He'd never know if he didn't go and find out. "I've ... I've got to go out, sweetheart. You'll be all right, won't you?"

"*Duh.* Where are you going?"

"To see someone."

"Is it Patrick?"

"Maybe." Mark grabbed his phone, his keys . . . Damn it, did he look presentable? He couldn't go in this shirt. He put the phone and keys back down again and ran upstairs to change.

Better. Now, where was he . . .?

Oh, bloody hell. Mark's spirits crashed. He couldn't go round and see Patrick.

He didn't have the first clue where Patrick lived.

Mark sagged, just as a text *bloop*ed through on his phone. He picked it up automatically.

It was from Fen. Got Ps add from Lex. 17 kite way. Ur wellcom.

Mark smiled and texted back. *I could kiss you.*

The reply came quickly. *Ew Dad gross.*

CHAPTER NINETEEN

Mark knocked on Patrick's door, his heart thumping somewhere in the vicinity of his mouth. Christ, what was going to greet him here? Patrick had seemed pretty angry last night. He'd *been* pretty angry last weekend.

But Lex had said he really liked Mark. Present tense.

The door opened, and Mark took a deep breath.

Then he shut his mouth with a snap. He hadn't been expecting to find himself facing a woman of around his own age.

"Yeah?" she said, smiling politely. Then her gaze raked up and down Mark, and she smiled more broadly. "What can I do you for?"

Oh God. Patrick had said he lived with his mother, hadn't he? Mark felt abruptly all of five years old, and barely managed to stop himself asking if Patrick could come out to play.

The smile was starting to waver again now. Mark cleared his throat. "Um, is Patrick in? I'm Mark Nugent."

Now the smile disappeared entirely. "Oh yeah?" she said, leaning against the doorframe and folding her arms. "And what do you want with my son?"

"I just wanted to talk to him."

She gave him a long, searching look. "Wait here," she ordered, and closed the door in his face.

God, what the hell had Patrick said about him? Mark didn't just feel like a five-year-old now. He felt like a five-year-old with a poor academic record who'd been sent to see the headmaster after he'd kicked a dinner lady in the shin.

Maybe this had been a mistake. He should have waited. Let Patrick cool down a bit first before attempting to explain. Mark looked around nervously.

Straight into the eyes of the next-door neighbour, who was evidently just going out. "You're a new one," the man said gruffly. He was in his sixties or seventies, Mark judged, with a grizzled, jowly face and mournful eyes. "Chucked you out already, has she?"

The man thought he was here for Patrick's *mother*? "It's not . . . I'm not . . ."

"I see 'em all come and go, I do," the man said, locking his door with fumbling, bloodless fingers. "Never last long. No surprise that boy's turned out the way he is."

Mark's anger rose. "I *beg* your pardon?"

"You 'eard me. Oh, I'm not blaming *her*. It's your lot what done it. Young lad wants a bit of stability in his life." He set off down his garden path with an unhurried, rolling gait. Mark watched him go. Good God. If the man thought Mark was a bad influence on Patrick when he was under the impression he was going out with his mother, what would he think if he knew the truth?

Whatever that was. Mark whirled as the door opened once more. Patrick stood there, looking wary. "Yeah?"

"I want to explain."

Patrick's expression didn't change. "Boyfriend gone home, has he?"

"Yes—no! David's not my boyfriend. Never has been." Mark held his breath. Would Patrick believe him?

Unexpectedly, Patrick smiled. His deep blue eyes crinkled up at the corners, and Mark's heart once again flirted with tachycardia. "Yeah. I know."

"You know?"

"Yeah. Just got a text from Lex."

"Oh?"

Instead of, as Mark had hoped, interpreting *Oh?* as *A text? About me? What did it say? Was it good? What did it* say? and then answering appropriately, Patrick just nodded. "Yeah. You coming in?"

"Um. Of course." Mark couldn't stop himself from looking around nervously as he stepped into the narrow hallway.

"It's all right." Patrick seemed amused. "I've told Mum not to bite. Cup of tea?"

"Yes. Please. Or coffee. Whichever's easiest. Actually, water would be fine." Mark followed Patrick into the kitchen, trying to wipe his palms on his trousers unobtrusively.

Which was ridiculous. He'd rushed over here, desperately hoping Patrick would listen to him and they might finally get together, and now it looked like that might actually be going to happen. Why the hell was he still terrified?

Patrick filled the kettle and put it on to boil. Then he turned and leaned back against the kitchen counter, his arms folded. For a moment, the resemblance to his mother was uncanny. "You gotta see it from my point of view," he said, his tone reasonable. "You tell me you're not out to your daughter. I might not like it, but I accept it. Then I come round to offer a bit of moral support and find a fit bloke on his knees to you offering, well, *im*moral support. Right where Fen could walk in at any minute and all."

"There was nothing going on!" Mark flushed. "David's just a bit . . . full-on. And, well, acting under a misapprehension."

"Yeah, seems like there's a lot of that going around."

Mark wondered what he meant but didn't quite like to ask. "You see, he's always been a bit, well, flirtatious. But I thought it was just his way. I mean, *I* thought *he* thought I was straight. So obviously he couldn't really mean anything by it."

"But?" The kettle, clearly in a hurry to get this over with, was starting to boil already. Patrick unfolded his arms and got out a couple of mugs, still keeping his body half-turned towards Mark.

"It, um, turned out he knows. About me, I mean. And so does Fen." Mark's face burned at the thought of the two of them *discussing* him. While eating popcorn. And watching Disney DVDs. "Um, you probably know this already."

"Not all of it. Not by a long chalk. This is the text I got." Patrick dug in his back pocket for his phone, thumbed it on, and showed Mark the message: *Mark n is single and not a shit. Tru dat.*

"'Tru dat'? Do people still say that?" Mark had always thought, based pretty solidly on what Fen had told him, if he'd heard of a bit of slang, it was already obsolete. Then again, that probably wasn't the most important thing about this ringing endorsement from someone Mark couldn't help thinking of as Fen's person-friend. "Um. So you believe me?"

"Yeah, I believe you." Patrick ran a hand over his hair, letting the hand rest at the back of his neck for an instant. The gesture was curiously mesmerising. "And, look, I'm sorry I went off on you like that. Shouldn't have jumped to conclusions."

"No, no. Quite understandable."

There was a pause.

"So, your daughter knows you're gay?" Patrick prompted.

"Oh—yes. Sorry." Mark grimaced. "Apparently, I'm a lot less subtle than I thought. And, well, she's fine with it."

"Fine in theory? Or fine with you actually having a bloke?"

"The, um, latter." Mark decided it might be best not to go into just how upset Fen had been about it not working out with David. "You and Lex work together, is that right?" After he'd said it, it sounded a bit lacking in context. He'd been meaning to go on and say he thought Lex had been putting in a good word with Fen for Patrick, but on reflection, it might have sounded rather like Mark had been assessing Patrick's suitability for boyfriend material by checking his references.

Oh God. Boyfriend. Mark swallowed.

Patrick was looking at him intently, a smile on his lips. "Yeah. Me and Lex work together. And sometime you've gotta tell me the rest of that conversation I just saw going on in your head."

"Sorry." Mark managed half a laugh. "It's just . . . I haven't been out with a man for nearly twenty years." And, oh God, what an appalling thing to say right now.

Twenty years ago, Patrick had been five.

From his slight wince, instantly suppressed, Patrick had just had the same thought. "It's not that complicated, you know."

"No?"

"Nah, you just find someone you get on with and take it from there."

Mark took a deep breath. "Well, we seem to get on all right. More or less. Despite . . ." He waved a hand vaguely.

"Me flouncing off like a jealous queen?"

"That wasn't what I was going to say," Mark protested.

Patrick stepped towards him, a smile on his lips. "No? What were you gonna say?"

"Nothing complimentary to myself, so I think, on reflection, I'll keep quiet." Because Mark might not be very practised at this sort of thing, but he had a fairly good idea that now probably *wasn't* the best time to remind Patrick he was a paranoid closet case theoretically old enough to be his father.

Patrick's smile broadened, and he took another step closer. "I can think of better things to do than talk." He licked his lips, and Mark was pretty sure he was doing it deliberately. Mark let his own lips fall open slightly, his whole body tingling and his heart racing in anticipation of Patrick's touch. Oh God. *Finally*.

The door burst open, and Patrick's mum bustled in. "Ooh, has the kettle boiled? Cheers, love, I'm gasping for a cup of tea." She gently elbowed Mark and her son out of the way, grabbed one of the mugs, and popped a teabag in, then filled it from the kettle. "You might wanna put a bit more water in there. Don't think it's gonna run to two more cups." Milk splashed in next, then she leaned back on the kitchen counter holding the mug in both hands and smiling at them. "Right, what have I missed?"

Patrick rolled his eyes. "The bit where Mark and me were plotting to smother you with an oven glove. But I can demonstrate, if you like."

"No, that's all right, love. You just carry on with what you were doing."

She looked like nothing short of a major natural disaster would force her to leave them alone again. Mark's nerve broke. "I'd better be getting back, anyway. Fen . . ." He gestured vaguely.

"That's your daughter, right?" Patrick's mum put in, her voice chirpy. "How old is she?"

"Fourteen," Mark said reluctantly.

"Fancy that. Only eleven years between her and my Patrick."

"Mum," Patrick said. "Be nice."

"I am being nice. I'm making conversation, aren't I?"

"Be *nicer*."

She ignored him, turning back to Mark. "You didn't grow up in Brentwood, did you? Only I wondered if we might have been at school together—"

"*Mum!*"

Mark coughed. "I really have to go. Thanks for the, er . . ." He waved a hand to indicate the drinks they hadn't, in fact, had. "I'll see you, um, sometime?"

"I'll walk you out," Patrick said firmly. "Mum, stay here."

"Nice meeting you, Mrs., um . . ."

"Owen," she reminded him, her eyes sharp.

"Don't let her get to you," Patrick said in a low voice when they reached the front door. "She just gets a bit protective."

"No, it's quite all right. Understandable, really." Guilt was kicking in. "After all, what mother wants her child to get involved with someone her own age?"

Patrick looked a bit spooked at having it all laid out so plainly. "You're still younger than her, right? She's forty-four."

Mark nodded. "Five years." It didn't seem like a lot. "Right. I'd better be off." He turned to go.

"Are you busy tonight?" Patrick said. It came out a bit quick, like he'd had to steel himself to ask.

"I—" About to say no, Mark caught himself and made a face. "I don't really like to leave Fen on her own two evenings in a row. Even if she *does* tend to stay in her room and leave me on my own," he added ruefully.

"How about I come round to yours, then? Keep you company while your daughter's ignoring you?"

"Are you sure you don't mind? You won't find it a bit boring, just staying in and watching TV on a Saturday night?"

"What, just cos I'm under thirty I ought to be out clubbing? Never been all that keen on that sort of thing." Patrick smiled. "And I reckon the company'll make up for it. I'll come round about eight, yeah? After dinner. Mum's making cottage pie, it's a thing."

"It's a date," Mark said firmly, and left so he could panic in private.

CHAPTER TWENTY

Patrick found his mum chopping carrots a lot more forcefully than she usually did. He stood and watched her a mo, wondering if their scarred old wooden chopping board was ever going to recover.

"Wanna help?" she asked without looking up.

"No, ta, but I do want a word. And no trying to get out of it."

"You want a word, do you? *You* want a word with *me*?" Mum jabbed the knife viciously into the final carrot—which was just the right size and shape to make Patrick wince—and left it there. The knife stood upright for a moment before falling slowly over onto the chopping board as the carrot rolled over. She put her hands on her hips. "Any of those words include what the bloody hell that man's doing round here slobbering over you when he's old enough to be your *father*? Not to mention, I have it on good authority he's a lying bastard."

"Piece of shit," Patrick said mildly.

"What?"

"That's what I called him. 'A lying piece of shit.' And he's not, all right? It was just a misunderstanding."

"Oh yes? So *he* says."

"And Lex says so too."

That took some of the wind out of her sails. Mum liked Lex. "So he's a charmer, and he's twisted Lex round his little finger too." She said it defiantly, but there wasn't a lot of conviction in there.

Patrick laughed. "He's really not, Mum. What, you think he's some suave, sophisticated con man? Trust me, you're not seeing the real Mark."

"I still don't see why *you're* seeing him," she grumbled.

"Cos I like him, all right? He's different."

"It's my fault, innit?"

"What?"

"Letting you grow up without a father. I should have tried harder with your dad—"

"Over my dead body— No, wait. Over *his* bloody dead body, the shite."

"—or Lenny, remember him? Back when you was a nipper. He wanted to marry me."

"Yeah, so he'd have someone to wash his socks and go and visit him in the nick. He'd have been as bad as Dad if he'd only had half a brain."

"That's not fair. He never knocked me about, Lenny didn't."

"Great, Mum. Really high standards you've got there. It's nothing to do with me not having a dad, all right? Mark's not like that."

"Like what? A decent father?"

"Oi, stop that. He's not like a father figure to me or anything. It's like . . . when I'm with him, I don't feel like he's older." Patrick laughed softly. "Sometimes I feel like *I'm* the older one. He's never been out— never been with anyone except his ex-wife, from what I can tell."

"Oh, love. How d'you know he's not just using you to get his confidence up? Dipping his toes in your waters, and then once you've taught him how to swim, he'll be off diving into every ocean in sight?"

"Cos he's not like that. I trust him, Mum."

She picked up the knife and started chopping again. "So when are you seeing him again?"

"Tonight. *After* I've eaten that delicious dinner you're slaving away over," Patrick added hastily. "So no need to shove that carrot where the sun don't shine."

Patrick got to Mark's house pretty much dead on eight o'clock. Mum hadn't exactly given her blessing, in the end, but she'd stopped trying to persuade him out of it, which was *almost* the same thing.

Course, now he was about to face another possibly hostile female relative. But Fen'd be all right—wouldn't she? At her age, there probably didn't seem that much difference between twenty-five and thirty-nine—it was all just *old*. He hoped.

He'd tried ringing up Lex to get a bit more info, but they weren't answering their phone. Probably busy with the boyfriend. So yeah, Fen was an unknown quantity. He could deal with that, though.

He took a deep breath and knocked sharply on the door.

Mark opened it with a smile that did a bloody good job of knocking all Patrick's worries clean out of his head. "Glad you could make it," Mark said as he stepped back to let Patrick in the hall.

"No problem."

"Come through to the living room. I'm afraid I owe you an apology."

"Yeah?"

Mark made a face. "Fen's watching *Scraping the Barrel*—you know, that awful reality show where they take all the talent show no-hopers and send them to boot camp to try to teach them to carry a tune. Apparently the terminally deluded are the one group it's still socially acceptable to poke fun at."

"Oh yeah, I know that show," Patrick said.

Mark froze. "Um. You're not a fan, are you?"

Patrick had to laugh at his horrified expression. "What, deal-breaker, is it? Nah, don't worry. Mum likes it, that's all. Makes her feel she's not doing too badly, she reckons."

Fen looked up as they walked in the living room.

"You remember Patrick, don't you?" Mark said, his hand hovering so near the small of Patrick's back he could feel the heat from it, yet still not actually touching.

Fen nodded but didn't say anything.

"Hi," Patrick said.

She bit her lip and looked back at the screen, where one of the contestants was being forced to sing "Three Blind Mice" over and over again in front of a jeering audience until they either got it right or broke down in tears. Patrick wished he knew if she was being deliberately unfriendly or just shy.

"Drinks?" Mark sounded a bit desperate.

"Cup of tea would be great, thanks."

"Fen?"

"Hot chocolate. Please. With marshmallows."

Patrick wasn't sure why Mark winced at that. "Sorry, darling, we're out of marshmallows."

"Oh. Squash, then."

"Right." Mark disappeared.

Patrick tried not to feel like he'd been thrown to the lions. He sat down gingerly on the sofa and watched the telly for a couple of minutes, but it was hard to get really involved in it what with the way the hair on the back of his neck was prickling.

Fen was staring at him. Patrick thought about just staring back, but it seemed a bit mean. And, well, he was trying to establish himself as one of the adults here. "School all right?" he asked, thinking a bit of conversation would definitely help. The contestant on screen had gone for the ugly sobbing option, which wasn't doing a right lot for the atmosphere.

She shrugged. "S'pose."

"Made any friends?"

She shrugged again. "S'pose."

Christ, had Patrick been this difficult as a teenager?

Yeah. Yeah, he probably had. Mum could probably go on for days about it, which was why he was never gonna ask her. Patrick smiled. "Good to see you getting friendly with Lex. They had a rough time at school—it's left 'em a bit wary about people." Well, people who weren't big, bearded bikers, when Lex's self-preservation circuits tended to short-circuit big time.

Fen leaned forward, tucking her hair behind an ear dotted with cute little sparkly studs. "Have you met Lex's boyfriend yet?"

"Not yet, no. Why, they said anything that's got you worried?"

"No . . . It's just, Lex seems so totally into him, you know? And it's, like, really soon, and they still haven't met any of his friends, and I'm just worried, you know? But, I mean, it's probably nothing."

Patrick frowned. "No, I know what you mean. Not sure there's anything we can do about it, though. 'Cept be there for Lex when they need us. *If* they need us," he added optimistically. "He might be all right, this bloke. Just give it time."

Fen nodded slowly. "Do you like going to the theatre?" she asked out of nowhere.

"Yeah. Do a bit of acting myself, actually. I'm in the Shamwell Amateur Dramatics Society, like Heather who runs your theatre group."

"Yeah?" Fen perked right up at that. "Can we go and see you in a play?"

"Next time I'm in one, yeah. You know, if the group works out for you, you should join. They're always after more young actors." Well, if he was honest, probably not *that* young, not for most of the plays they did, but there was still stuff she'd be able to get involved in, like props and scenery.

Patrick looked up as Mark came back into the room, carrying two steaming mugs in one hand and a glass of orange squash in the other. "Ah, cheers."

"Dad, can I join the Shamwell Amateur Dramatics Society? Patrick's a member, and so's Heather who does theatre group."

Mark blinked, and looked pleased. "Of course you can—if you're old enough?"

He looked at Patrick, who nodded. "Yeah, she wouldn't be the youngest. Everyone calls it the Sham-Drams, by the way. Bit less of a tongue twister."

"So . . . do you act?" Mark asked, sitting down.

Patrick cradled his mug of tea. "Yeah, but I haven't done anything for a while. Had to take a break after last summer." He slapped his leg, then realised that wouldn't mean anything to Fen. "Broke my leg playing cricket," he explained. Then, cos he thought she'd appreciate it, he added, "Nasty one too. Had the bone sticking right out through the skin."

She shuddered, wide-eyed. "Did it hurt?"

Patrick had to stifle a laugh, and from the look of him, Mark was having similar trouble. "Yeah, just a bit. Wanna see the scar?"

Patrick pulled up his trouser leg and got a weird sense of déjà vu as she reached forward to run a finger over it, just like her dad had done.

"I broke my arm when I was little," she said, then added in a disgusted tone and with a face to match, "*Dad* tried to rub it better."

Okay, there was no holding back the laugh that time. "Let me guess, didn't really help?"

"Now hold on a minute," Mark protested with a mock grimace. "She fell off her bike when it was *stationary*. How was I to know she'd broken a bone? I wouldn't have thought it was even *possible*." He gave his daughter a fond look, like he was proud of her for defying probability like that.

"Yeah? A bit accident prone, are we?" Patrick teased Fen.

"*No.*" She gulped some squash. "Ask Dad who broke a window teaching me how to play cricket when I was six. *Twice.* And he made me take the blame for the second time."

Mark's face was definitely a bit on the pink side. "I did not *make* her take the blame, all right? Payment was involved. Five pounds, as I recall. And two Cadbury's Creme Eggs."

Patrick shot him an amused look. "Sorry to break it to you, but the parenting halo's still starting to look a bit tarnished."

Fen giggled, then gave him a serious look. "Dad said you work for a charity. Helping disabled people."

"Yeah, that's right. SHARE—it's for adults with learning disabilities. Helping 'em be as independent as possible. A lot of people forget it's not only disabled kids who need a bit of support. I just do the fundraising, though—I leave the actual helping to the people who're qualified for it."

She nodded. "We're going to do the fun run, me and Dad. The 10K."

"Yeah? Lex handles all the online registrations, so I didn't know you'd signed up. Glad to hear it." Patrick smiled. "Hope you're getting him in training."

"He *says* he goes running when I'm at school."

"Excuse me?" Mark gave her a mock glare. "What do you mean, *says*? I *do* go running while you're at school, madam. You could have a bit more confidence in your father. What do you think I do all day, anyway?"

Patrick laughed. "Probably best not to ask that."

Fen giggled again. The lack-of-talent show ended, and she uncurled herself from the sofa. "I'm going upstairs, right?"

Mark, flicking through TV channels, just nodded vaguely.

Fen tutted. "Dad? I said I'm *going upstairs*, all right? I'll probably just go straight to bed, you know, when I'm ready." She waited a moment, clearly decided it hadn't sunk in, and added, "So I won't be downstairs again, 'kay?"

Patrick had to hold back a laugh when the penny visibly dropped in Mark's brain and he went a bit pink.

"Oh. Right. Well, good night, then, darling."

"Night, Dad. Night, Patrick."

Well, that hadn't gone too badly. And now here he was. With Mark.

Alone.

CHAPTER TWENTY-ONE

Mark experienced mixed emotions on watching Fen leave the room, supposedly exhausted from all that demanding TV watching. On the one hand, he was proud of her thoughtfulness in letting him have some time alone with Patrick. On the other, he was absolutely mortified that his child was bent on facilitating his love life. On the *third* hand, and he realised this metaphor was starting to get a little out of, hah, hand, there was a strange, anticipatory fizzing inside him he wasn't sure he'd ever felt before that was so overwhelming, he almost thought of calling her back.

Mark had finally found a channel that was showing some golf tournament, which he felt would be a much better backdrop for romance than, say, the blood-gore-and-screaming hospital drama that had come on straight after *Scraping the Barrel*. He wondered which bright spark in scheduling had decided to follow that bit of car-crash telly with a programme which featured *actual* car crashes.

"She's a good kid," Patrick said into the sudden silence.

"Yes. Yes, she is." Mark really didn't deserve her.

"It's great, you and her having all those memories together," Patrick said. He sounded almost wistful, but then perhaps he was thinking of his own father.

The fizzing subsided a little. Mark felt like an imposter. "Yes, but . . . they're all from a long time ago."

"So? At least she's got good memories of you." Patrick grinned. "Although bribing a kid to take the fall for a broken window, that's low."

"Clearly you haven't met my ex-wife." Mark shook his head, smiling back. "No, that's not fair. But I was still trying to make things work with her, and we'd been going through a rough patch, so . . . All turned out to be a waste of time, in the end."

"Well, at least Fen got five quid and some chocolate out of it," Patrick pointed out.

"There is that. Um. Would you like a real drink now? I've got bottled beer—just some stuff that was on offer at Waitrose, but it's fairly drinkable. Or there's wine."

"Wine'd be good. I like my beer draught, you know? But with wine, I'm not fussy."

"Wine it is, then," Mark said. Thank God. Not only was the prospect of his preferred brand of Dutch courage a relief, there was something more intimate about sharing a bottle of wine. Or did he only think that because he'd never been, well, *intimate* with a beer drinker before? "Shiraz okay?"

"Told you, mate, I'm not fussy. I grew up drinking the stuff Mum buys cheap at Asda." Patrick leaned back in the sofa, resting an ankle on the opposite knee.

Mark's heart beat faster as he went to get the wine from the kitchen. His hands slipped a little as he uncorked it, but he had himself back under control by the time he was back in the living room, bottle and two glasses in his hands. He even managed to pour the wine without clinking the bottle top on the glass.

"Hey, calm down, all right? I'm not gonna jump on you." Patrick's eyes twinkled.

Mark laughed ruefully. "God, am I that obvious? It's just—"

"I know, all right? Never done this before. Don't worry about it. We don't have to do anything, if you don't wanna."

"I wann—I mean, I want to," Mark said fervently. He took a fortifying swallow of Shiraz. "I'm really much better with women." It just slipped out. Mark cringed inside.

Fortunately Patrick laughed. "Yeah, girls are easier, some ways. You grow up, nearly everything you see on the telly and in films— yeah, and in real life too—it all tells you how to treat a woman. Or how not to," he added, his face darkening for a moment. "Even when there is gay stuff, a lot of it's issue-driven. You know—if a character's gay, there's gotta be a reason for it."

Mark nodded and took another gulp of wine.

Patrick was silent a moment before he spoke again. "So how come you never, you know, experimented or anything?"

The fizzing, this time, was definitely uncomfortable. "I did. Sort of." Mark's heart was racing. He put his glass down, although reluctantly. "You asked me, a while ago, how many boyfriends I'd had before I was twenty-one. The answer is one." Mark hardly got the word out through a throat that seemed to have closed up. "Just one." He shrugged jerkily. "It didn't last long. My dad saw us, and, well, made it clear it wasn't acceptable. And we had to move again soon after that, anyway." He took a deep breath and wiped his hands on his trousers. There. He'd said it. It hadn't been so bad, not really.

Just . . . It had just been so long since he'd spoken about Ray. That was all.

Mark realised Patrick hadn't replied, and looked up. Those sharp blue eyes were piercing into him. "What happened?" The tone was low, calm, but he looked almost angry.

"What I just told you. I was sixteen; he was twenty-three. Dad broke his nose and told him if he saw an effing poofter like him hanging around his son again, he'd be carrying his balls home in a bag."

"Christ. What did he catch you doing?"

"Talking." Mark took another deep breath. "It was late, and Dad was walking back from the pub with a couple of mates, and there I was with Ray. Standing under a lamppost like a couple of idiots in a bloody spotlight. I suppose he thought he had to take a stand. Everyone knew Ray was queer, so . . ." He swallowed. "After Dad knocked him down, the men with him put the boot in. Cracked a couple of ribs."

"Bloody hell. Did he report it?"

"Of course he didn't! I told you, I was *sixteen*. What the hell do you think would have happened if he'd brought the police in?" Mark looked Patrick in the eye. "You don't get it, do you? This was over twenty years ago. It wasn't like it is now. Best-case scenario, they'd have sent him home with a warning not to waste police time. Worst-case . . . Worst-case, he'd have been branded a paedophile, and he'd have been lucky if he only got bricks chucked through his windows. Dad . . . I thought he was going to wallop me too, but he just took me home, sat me down, gave me a beer, and asked me if that was what I wanted my life to be like."

"So basically this Ray got beat up to teach you a lesson?"

Mark's stomach lurched. "I . . . Oh God." He'd never thought of it that way. Why the hell had he never thought of it that way? "Maybe. God. I only wanted . . . He was the only gay man I knew. You couldn't miss him—he was so bloody camp, he probably had tent poles instead of bones. So when I realised I was, well, confused, he was the one I went to speak to about it. I liked him, although we never did much more than kiss." He licked his lips, only realising he was doing it when he saw Patrick staring at his mouth. Mark gave a shaky sigh, feeling hot and cold all over. "Sorry. That's rather killed the mood, hasn't it? This probably wasn't what you were expecting, coming round tonight."

Patrick leaned over and put a hand on Mark's arm. "No. But I'm glad you told me." His other hand came up slowly to Mark's face, as if Mark were a nervous cat that needed to be gentled. "Can I kiss you?"

Those startlingly blue eyes were only inches from Mark's own now. He felt confused, off-kilter. He hadn't expected—he wasn't sure what he'd expected. But something in Patrick's intense gaze seemed to say he knew what it meant to Mark to finally get his past all out in the open between them. It even seemed to suggest it meant something similar to Patrick to have been the recipient of his confidence.

Was he reading too much into a pair of blue eyes that darkened as he looked at them?

Did it even matter?

Before he was aware he'd formed the thought, Mark found himself leaning across the final few inches to press his lips to Patrick's. They were soft, and dry, and oh God, perfect. Patrick's mouth was rich and spicy like the wine they'd been drinking, and far more intoxicating. Mark leaned further into the kiss, the angle awkward where they sat side by side on the sofa. He wanted to get closer to Patrick, but their legs were pressed together as it was, so how—

Yes. God, like that, he realised as Patrick slung a leg over him to straddle his lap. It was still almost chaste, no . . . bits rubbing together, but it was *glorious*. Patrick hadn't shaved, and the light stubble that'd given him a wickedly rakish air now rasped deliciously against Mark's face. Ellen hadn't much liked—and God, no, he wasn't going to think about Ellen right now. He was with Patrick, whose hand on the back of his neck was soft, yes, but firm and strong. Steadying. Patrick's waist beneath his hands was trim but decidedly masculine, and the thighs that trapped his own were thick and muscular. Even the smell of him was all male—musk mingled with something dry and citrusy, as if he'd splashed on cologne before coming down here.

Mark wanted more—God, how he wanted more—but he also wanted this never to stop, ever. He made a soft sound of complaint as Patrick drew back from the kiss, breathing heavily.

Patrick laughed. "Christ, that Ray bloke must have been a bloody good teacher. Think maybe we'd better cool it a bit, in case Fen changes her mind about going straight to bed?"

Mark blinked and drew in a few deep breaths of his own. "God. Fen. Yes." Thank goodness one of them could still think straight.

Patrick sat back down beside him, laying a proprietary hand on Mark's thigh. Mark covered it with his own hand, linking their fingers together. God, it felt good.

"Prob'ly best we don't go too fast anyhow, yeah?" Patrick said, in the sort of tone that suggested he wouldn't mind if Mark disagreed.

Mark wanted to disagree. He wanted it so much it hurt, but he couldn't help feeling a shameful knot of relief that they weren't, apparently, going any further tonight.

Maybe Patrick had been right about him having some issues about being gay.

"You know," Patrick said after a bit. "What you just told me about your dad, him beating a bloke up, talking like that . . . That's really not the sort of family I reckoned you came from."

Mark's heart sank. He'd thought they'd finished raking over the muck in his past for now, but then again, wouldn't it be less painful in the long run to rip the scab off all in one go? "That was pretty much the point." He felt suddenly tired, and he probably wasn't making a lot of sense. "He . . . Dad was the sort of man who could get along with anyone—anyone who hadn't known him for long, that was. He'd suss people out, drop his accent up or down a couple of notches. Make them feel like they'd grown up together, no matter who it was. I used to get a clip round the ear if he caught me dropping aitches at home—

"He hit you?" Patrick's voice was sharp.

"No—well, not really. It was just a reprimand. He wasn't a violent man."

"So you'd do the same to Fen?"

"Of course not! But . . ." Mark wasn't quite sure how to finish that sentence. "Anyway," he went on quickly, "he said if I started out well-spoken, it'd be easier for me. But half the time, he spoke like an East End barrow boy himself."

Patrick was frowning. "I don't get it."

Mark steeled himself to look Patrick straight in the eye. "That was how he made a living. Conning people. I mean, I don't think he saw it that way. He just saw it as good business sense. Being savvy. But he'd get them to invest in his schemes—he could talk a donkey into sawing its own hind leg off and handing it to him—and for a while, we'd have plenty of money. Until the scheme failed, or someone started to get a bit impatient to get some kind of return on their investment. And then it'd be *Pack your bags, son, we're moving on*."

"Where was your mum in all this?" Patrick's tone was neutral, not condemning.

"She died when I was eleven. I think . . . Maybe he wouldn't have been so focused on the wheeling and dealing if she'd lived. I don't know. Maybe that was just the way he was. I don't really remember much from before she died." Mark gave a humourless smile. "Ellen used to say I was suppressing things because it was too painful to remember her. Maybe she was right. I mean . . . He wasn't a *bad* father. I wouldn't want you to think that. I'm sure he wanted the best for me."

"Just wasn't that great at providing it?"

"He did try. He used to say he'd never denied me anything, and it was true, in a way. It was just that a lot of his promises had a way of not coming true."

"From the way you're talking, I'm guessing he's no longer with us?"

"No. He was diagnosed with cancer while I was at university. Died about a year and a half before Fen was born."

"Must have been rough, having to worry about your dad while you were studying. Still, you must have done all right—got your degree, yeah?"

Mark nodded. "No credit to me, really. He, well, he put up a good front. Nobody knew how ill he was. I suppose he thought no one would have confidence in a dying man. And, well . . . I was young, and there were a lot of distractions. You know what it's like at uni." He still felt guilty about it.

Patrick shrugged. "I never went to uni. Didn't fancy the debt and wanted to get out in the real world. No offence."

"None taken. I'm not sure I'd have gone if they'd been charging fees to students in my day." Or if his father hadn't managed to fiddle the form somehow so he'd got a full maintenance grant with no parental contribution, but Mark decided not to mention that. He had a feeling Patrick, with his social conscience, wouldn't approve.

"What did you study?"

"Maths." Mark said it self-deprecatingly, bracing himself for the usual response of *You must be so clever*, which he'd never really known how to answer. On occasion, he'd just gone with a simple yes, but this wasn't a conversation he particularly wanted to shut down.

Patrick didn't disappoint. "Ooh, bright lad. You're an accountant, yeah? At least, that's what Barry said."

"Ah, yes. That's right." He'd started out as an accountant, before choosing to specialise in tax. Mark wasn't sure Patrick would be all that interested in his many years of studying and exams, however. "I'm not sure it'd have been my choice, necessarily, but I didn't have strong views either way and, well, Dad was keen for me to go into it. 'Got to know the rules before you can work around 'em,' was what he said."

"And you didn't wanna upset him while he was ill, yeah?" Patrick guessed correctly. "Was it hard when he died? Shit, sorry, that must sound like crap. Course it was hard." He ran a hand over his hair. "Just—think I mentioned my dad's a right shite, yeah? Sometimes I wonder, you know. If I'll regret stuff when he goes. Sorry."

Mark thought about his father's death, and the mess of guilt and regret he'd had to untangle afterwards. "I don't think anyone really knows until it happens. But, for what it's worth, I don't think he deserves a reconciliation. Not from what you told me."

"Wasn't sure you'd remember all that. You were a bit under the influence at the time." Patrick gave him a half smile that was teasing and charming all at once.

"And you weren't?" Mark raised an eyebrow.

"What, me? I can hold my drink, I can."

"So all that business in the gents' that night—that was you being entirely sober, was it?"

"Well, maybe not totally sober. Christ, that was fun, though. The look on that bloke's face." Patrick laughed. "Yours too, come to that." His face straightened. "So are you okay with it now? Us, I mean?"

Mark ruthlessly suppressed the stray bolt of panic that shot through him for an instant. He swallowed. "Yes. I think so. Yes," he said again, more firmly this time.

Patrick gave him a shrewd look. "In public? Telling everyone in the Spartans you're my bloke?"

Mark grabbed the wine bottle and refilled their glasses. "Just let me get a pint in first, all right?"

Patrick grinned and clinked their glasses together. "I'll drink to that."

He stayed another hour or so, then left, saying his mum was expecting him. Mark suspected it had more to do with the kisses getting a bit heated again. And while Mark's baser half wanted to tell him *No, come back, I'm a grown man, for God's sake*, his more sensible and, dare he say it, more romantic half was relieved and delighted that Patrick had meant it about not pushing the pace.

It was a big thing—all puns aside—to have sex with another man for the first time. Kissing, well, he'd done that before. But while he had no doubt it was what he wanted, Mark couldn't help feeling a certain amount of trepidation at the thought of crossing his own personal gay Rubicon.

After Patrick had gone, Mark buzzed around the house, too keyed up to settle to anything as mundane as reading or watching television. The very thought of sleep was laughable. He felt, right now, as if he could dash off a book in a night, if he could only settle to writing. Or phone up his former superior, Charles, and tell him exactly what he thought of his bigoted attitudes.

In the end, Mark got out his laptop and did a search for Ray Franzese. He could remember Ray telling him about his surname—he'd thought it was funny. *"Here I am, a British bloke with an Italian surname that means* French. *No wonder people don't know what to make of me."*

Right. Dad had known only too well what to make of him.

There were several people with the name Ray Franzese, all of them with profile pictures, thank God, so at least he'd know when he'd found him. Then again, would Mark even recognise him after all these years? He scanned through the images—too young, too black, too blond . . .

There. It had to be, although, Christ, what the hell had happened to his hair? But he was the right age, had the right look—crooked nose and all—and it was a wedding photo, with him standing next to a dark-skinned man of similar age and lack of hair, both of them smiling their bald heads off at the camera. Heart thumping, Mark scrolled down Ray's timeline, feeling uncomfortably stalkerish but unable to stop himself. Ray had married his husband, whose name turned out to be Ola, only last year—no, wait, that had been the conversion of a civil partnership to marriage when the law allowed, Mark realised after scrolling down further. They'd had a second ceremony, both of them dressed in traditional morning coats, top hats and all. They'd been together for . . . God. Twenty years now.

There were plenty of good-hearted comments from friends on the photos they'd posted, both of the wedding itself and of moments from their life together.

He didn't do too badly in the end, did he, Dad?

CHAPTER TWENTY-TWO

Mark saw Patrick several times over the following week—he seemed to be quite happy to drop round either for dinner or after they'd eaten, even though it inevitably meant spending time with Fen too. It was gratifying that she seemed to want to get to know him, although Mark wasn't sure he'd ever feel *wholly* comfortable with the way she continued to rather obtrusively leave them alone together after a while.

Still, it was probably better than going up to Patrick's house and being glared at by his mum. He was damn certain there'd be no tactful withdrawal of chaperonage there.

Thursday night, Patrick turned up a bit later than usual. "Hope it's not too late to come round. Kitchen disaster," he half explained as Mark stood aside to let him in. "Don't ask, and don't offer me any toasted bread products. I had to stay and help Mum out. No Fen tonight?" he added, seeing the empty living room.

Mark shook his head. "Apparently, she's actually been given some homework tonight, so she's upstairs on her laptop researching towns with a tourist industry. Or talking to her friends on whatever it is teenagers use instead of Facebook these days. One of the two."

Patrick grinned. "So, just you and me, yeah? Glad I came after all. Not that I'm only after your body. Wouldn't want you to think that."

"No?" Mark felt by this time he'd had plenty of leisure to think over the idea of having sex with a man, and he'd come to the conclusion that yes, he was fine with it, and could he be having it right now, please? He grabbed Patrick by the hips and pulled him close. "But you *are* after my body? In addition, obviously, to all my other fine qualities?"

"Fine qualities . . .?" Patrick's puzzled frown cracked into a laugh as Mark pinched his bum in retaliation. "Oh yeah. I am seriously, *seriously* after your body, Mark Nugent."

They kissed, Mark wondering if he'd ever get used enough to the taste of Patrick, the feel of him in his arms, to take it all for granted. Right now, every moment seemed like a gift. He was getting hard, and was desperate to know if Patrick was too. Maybe if he shifted their bodies just so—

Patrick broke away. "C'mon. How about we sit down and watch a bit of telly? Don't want you feeling like a booty call."

Mark would, right now, have been just *fine* with being a booty call. "If nothing else, it'd be a novel experience," he muttered, sinking down on the sofa beside Patrick.

Patrick slid an arm around his shoulders, and Mark settled a bit lower in his seat to make it more comfortable. He was slowly getting used to sometimes being the snugglee, and not just the snuggler. Or did he mean that the other way around? Of course, they were much of a height, which made it easier to switch roles. He wondered how it was for men with much smaller partners. Did they find themselves perennially the big spoon?

"Now that I can't believe," Patrick murmured in his ear.

Mark blinked, then realised what he was referring to. "Believe. I wouldn't say booty calls hadn't been invented—although, as far as I know, the term didn't exist—but they were a lot less prevalent back before I got married. At least, from the sort of girls I knew."

"And you never had a chance to get to know the right sort of blokes, yeah?"

Patrick had been flicking through channels and had apparently settled on a dull-looking programme about migrating birds. Mark frowned at the television. "You really want to watch this?"

A laugh tickled his ear. "Not a lot, no. You ready to be my booty call now?"

"God, you have to ask?"

This time, their kiss was richer, deeper. Patrick's tongue delved into Mark's mouth, sending a jolt straight through his body to his groin. Mark met the challenge with one of his own, light-headed with it all. He slid a hand up from Patrick's hip to his chest, and thumbed a nipple through the thin fabric of his shirt. Already peaked, it hardened under his ministrations.

Mark shifted closer, and Patrick leaned back, pulling them both down to lie on the sofa, Mark on top of him. He could feel Patrick's cock getting hard against his hip, and ground his own erection into the warm, perfect body beneath him—

"Dad?" It was Fen's voice, calling down the stairs. "*Dad*!"

Mark broke the kiss and closed his eyes briefly. "Sorry. It's probably just a spider in the bath, but I'd better see to it, whatever it is."

Patrick chuckled as they got up, straightening shirts and adjusting trousers. "Nah, it's okay. I'd better be going anyhow. But it's been great, yeah? I'll see you soon."

He left, Mark watching him go with an ache in his heart and . . . elsewhere, to the sounds of Fen calling "*Dad*! *Now, all right*? *DAD.*"

It was some small consolation that Fen had discovered a minor leak in the bathroom that might, if left to itself, have had serious repercussions for the downstairs ceiling.

Mark couldn't help wishing she'd given them just half an hour longer before reporting it, though.

Even five minutes would probably have done, damn it.

Next day, after a restless night with some dreams he would *not* want his daughter to know about, Mark was just starting to think about lunch when the doorbell rang. Opening it, he found Patrick on the doorstep, bearing a couple of paper bags from the village baker's shop and a hopeful expression. "Wanna do lunch?"

Mark smiled, his heart—and yes, all right, other parts—giving a joyful little leap at the sight. "Come in. I was just about to eat, so your timing's excellent."

Patrick grinned as he closed the door behind himself. "How hungry are you? Gotta eat this minute, or you okay to wait . . . for a bit?"

The glint in his eye left absolutely no doubt as to exactly *what* he meant a bit of. Mark swallowed. "I can wait," he said fervently, in a voice gone suddenly hoarse.

"Fen safe at school, yeah?" Patrick asked, stepping closer and slipping his arms around Mark's waist.

Mark nodded. "Not due back for hours. Come upstairs?"

"Mm, no hurry." Patrick nuzzled into Mark's neck and nipped at an earlobe playfully. "I told Lex I'd be taking a long lunch. Thought we could pick up where we left off last night."

"With a leak in the bathroom?"

"No, ta, I went before I came."

Mark drew back to stare at him. "What—not that *sort* of leak! That was what Fen was yelling about last night."

Patrick's smile was slow and lazy. "Uh-huh? So what am I gonna be yelling about today? Gotta say, I was hoping for something better than that."

"In that case," Mark said firmly, "let's go upstairs and give you something to yell about." He grabbed Patrick by the arse and pulled him close, unable to stifle a groan as their erections ground together. God, he'd never been so hard in his *life*. Patrick had grabbed him right back and was nipping at his neck again, none too gently.

"No one can see in your living room from outside, right?" Patrick breathed into his neck. "Unless they've climbed the fence and they're standing in your garden, in which case they deserve to get an eyeful, the pervs."

"No, but—"

"Thought we could make a few memories on that sofa of yours. Something to tide us over, nights when we don't get the chance to be alone."

"Oh God, yes." Mark barely heard the paper lunch bags hit the hall floor, too intent on dragging Patrick by the hand into the living room. Patrick kicked his shoes off as they went, leaving them who knew where, and by the time they'd reached the sofa, he was tugging his shirt over his head.

God, he was gorgeous. Lightly tanned skin, a hairless chest—did he wax?—and pale nipples that tightened as Mark looked at them, and tightened even more when he pinched and played with them.

"Been thinking about getting a piercing," Patrick said. "What do you reckon?"

Was it possible to improve upon perfection? Apparently Mark's cock thought so, twitching at Patrick's words. "Definitely worth thinking about," he breathed.

Mark stripped off his own shirt, feeling self-conscious and very, very hairy. Patrick didn't seem to mind, though. He ran his fingers through Mark's chest hair with a murmur of "Nice," then bent to kiss Mark's neck again. "What do you wanna do?"

God, what *didn't* he want to do? "I want to suck you," Mark blurted out, shocking himself with his bluntness.

"I'm good with that," Patrick said with a smile and undid his trousers. "Sit on the sofa, yeah?"

Mark did so.

Patrick pushed off his boxer briefs and climbed on the sofa to kneel astride Mark's lap. Suddenly, deliriously, Mark was faced with conclusive proof that yes, Patrick *did* wax.

Mark had never been this close to another man's hard cock before. Close up, it looked enormous, aggressively red, jutting proudly from between lean, strong legs. It looked *delicious*. The scent was driving him wild, so musky and male, with a hint of salt from the moisture glistening on the tip. Light-headed with desire, Mark slithered down on the sofa between Patrick's legs until the angle was just right, then gripped the base with one hand and reached out with his tongue for a taste.

He wasn't prepared for the jolt that ran through him, from his tongue through his chest and straight to his balls, as if Patrick had somehow plugged himself into the mains without Mark noticing. This was it. *This* was what he'd been missing all those years.

Heady as it was, it wasn't enough. Mark plunged his mouth over the head of Patrick's cock, revelling in the feeling of it filling his mouth, almost choking him. Patrick's gasp only fed his desire, and he sucked gently, then ran his tongue around the head. His hand slipped lower to fondle Patrick's balls, the hairlessness strange yet undeniably erotic.

"Fucking . . . Are you sure you haven't done this before?" Patrick panted.

Mark scrabbled at the fastenings of his trousers, finally managing to get them open wide enough to get his hand inside. He gripped himself firmly and started to stroke. He wanted to come with Patrick's dick in his mouth. He'd seen it in online porn, a man jerking himself off as he sucked his partner, and God, he wanted that. Wanted Patrick in his mouth as he came.

It wouldn't take much, he knew it.

Patrick was babbling, muttering *Yeah, fuck, God*—then he stopped.

A strange, jangly little tune had started playing.

It was a moment before Mark realised Patrick's phone was ringing. "'S okay," Patrick gasped. "They can leave a message."

Thank God for that. Mark started sucking again, the saltiness in his mouth intensifying, Patrick's dick hard as velvet-enclosed iron. This was heaven, this was *it*, this was—

There was a pounding on the front door. It sounded urgent, with a strong suggestion of *I'm not stopping till you answer*.

Damn, damn, *damn*.

Patrick hung his head and half laughed, half sighed. "Christ, does somebody up there hate us?"

Mark let Patrick's dick slip from his mouth. Patrick groaned, and not in a good way this time, swung his leg back over Mark, and stood up.

Damn it all to *hell*. Mark pushed himself up off the sofa, zipped up his trousers, and pulled on his shirt, not bothering to button it back up. Whoever was at the door could just deal with it—with a bit of luck, it'd turn out to be a delivery for next door or something, and they could get back to what they were doing. He hurriedly checked to make sure nothing was poking out where it shouldn't and there were no betraying stains, then ran to open the door.

"'Ullo, Mr. Nugent." It was Lex, wringing their hands and at least having the grace to look as embarrassed as Mark felt. "I'm really, really sorry, yeah, but I need Patrick. Urgent. It's the bloke from the council, and there's been a cock-up about the run, and he's gotta sort it out, like, right now. I wouldn't've interrupted otherwise."

"No, no, not a problem at all. Won't you come in?" Mark babbled, taking refuge in extreme politeness from the cringe-inducing mortification of his daughter's friend knowing exactly what he'd just been doing, and with whom.

"Nah, ta, I gotta get back, but you'll send him right over, won't you? I told 'em he'd only be ten minutes, see, and there's five gone already."

Mark nodded sadly. "He'll be right over."

CHAPTER TWENTY-THREE

The week leading up to the fun run started out well enough for Patrick, but went downhill rapidly. He had about a ton and a half of stuff still to do before Sunday, so of course the trustees of SHARE had decided Friday would be the perfect day for a meeting. He knew from experience it'd take up the whole afternoon, and by the end of it, they'd have got bugger all done. *And* it meant bringing forward the deadline for sorting out any last-minute problems with anyone who worked office hours, like the insurance company and the council— although he hoped to God everything was now sorted with the last lot at least.

His time spent with Mark was the one bright spot. They'd had a lazy Sunday together the previous day, taking Fen out to lunch at the Sticky Wicket. Mark had wanted to invite Patrick's mum along too, but Patrick had vetoed that one. He knew his mum, and while she was coming round to the idea of them being together, he wanted to give her a bit more time before he let her loose on Mark in public. Although, to be honest, he thought he might have spoken too soon once they were sat down at the table, Fen so bloody obviously on her best behaviour it made him want to hug her. Mum was a sucker for that kind of thing. Yeah, Fen'd bring her round if nothing else did.

Afterwards, they'd gone for a walk on the common, then sprawled around on the sofa at Mark's watching DVDs, all three of them. It'd been a good day, even if Patrick was getting seriously frustrated by the lack of alone time with his bloke. God knew he wouldn't have time to just pop round during the day *this* week. They'd both just have to settle for a bit of alone time by themselves.

Phone sex had been a nonstarter, Mark too bloody paranoid Fen would overhear. And, in any case, Patrick wanted to *be* there the first time he made Mark come.

They managed a couple of evenings together, but Patrick wasn't really on his game. He was just too bloody knackered. The last time he made it there, in fact, Fen had videoed him snoring on the sofa with her phone and sent a copy to Lex.

Of course, sod's law, he drove himself so hard during the week to get everything done by lunchtime Friday, he found himself with hardly anything to do for most of the morning—nothing that needed doing today, that was, and he was damned if he was starting anything new before the fun run was done and dusted—except look forward to the meeting with the trustees.

That was a passion killer if ever he'd known one.

"Right, wish me luck," he said in resignation, standing up after lunch to go to the meeting. It was going to be held at the Tickled Trout, as usual—catch the trustees squeezing themselves into SHARE's little office by the river. He rolled his shoulders to try to get rid of the stiffness that'd come from nowhere over the morning.

Lex grinned. "You know what? I changed my mind. If your bloke decides he's gonna keep you and you don't have to work no more, I don't want your job. I've seen the way them trustees look at me. Like they reckon I'm gonna run off with the collecting boxes."

"Nah, they're not all bad," Patrick said, trying to sound like he believed it. He knew they *meant* well. All right, most of the time he did. Most of 'em. Maybe not Onslow, who was a git if ever he'd met one. But the rest of 'em were human. More or less. "They just don't know what it's like doing the actual work."

Patrick ducked under the low lintel of the Tickled Trout's door and went into the main bar to find the trustees already sitting around their usual large, round table in the corner. Onslow looked at his watch as Patrick approached, despite the fact Patrick knew damn well he was five minutes early.

There were six trustees of SHARE, but only five ever made it to a meeting. Old Miss Wellbeck, who'd been one of the founders, was excused on grounds of age and general decrepitude, although Patrick had seen her around the village a lot lately, leaning on the arm of a dapper older bloke, and she'd seemed to have plenty of spring in her step these days. The ones who always turned up were the vicar; Mrs. Ormley, the school receptionist; Roger Hunstanton, who Patrick knew from the Sham-Drams and who was a total dick; Trevor Williams, who had ambitions to be a dick but would never, ever make it because even a dick had to be able to stand up for himself now and then; and Onslow, who thought UKIP was a decent enough political party but they didn't go far enough in their policies.

Patrick had often wondered what the lot of them, the vicar and Miss Wellbeck excepted, were doing as trustees of a charity, seeing as when it came to the milk of human kindness they were all pretty much lactose intolerant. Still, fair dues, they gave their time for nothing, and a charity as unfashionable as SHARE probably had to take what it could get.

The vicar always chaired the meeting, due to some long-standing tradition which totally ignored the fact he was the person least suited for the job. Mrs. Ormley always took minutes due, Patrick privately thought, to being female. How come she never seemed to mind was beyond him.

Despite the fact they'd all been handed a paper copy of the agenda on arrival, Mrs. Ormley insisted on reading it out with irritating slowness. When she finally got to item nine, the last on the list, Onslow coughed. "I have an item for Any Other Business. I wish to discuss staffing."

Patrick frowned, but before he could say anything, the vicar spoke up, which was a first. "Really? I'm sure I speak for all of us here—not that I'd presume to speak for everyone else, of course—"

Onslow coughed again, louder this time. "Mrs. Ormley, if you would be so good as to note it on the agenda?"

"Of course, Kenneth," she said with what was disturbingly close to a simper.

Patrick wondered what the hell Onslow was up to. He couldn't believe the bloke wanted to increase staff, but he'd actually been grudgingly supportive of getting an admin assistant in six months ago, which had led to Patrick hiring Lex. Why would he change his tune now?

The memory of what Lex had said sent an uneasy shiver down his spine. *"I've seen the way they look at me."*

Shit. Onslow didn't like who Patrick had hired, did he?

The journey down points one through eight on the agenda went with the usual frustrating stop-start approach, dithering from the vicar, and obstructiveness from Onslow and Hunstanton. It was all routine stuff, with the same old arguments they had every two months at these bloody meetings, half of which didn't even concern Patrick cos it had to do with spending funds, not raising 'em. His eyes had seriously glazed over by the time it got to item number nine.

Onslow coughed. Patrick was seriously tempted to offer to nip over the chemist's shop and get him some lozenges, 'cept if he did that, he'd be even more tempted to just not come back. "It's come to my attention that we may have been a little hasty in employing an administration assistant. I'm really not sure our funds allow it."

"Oi, now wait a minute," Patrick said. "We went through all this six months ago, and you *know* the numbers make sense. More staff means more funds raised."

"Ah, but . . ." Onslow looked around the table at each of them in turn. "Does it? It's come to my attention that the . . . person currently holding the role is not working as many hours as we might wish. I'm sure you're all aware that in the current climate, with budgets for government services being squeezed ever tighter, we need to make sure every penny of our own funds is spent as wisely as possible."

"Lex has medical appointments," Patrick said shortly. "They made it clear when they interviewed, all right?"

"Yes, but it's not exactly a *health* issue, is it? Now, I have every sympathy with the individual concerned—"

Yeah, right, Patrick thought sourly.

"—but SHARE does not exist to help individuals with that sort of problem. Is it fair to the people we were set up to help to continue in a course of action that is to their detriment? I'm sure we're all aware the Home Farm Market Gardening project, to name but one, now relies solely on charity funding, and there's a chronic shortfall of Supported Housing places throughout the district."

There was a general chorus of muttered approval from the trustees. Even from the bloody vicar. Didn't he see this was blatant bigotry, just dressed up as concern for the charity cos even Onslow knew that sort of thing didn't fly anymore? And yeah, so maybe everything he said about the state-funded programmes being cut back and all was true, but that didn't make it Lex's fault.

Patrick leaned forward to make his point. "Lex works hard. Just cos they sometimes have to have time off doesn't mean they don't make it up later. I dunno what I'd have done without Lex, sorting out this fun run." For which none of *them* had bothered to sign up, he'd noticed.

"Well, well," put in the vicar, looking at his watch. "Perhaps we could address the matter after the run? I could be free this time next week, if that's acceptable with all of you?"

Great. Patrick could see how it'd go. Next week, they'd ask him if he had any big events coming up. He'd have to say no, because this was the big one until the autumn, when they had a ball planned. And then they'd say, *Right, so you don't need an assistant, do you?* And that'd be it, and there'd be one more person signing on for the dole.

Christ, how was he gonna tell Lex?

And why the bloody hell did all this have to happen *now*?

CHAPTER TWENTY-FOUR

Mark was surprised—and pleased, if embarrassed—to be greeted with a rousing cheer when he turned up to the Spartans meeting on Friday night. As the fun run was on the coming Sunday, their fortnightly meeting had been pulled forward. Much to the annoyance, apparently, of the local poetry society, who were used to having the upstairs room at the Three Lions to themselves Friday nights.

"Best induction effort ever, that was," Barry said, and there was a chorus of nods. "You've raised the bar there, mate, and no mistake. We were raking it in with the charity buckets, and we had half a dozen people asking about membership. Most of 'em not eligible on account of being female, unfortunately, but you can't have everything."

Si laughed, his big black beard shaking. "Oh yes, and most of 'em over fifty."

"Not all of 'em," Rory put in glumly. "My ex-missus was asking if you were single."

Jolted out of his disbelieving high (*They like me, they really like me*), Mark swallowed and darted a glance over at Patrick, whose face gave away nothing of his wishes. "Sorry. No," he managed. Rory looked a bit more cheerful.

Mark wasn't sure if he was relieved or disappointed when Patrick didn't jump in with *Actually, he's with me*. They'd seen each other a couple more times this week, but Patrick hadn't had a lot of time to spare, with the fun run coming up on Sunday.

At least, Mark hoped it was that, rather than him having changed his mind about Mark.

No, that was paranoia. The time they'd spent together, while definitely frustrating in one particular way, had otherwise been, well, nice—sitting side by side on the sofa watching television with Fen, sneaking kisses whenever she left the room and then laughing about it like schoolboys. Particularly when she gave them withering looks on her return and came out with things like "I do know what you're doing. I'm not a *kid*." It'd been fun. Cosy.

Taking her out last Sunday had been wonderful too. Like having a family again, only this time, one that worked. If they'd bumped into anyone from the Spartans while they were out that day, Mark didn't think he'd have been able to restrain himself from proudly announcing their couple-dom.

Patrick—Patrick had been marvellous. Great with Fen. Maybe there wasn't the instant connection she'd had with David, but she seemed to like him well enough. Apparently, Lex's endorsement was worth a good deal. Or maybe it was just that Patrick was, well, *Patrick*.

Possibly Mark was biased there, however.

Barry rapped on the table, startling Mark out of his reverie. "Right. Main, and pretty much only, item on the agenda: the SHARE Fun Run. Patrick, want to say a few words?"

Patrick stood up. He looked tired. "Cheers, Barry. Yeah, well, it's all looking good. Rory, you're still on to man the bouncy slide, right?"

Rory nodded. "Me kids'd never speak to me again if I backed out now. Course, I'm gutted I won't be able to do the run," he added, actually looking pretty smug about it.

"Yeah, right." Patrick's dry tone clearly showed he had Rory's number. "Thanks to everyone who's signed up as a marshal—we've got plenty of those now, so the rest of you are just gonna have to run it."

There was a chorus of groans from the less fit members of the group.

"Ah, ya lazy bastards," Kevin shouted over them. "I'm running the 10K and I've got both my littl'uns signed up for the 2K."

That was optimistic of him, seeing as only one of them was old enough to walk. Mark supposed Mrs. Kevin would be called on to don her martyr's halo once again and push the littlest one around the course in a buggy.

"I'll be running the 10K too," Mark said by way of moral support.

"That's right, show the rest of us up even more," Rory said with a grin.

They got into the nitty-gritty of the day's organisation, which proved to be both nittier and grittier than Mark had expected. He'd had no idea what a mammoth task it was, organising people to run a few miles across country, and how hard some people involved could be to wrangle. While his respect for Patrick had gone up a notch or two over the last week, Mark noted with concern that Patrick was quieter and more serious than usual. The pressure of bearing ultimate responsibility for the success or failure of the run seemed to weigh heavily on his shoulders—but then, they were quite young shoulders, weren't they?

He'd offered to help, but Patrick had said that at this late stage, there was very little he could do without Patrick having to spend hours he didn't have catching Mark up on everything first. All the helpers' roles had been filled weeks ago.

Mark would just have to make sure he made a damned fine showing in the run itself, that was all.

Barry stood up. "Right, lads. Meeting's over, it's Friday night, and by Spartan law, we will stand and drink until we can't stand up anymore. Are you with me?"

There was a general indication of approval for that plan. Mark glanced at Patrick, thinking if Patrick was agreeable to sloping off early, he'd definitely be on board with that plan, but Patrick just gave a tiny shrug.

Beers it was, then. Mark didn't mind. He was on top of the world—feted by his fellow Spartans and, well, if not in love, certainly a fair way along the road to it. And he'd even managed to have a perfectly civil conversation with Patrick's mum the previous evening, having met her by chance at the Shamwell Area Preservation Society (SAPS) meeting, where he'd inadvertently let slip he was a chartered accountant and somehow found himself co-opted on the spot to become treasurer.

He hadn't minded that either, despite how clearly relieved the previous incumbent had been to give up the role. It was good to get involved with village life. To give something back. His book on tax avoidance wasn't going at all well—in fact, he wasn't sure he even wanted to write it anymore—so he had plenty of time on his hands. Why not use it for the benefit of the community?

Mark managed to snatch a few words with Patrick on the way down the stairs. "All right?" he asked, hoping Patrick would get that he meant it to be all-encompassing, from the general state of Patrick's health to his reaction to Mark's failure to out them as a couple.

Patrick's smile looked tired. "Yeah. Rough day, though. Had this git on the committee trying to talk the rest of 'em into sacking Lex."

"Seriously?" Mark was appalled. "On what grounds?"

"Trying to cut costs, *he* said." Patrick snorted. "'Cept he was all for expanding the staff *before* we hired Lex. Like Lex doesn't have enough to deal with without bigoted sods like that."

"They can't just sack Lex," Mark said confidently. "Charities are subject to employment protection laws, the same as any employer."

Patrick stared. "And you really reckon Lex'd go to a tribunal and make 'em spend all the money we've been raising on legal fees? Make the people SHARE helps go without support so they can get their rights?"

Mark opened his mouth, then shut it again. "That's unfair," he said at last.

"Yeah, welcome to the real world."

"But there must be something that can be done—"

"There's nothing, all right? Not without—" Patrick's voice, which had been rising, stopped suddenly. He closed his eyes. "Shit. Just ignore me until I've got a couple of beers down me, all right?"

Well, bugger that. Mark wanted to talk some more, but they got separated in the pub. Mark was dragged off by Si, who was insistent on buying him a pint for reasons unknown, and Patrick got collared by Barry. Presumably he had some more things to sort out about the fun run again, although God knew Mark had thought they'd talked it all to death already.

Si just seemed to want to talk about the Six Nations rugby, and whether it'd been better when it was still the Five Nations, or even the Home Nations, which none of them was actually old enough to remember. Not that Mark had ever been particularly keen on rugby in any case, so why Si had chosen him to talk to about it he had no idea.

Alasdair kept giving Si annoyed looks, though, as if he'd wanted to talk about something else entirely.

When, after two more rounds of drinks, Patrick was *still* cornered at one end of the bar by Barry's bulky figure, Mark thought he'd better mount a rescue. He was, in any case, getting a little unnerved by Alasdair's behaviour and the way Si kept insisting on buying his beer.

Barry and Patrick seemed to have moved on from the fun run. Barry was gazing at Patrick with big, soulful eyes. "Nobody ever calls me Baz, or Bazzer. I'd make a great Baz. Wouldn't I?"

Patrick didn't roll his eyes, but he gave Mark an exasperated glance. "Yeah, but mate . . . You always tell people your name's Barry. So that's what they call you, innit? Like I'm Patrick, not Pat or Paddy or any of that crap."

"Yeah, but . . . 's different, innit? Patrick's a good name. Solid. Barry's just . . . 'S like Gary, or Harry, or even bloody Larry, 'cept they're all short for something, ain't they? They all got proper names attached. Barry's just . . . *Barry*."

"I thought it was short for something," Rory said, huffing a bit as he climbed up on a barstool next to them.

"Yeah? What d'you reckon, then?" Barry demanded, his tone belligerent. "Barreth? Barold? Sodding Barrence?"

Rory scratched his head. "Nah . . . Bartholomew?"

"That's Barty."

"Barnaby?"

"*Barney*."

Barry was looking like he was a bit close to thumping the table when Patrick stepped in. "Finnbarr."

Two pairs of bloodshot eyes turned to stare at him. "What?" Barry demanded. "Are you twisting my spanner?"

Mark stifled a laugh.

Patrick didn't look like he was amused. "It's Irish, innit? Like Patrick. And it's what Barry's short for."

"Not on my bloody birth certificate it ain't." Barry fumbled out his credit cards. "See there? Says B. Thompson. *B*. Not effing *F*. Oi," he added in Mark's direction, having finally noticed he was with them. He grabbed hold of Mark's arm. "That look like an *F* to you?"

"Ah . . . no?"

Barry slapped the table. "See? My name ain't short for Finnbarr. It ain't short for nuffing."

"I knew a Barrington once," Mark said warily. "American, obviously."

There was a silence, then Barry started nodding slowly. "Barrin'ton. Like it. That's a good, strong name, that is. That name's got class. *And*," he added, leaning forward to wag a finger at Patrick, "it starts with a *B*."

"Not gonna argue with you over that, mate," Patrick said. His faint emphasis on the *that* seemed to suggest they'd not been seeing eye-to-eye on everything tonight. "Right. Barrington it is. Think I'll call you Barry for short, though—that all right with you?"

"Course it is." Barry gave a little wave like the Queen on a walkabout. "*Course* it is." He frowned. "How'd we even get onto this, anyhow? We was talking about this fun run of yours. Something I gotta ask you . . . What was it? Oh, yeah—you're gonna sort out chairs for the marshals, right? Cos if I wanted to be on me feet all flippin' morning, I'd be doing the run, now wouldn't I?"

Patrick closed his eyes for a moment, the tiredness all too evident again, but shrugged at Mark, as if to say, *What can you do?* "Barry, we've been through this, all right? You wanna take a fold-up chair to sit on, that's fine by me. But you take it *yourself*."

"Yeah, but—"

Mark gave Patrick a sympathetic look and took his pint over to rejoin Si and Alasdair, not without a glance back over his shoulder. Barry seemed to have moved into belligerent-drunk mode now, from the vehement hand gestures. Should Mark have stayed?

No. Patrick was a grown man, for heaven's sake. If Mark kept hanging around him as if he needed protecting, it'd just look ridiculous. And, well, obvious that there was something going on between them. Which wouldn't be a problem, really, as Mark had told Patrick he didn't want to hide their relationship—but there was a difference between the other Spartans finding out about it by being told and by watching Mark hang around Patrick like a lovesick teenager.

Alasdair nudged Si as Mark sat down with them. "Go on, then. Fucking *ask* him, for Christ's sake."

Mark had *known* there was something going on there. Were they finally going to get to the point?

Si leaned forward, a serious look on his face. "Spartan, what is your profession?"

Mark blinked, then laughed. "War?"

Alasdair made a frustrated sound.

Si nudged his mate, none too gently, until he shut up. "No, see, I'm being serious here. What is it you do for a living? Cos Patrick said you was an accountant, but Alasdair here says *you* said you're something else."

"So you want to know my actual profession? Well, still war, I suppose, but only on the tax man. I started out in accountancy, but I've spent most of my working life as a tax advisor." He was quite proud of himself for modestly leaving out the *chartered* bit.

"Tax advisor, is it? So you tell rich people how to get away without paying their taxes, is that right?" Si seemed disappointed, which stung a little.

"Rich corporations, actually, but yes. I know tax might sound a bit dry, but it's actually a fascinating subject—utilising legal loopholes in an innovative way to help the client. I've personally managed to wipe out more than one multimillion-pound tax liability—got some very nice bonuses for it too. Well, the clients were grateful, of course. It made a sizeable difference to their bottom line. All aboveboard, obviously," Mark added hastily, as Si still wasn't looking as impressed as he might have hoped. "I wouldn't want you to think I was involved in tax *evasion*."

"No, I don't s'pose you would," Patrick's voice said from over Mark's shoulder. His voice sounded flat and hard.

Mark turned. Patrick was looking straight at him, his expression cold. Mark wondered desperately what he'd said.

"Let me guess, you've got private medical cover?" Patrick asked, then went on without giving Mark time to say, *Well, yes, doesn't everyone who can afford it?* "So it wouldn't have occurred to you just what a *sizeable difference* all those millions in lost tax might have made to the National Health Service? The hospital my mum works in—"

Bugger.

"—has had to close down wards cos they can't afford to keep them open. And there's people having their operations put off for nigh on *years*. All right for you, maybe, but it's not much fun for grannies who can't get out to the shops because they've been waiting a year and a half for a new hip. Not to mention all the people SHARE helps who've had government funding for help slashed over the last few years."

"Now just wait a minute," Mark said, the hollow space that had opened up in his stomach rapidly filling up with anger. "These are *legal* loopholes. In some cases, government-sanctioned schemes."

"*Legal* isn't the same as *moral*." Patrick leaned on the back of Si's chair, his eyes as glacial as his tone, while Si shrank away.

At any other time, Mark might have found it amusing to watch a six-foot mountain of a man trying to disappear into the furniture.

Now, though, Mark met Patrick glare for glare. "And a successful company has the moral obligation to bankrupt itself to take care of all the people who haven't made adequate provision for their future?"

"What, so it's the old folks' fault they never made enough money at their jobs? Or the parents of disabled kids who haven't managed to put away enough to support them all through their adult lives?"

"I'm not talking about people with disabilities. *Clearly* that's a special case. But for ordinary people—where the hell do you think this country would be if everyone was content to chug along at minimum wage?" Mark barely managed not to thump the table with his clenched fist. "Or worse, on benefits? They could have got an education, advanced their careers. *Some* people work hard to better themselves—"

"Yeah, well, it's easy to see you had everything handed to you on a plate. You don't know what it's like for people stuck in the poverty trap—"

"Oh, don't give me that bollocks." Mark was livid. Patrick damn well *knew* that wasn't true. "Anyone can—"

Mark jumped as Alasdair cleared his throat. "Ladies, please. Let's keep it friendly, all right?"

Patrick clenched a fist, then unclenched it again. "Fine. Whatever. But I've had a fucking awful day, so I'll leave you to it. Don't wanna waste any more of your time." He looked up at Mark as he said it, his eyes stony, then turned on his heel and left.

Mark was so furious, he could barely see straight. Just what the *hell* made Patrick think he had the right to criticise Mark for his choice of career? In front of *everyone*? To think Mark had actually been beginning to fall in love with him.

Si's voice broke the silence. "So I'm thinking it's probably not the best time to ask you if you'd like to take over as Spartans treasurer?"

CHAPTER TWENTY-FIVE

People seemed to scatter away from Patrick's path as he stormed out of the Three Lions. Good. Anyone who got in his way right now was just asking for it, and he'd fucking well make sure they got it too.

The worst thing, the absolute worst, was realising how wrong he'd been about Mark. All that stuff Mark had told him about his dad being on the make—he'd said it like he disapproved. Like he was different. Like he was a decent fucking human being. It was like they'd said about Patrick when he was young, wasn't it? The apple never falls far from the sodding tree, and Christ, if any of *them* showed their faces around here tonight, he'd take great pleasure in proving them right by punching their fucking lights in . . .

Fuck.

Fuck, fuck, fuck. Patrick stopped walking, breathing hard, and leaned over, bracing his hands on his legs. He should have stopped after that last beer, he knew he should have. He'd been matching Barry pint for pint cos after the day he'd had, that was the only way he could face the bloke's whinging . . .

Shit. He wasn't being fair. He knew it and he hated it, but sod it, why did he even *have* to be fair all the time? It wasn't like any other bugger bothered. There was Lex about to lose their job—how fair was that? It was like he'd told Mark—welcome to the real world.

It hurt, it fucking *hurt*, to find out Mark was just another of those smug corporate bastards who didn't care about anyone so long as they got their fucking bonuses. And he'd lied again, hadn't he? At least, maybe he hadn't lied last time, but he had this time. He'd said he was an accountant, not a fucking professional tax fiddler.

The neighbour's cat was in the front garden again, but this time it took one look at Patrick and fled, scrambling over the fence with a skitter and a scritch of claws.

"'Ullo, love," Mum said as Patrick walked into the kitchen, still in his shoes cos if he tried to kick them off now, he'd probably kick 'em right through a window. Then she looked up at him from the cup of tea she was stirring, and just for a moment, her eyes went wide.

"What?" It came out a bit sharper than he meant it to.

"Nothing," she said, and carried her mug out to the living room, her head down.

Patrick wanted to smash something. Kick the cupboard doors in, throw a mug on the floor, lob a saucepan through the fucking window.

Instead, he just stood there, breathing hard, fists clenched, until the white-hot rage died down like it always did, leaving him shaky and exhausted.

Then he took off his shoes, put them neatly by the door, and padded into the living room. "I'm not him," he said softly.

Mum smiled, her eyes looking a bit wet around the rims. "Course you're not, love." She stared down into her mug of tea for a moment. She hadn't drunk any yet, but she had both her hands wrapped around it like she was feeling cold. "You look a lot like him, though. Always was a good-looking sod, your dad." Then she looked up at him. "Come and sit down, love. You can have my tea. I'm not that thirsty after all."

Patrick sat down, wishing he was still young enough to put his head on her lap for a stroke. "It just all went wrong tonight. Everything. Barry was getting on my tits with his stupid first-world problems—I mean, Christ, moping about not having a nickname? What fucking planet does he think he's on?—and Mark . . ." He couldn't go on.

Mum slipped an arm around his shoulders and gave him a hug. "And you're all stressed out over this bloody run—which, don't get me wrong, is a really good thing, and I completely support you—so you had a couple of beers too many, and you said a few things you shouldn't have?"

"I dunno, Mum. Shouldn't I?" Patrick wasn't sure, not right now. "You know I said he was an accountant? He's not. He works in tax, telling people like that smug arse on the telly how to cheat the country."

Mum frowned. "Don't they all start out as accountants, though? Anyway, he's not working now, is he?"

"No, but he still acts like there's nothing wrong with it."

Mum looked at him, took a breath like she was about to say something, then closed her mouth.

"What?" Patrick asked a bit sharply.

"Nothing, love. Want a biccy with that tea?"

Patrick shook his head. He sipped his mum's lukewarm tea, stared at a comedy rerun he'd seen twice already, and tried not to think about anything at all.

CHAPTER TWENTY-SIX

Mark hadn't stayed at the pub long after Patrick had left. For a start, he'd found it extremely difficult to form a polite answer to Si's attempt to offload his duties as the Spartans treasurer. Or to any other conversational overtures, for that matter.

He walked home alone, feeling humiliated, and betrayed, and very, very angry. How could Patrick have spoken to him like that? In front of everyone? Hadn't Mark just done what he'd been trained to do, to the best of his ability? Okay, so maybe his job hadn't been as directly socially valuable as raising money for disabled people, but damn it, it wasn't just a matter of taking money out of the country's coffers and giving it to corporate fat cats. Those companies had shareholders, and some of them were those very same little old ladies sitting at home waiting for a hip operation. They had employees, whose jobs depended on the company making enough money not to decide to take their business to a country with laxer tax laws. He'd done *nothing wrong*, damn it.

And he really wished he'd thought of all these arguments back in the pub.

What would have been the use, though? Patrick hadn't been listening to him—at least, not after the first, disastrous bit of overhearing. Which, by the way, was a fine way to go on for someone so supposedly moral—listening to other people's private conversations.

Mark walked on, cursing the clean streets one always seemed to see in the village. Where the hell was a discarded Coke can when he desperately needed something to kick?

All right, *fine*, maybe the middle of a pub after a Spartans meeting wasn't exactly *private*, but surely the decent thing to do was to announce one's presence in some way, before the people holding the conversation said things they might have phrased a little differently—or not at all—if they'd realised who was listening?

He reached his front door and let himself in quietly, mindful that Fen might, for whatever bizarre reason, have decided that tonight was the one night of the year she actually wanted to go to bed early.

No such luck.

"Dad?" Fen's face, oddly young when scrubbed of makeup, looked down the stairs at him from halfway up. "Is it just you?"

Mark tried to smile. "Why, hoping I'd run into David and brought him home, were you?"

"*Daa*-aad. I know you're not going to be bringing David round now you're going out with Patrick. He'd be well jell."

Mark gritted his teeth. She'd have to know sooner or later. "Well, actually, I don't think that's going to be a problem."

Fen stared. "What do you mean?"

"We had a, well, a difference of opinion."

"What do you *mean*?"

"Apparently we have some fundamental disagreements about what's an acceptable way to talk to someone you're in a relationship with." Fen's eyes went wide, and Mark tried to even out his tone so as not to frighten her. But damn it, it was hard. "*Apparently*, Patrick thinks it's just fine to rip apart my career choice in front of all our friends. Oh, and that I'm single-handedly responsible for all of society's evils, but I suppose that goes without saying."

Fen stared at him some more. "Are you still going out with him?" she asked finally, in a very small voice.

That was when it hit him. It was over. Over for good. "No," he said, his voice no louder than hers.

Fen's face crumpled. "Why do you have to ruin *everything*? I *hate* you!"

Mark stared as she ran back up to her room, leaving him alone with an emptiness that seemed to ache as it spread.

CHAPTER TWENTY-SEVEN

S unday morning dawned bright and clear, thank God. Patrick sent a mental *Cheers, mate* to the bloke upstairs. Not that the run would have been cancelled for anything short of an actual apocalypse, but good weather made a lot of things much, much easier. And a lot more pleasant.

By the start time, eleven o'clock, the runners were not so much lined up as sort of milling around, chatting, but they were nearly all more or less in the right place. It'd do. Patrick took a moment to be frankly amazed how many people had turned up for what had started out as an idea over a pint and had turned into the biggest fundraising event he'd ever organised. Half the runners here were from Bishops Langley. Most of the people in that place liked to act as if they hadn't even heard of Shamwell, let alone ever wanted to go there.

Patrick nodded to his mum, who was waiting to start the race. She'd insisted on turning up in top-to-toe Lycra, even though she wasn't actually running, but she looked pretty good in it, her figure just on the voluptuous side of slender that a lot of blokes seemed to go for. Patrick hoped it didn't mean she was on the pull. With her usual luck, the bloke'd turn out to be a right waster, and they could do without both of them having disastrous love lives at the same time.

Mum blew a piercing burst on the referee's whistle she'd borrowed from the kiddies' footie club chairman, and the first Shamwell Charity Fun Run was off.

It wasn't exactly the London Marathon, but it still took a fair bit of time for the last of the runners (Rob, shepherding all thirty-one of his class of seven-year-olds like a flock of brightly coloured, slightly more woolly-headed lambs, bless him) to make it over the starting line. Mum turned to Patrick with a big smile. "Well, the weather's fine, there's loads of people running, and the ice cream van turned up on time. It's all going really—"

Just as Patrick interrupted her with a hasty "Don't jinx it!" there was a loud cry of "Man down!"

Patrick groaned.

Mum cringed. "Sorry, love. Still, look on the bright side, it's probably not another broken leg." She caught Patrick's horrified look. "All right, shutting up now."

Patrick set off at a fast jog to where a small crowd, mostly consisting of children, was clustered around a figure on the ground barely three hundred yards from the start line. As he neared them, a girl of ten or so broke away from the group with a disgusted cry of "Come on, Charlie, it's boring. There's not even any blood."

That was a good sign. He hoped. At least he could see the man on the ground now.

It was Mark. Patrick's gut clenched up. "All right there?" he called.

"Sorry," Mark said, clutching his ankle. "Think I've sprained it. Great start, eh?"

Patrick wasn't prepared for the heady wash of relief that swept through him. For a moment there, he'd almost felt the horrible, twisting snap as his foot turned under him, and the searing agony of bone ripping through flesh. He couldn't face Mark going through that . . . No. He was just relieved the bastard wasn't seriously injured and likely to sue. All right, the event was insured anyway, but even so, that would have been the last sort of publicity SHARE needed. Yeah, that was it. He'd just been worried about SHARE.

Patrick pasted on a sympathetic smile. "Nah, could have been worse. Trust me. Come on, let's get you up." It was weird, talking to the bloke again. Patrick hadn't seen him since Friday night.

He'd been busy. Preparations for the run, and all that. And okay, maybe it hadn't all been *strictly* necessary, but you could never check stuff too many times, could you?

He put out a hand, and after a moment, Mark grasped it. Together, they got him on his feet—well, *foot*, as he hissed in pain when he tried to put the other one down. "Think I'm going to need to sit this one out after all."

"No problem." Patrick hesitated, then thought, *Sod it*, and put his arm around the man. "Come on, I'll help you over to somewhere you can sit down."

It was like the three-legged pub crawl all over again. Only Mark was holding on to him even tighter, and instead of the buzz from flirting with a hot bloke he was pretty sure was into him, Patrick was queasy with the knowledge this was all he was ever likely to get.

The safest place to go, at this end of the course, was back behind the start line. Patrick helped Mark back there, then glared at Barry until he shifted his arse off the folding chair he'd brought.

After he'd eased Mark down onto the seat, he glared at Barry some more. "You're not even supposed to be here, mate. You're supposed to be marshalling on the turn into Carver Lane."

Barry's brow furrowed. "You sure about that?"

"Course I'm bloody sure. Why would we want a marshal right at the start?"

"Uh . . . Oh, bloody hell. Not gonna get there now, though, am I? Shit, sorry about that."

"Nah, you'll be fine. Just cut across the field and you'll make it there before most of 'em." Patrick gave him an evil grin. "Might wanna run, though."

It shouldn't really have been so satisfying to watch Barry scurry across the field in a half jog, which was probably quicker than he'd moved in years. But, bloody hell, Patrick enjoyed the sight.

Then he turned back to Mark. "You need anything? I'll get the St. John's Ambulance people to come over and have a look at you, but do you need a drink? Want me to find Fen?"

Mark huffed a rueful laugh. "She was running ahead of me. Probably miles away by now. I'll just wait for her to get round to the finish. You should get off and do what you need to do."

Patrick shrugged. "Not a lot to do right this minute. But I'll get the St. John's Ambulance guy over." His feet didn't seem to wanna move, though. It felt weird, just leaving Mark like this.

There was a long pause.

They both spoke at once, then broke off, embarrassed.

"Look, I wanted to—"

"Patrick, can we—"

Mum put a hand on Patrick's shoulder. "Why don't you let me take care of Mark? Only there's this bloke at the desk complaining the start time was put wrong in the parish newsletter. Thought you might want to deal with *him* yourself."

"Uh, Mum . . ." Patrick had a pretty good idea Mark would probably prefer to crock the other ankle as well rather than spend time with Mum.

"It'll be fine," she said brightly. "Won't it, Mark?"

"Yes, that's fine," he said.

Huh. It'd sounded sincere enough. True, it'd come out sounding pained, but then, the bloke was, actually, in pain.

"You sure?" Patrick would've had to been a total bastard not to give him one last chance to back out of it.

"Absolutely. You get off—you must have a million and one things to do."

Patrick nodded and jogged off. There was a shitty little part of him that was relieved.

He still didn't know what he wanted to say to Mark.

CHAPTER TWENTY-EIGHT

After coming an ignominious cropper on the fun run, right in front of the one man he'd wanted to impress, Mark was heartily glad to limp through his own front door. Patrick's mum, who'd insisted he call her Jen, settled him on the sofa with his foot up and a pack of frozen peas wrapped in a tea towel on his ankle. Then she made him a mug of tea and sat down with her own mug, facing him.

Mark's stomach gave a queasy lurch. He had a feeling he knew what was coming.

Jen took a slurp of tea, then put her mug down very deliberately on the table. "You know, you're not at all what I was expecting," she said. "I mean, I know we haven't spent a lot of time together, but I like to think I'm a good judge of a bloke."

It was a close-run thing, but Mark just about managed to turn his incredulous snort into a plausible cough. He'd heard *plenty* from Patrick on the subject of his mum's taste in men.

At any rate, her eyes narrowed only marginally before she went on. "Everyone was impressed with you at the SAPS meeting too. And not just cos you were the best-looking one there. You seem like a decent sort of bloke, willing to give up his time and muck in and help, and you're pretty good at not putting people's backs up while you do it, which, believe you me, is rarer than you think. So I'm wondering, how's it all fit in? How come you've managed to upset my little boy so badly?"

Upset? Did that mean Patrick was sad, like . . . like Mark was? Or did it just mean he was angry? Which, for that matter, Mark probably still should be as well, except the sadness seemed to have smothered the anger, somehow. Mark wished to God Jen would be a little more precise with her words. He swallowed. "We just had a disagreement. A matter of principle."

"Mm. Heard." She took another slurp of tea. "See, what you gotta understand about my boy is, he's been under a lot of stress this last week or so. And he can get a bit worked up about his principles."

Mark shrugged helplessly. "He thinks my choice of career is immoral." And had said so. Loudly. In front of all their friends. In the space of an evening, Mark had gone from man of the hour to villain of the piece. Even now, it hurt Mark to think about it, no matter how much his conscience told him it was just his pride that was bruised.

"Well, maybe he has got one or two problems with what you used to do for a living. But I'll tell you this, most of what he said to you, he regretted by the time he got home. His dad was like that," she said unexpectedly. "'Cept he'd lash out with fists, not words. He may have been dealt a rough hand, my Patrick, and in more than one way, but he does a bloody good job with what he's got, and he never takes the easy way out."

She stood up. "Now, anything else you need, or can I get back to make sure my little boy's not having another crisis?"

"I'll be fine, thank you." Mark was suddenly desperate to be left alone. He needed to think. Was it possible she was right? That his choice of career wasn't the absolute deal-breaker for Patrick it'd seemed? The depression that had settled on him through the Patrick-less weekend was pierced by a tiny shoot of hope.

"You know, I could probably borrow you a walking stick," Jen said, picking up her mug. "Help you get around a bit easier."

Mark winced. What would she suggest next? Carpet slippers and a place in a bloody retirement home?

Jen sighed. "*But* I can tell you're gonna do the typical man thing and insist on managing without. If you change your mind, call me."

Mark decided not to remind her that he didn't have her number. "Thank you."

"Or you *could* always call Patrick." Smiling, she left.

Fen didn't turn up for hours. And although he knew there was a barbecue after the run, and hadn't expected her back for lunch, he *had* expected her back rather earlier than their normal teatime.

"Darling, you're back." Mark didn't manage to keep the relief out of his voice, but then, he wasn't trying all that hard.

She frowned at him. "What's wrong with your leg?"

The peas had thawed hours ago, so he'd made do by keeping his foot elevated with the damp tea towel draped over his ankle. "I twisted my ankle."

"Oh, *Daa*-aad. How far did you get?"

"About a hundred yards. I take it your race went a bit better?"

"Yeah, I got a really good time. I was *nearly* under an hour, *and* we got held up going over the stile. One of Lex's mates fell off it and landed in a cowpat. It was dead funny. I mean, they weren't hurt or nothing. Just really smelly."

"*Anything*," Mark corrected absently. "You were with Lex? I don't remember seeing Lex there."

"No, they were on the finish." That'd been the other end of the field in which they'd started the race. "But Kai was running."

"Kai? Is that a girl or a boy?"

She rolled her eyes. "*Daa*-aad. What's for tea?"

Mark gave up. "Whatever you're cooking, with me laid up like this."

Her face lit up. "Yay! Pizza!"

What with her now apparently no longer hating him, Mark had been hoping for a cosy evening together in front of the telly. He'd even suggested a DVD, when she gave him a shifty look and said she "had" to go out.

"Go where?"

"To see Lex," she said, not meeting his eye. "I'll only be an hour."

Mark looked at his watch. It was only seven o'clock now, so he supposed that wasn't unreasonable. "See that you are."

"Whatevs," Fen said airily. She jammed on her Doc Martens and slammed out of the house.

Mark was left to think dark thoughts about who this Kai might be, and how on earth he could find out without actually stalking his daughter.

CHAPTER TWENTY-NINE

Patrick was all kinds of knackered when he finally got home after the medal presentations, the barbecue, and the unavoidable clear-up. He'd been buzzing all through it, though, lifted by all the smiles he saw and the congratulations people kept chucking his way.

Walking through his front door, the crash hit. He barely had the energy to trudge to the sofa and collapse on it.

Mum gave him a smile and a hug. She'd helped for a while with the clear-up, but he'd sent her home after a bit cos it was his job, not hers. "Hungry?"

About to say no, Patrick was surprised to realise he was absolutely bloody ravenous. Come to think of it, he never had managed to get to the barbecue to get some lunch. "Starving. Any chance of a sarnie?"

"Course, love. You did a really good job today," she added, heading out to the kitchen. The smell of bacon cooking drifted in soon afterwards, making Patrick's stomach practically turn itself inside out, it was rumbling so hard.

"You're a lifesaver," he groaned when she came back in with a large plate of bacon butties.

After he'd eaten, Patrick had just enough strength to drag himself upstairs to change into slobbing-out clothes, then he slumped back on the sofa in front of the telly and thought about never moving again, ever.

Just as he was starting to feel vaguely human again, the doorbell rang. Patrick's heart leapt for a moment, before he realised there was no way short of divine healing it was likely to be Mark.

Mum gave Patrick a funny look when she came back from answering the door. "There's a *young lady* to see you."

Patrick gave her a funny look right back. "Who?"

"See for yourself, love." Mum stood back and let Fen into the living room.

Patrick felt a bit caught off guard, sprawling there on the sofa in his saggy trackie bottoms and old T-shirt, with his feet up on the table and a hole in his sock. He sat up straight and put his feet on the carpet. "Fen?"

She sent a distrustful look Mum's way. Mum just held her hands up in surrender, smirked at Patrick, and left.

"It's about Dad," she started. Then stopped.

"Yeah?" Patrick encouraged her cautiously, not sure if she was going to tell him she missed him, or to piss off and never darken their door again.

It was like he'd thrown open the floodgates. "Look, just fix it, all right? He was happy with you, and now he's not. He's spent the whole weekend moping about looking sad, and it's horrible. And he came back from your fun run all hurt, and you didn't even bring him home. And I know he said you said horrible things about him, but he still likes you anyway, so just come and say sorry, and it can go back to how it was, all right? Cos I *hate* it the way it is now. So *fix it*."

"Look, it's not that simple, all right?" Patrick ran a hand over his hair. "You know what he does for a living? Used to do, I mean?"

"Um. He works out people's taxes? So?"

"Well, for a start, he never told me that. He said he was an accountant."

Fen nodded. "He is. He's always going on at me about how he'd never have got such a good job without spending, like, years and years doing exams and getting fifty million letters after his name. Like not having a life is a *good* thing. He tried to teach me double-entry bookkeeping once so I could keep track of what I was spending. It was *so boring*. I mean, God, what's the point of writing everything down *twice*?"

Huh. "Well, okay. But the tax thing, see, me and him have got a few differences about."

"*So?*"

"Well, some of us think people should pay what they owe. Otherwise, there'd be no money for schools and hospitals and programmes for disabled people."

Okay, that one hit home. Her forehead creased in a frown. "So Dad told them to pay less than they owe?"

"Well, sort of. He found all these loopholes in the laws that meant they wouldn't have to pay so much."

Her jaw set. "They should make better laws, then."

"Well, yeah, but—"

"So you dumped him for just doing his job? Which he's not even *doing* anymore? That's *so unfair*."

"I didn't dump him, all right!"

"No, you just were all mean to him and then never said sorry. That's like constructive dismissal."

"How do you even know what that is?"

"David said. And we learned about it in school, anyway. In PSE— you know, those lessons where they teach you about sex and life skills and stuff? It was in the bit about discrimination. Which is totally what they're doing to Lex, so you'd better make them stop it, all right?"

"Me? What am I supposed to do? I don't make the decisions about who gets hired."

"No, but you could tell them if Lex goes, you'll leave too. Lex told me they saw the accounts, and you've made loads more money for SHARE than the last person who had your job. And you've been there years. They won't want you to leave and have to get someone new in and train them up and stuff."

Could it be that simple? Patrick was so used to the trustees laying down the law from above, he hadn't stopped to think he might have a bit of power over them too. Could he risk it, though? Mum'd have a real struggle paying the mortgage on her own.

Fen was looking at him sharply. "Or is it only Dad who's supposed to give up his career for what you think is right?"

Ouch.

"So what did Mark's little girl want with you?" Mum asked after Fen had stomped off, her chin high. "She's all right, that one. Ever so polite when I opened the door, all *Sorry to bother you, Mrs. Owen* and that."

Patrick looked away. "Told me off for being mean to her dad."

"That's sweet. You can tell they're close, her coming rushing round to defend him. Like I always say, it's bollocks that single parents can't bring kids up right."

"Yeah, but . . ." Patrick ran a hand through his hair. It just flopped lankly afterwards, as if standing up in its usual style was just too much effort right now. Christ, he needed a shower. "I know what I said . . . I shouldn't have spoken to him like that. And maybe he didn't actually *lie* to me about what he did for a living. But . . ."

"But what, love?"

He sighed. "Well, what do you think about the fact he used to help people cheat the taxman? And yeah, I know it was all legal."

Mum perched on the arm of the sofa and levelled her gaze at him. "You know that comedian you don't like? He was on the news earlier. Paid back half a million quid in tax, *and* he said he was sorry."

"So?"

"So people change. And, more to the point, he didn't have to do that, this comedian. Wasn't like he'd broken the law or anything. You know what your problem is, my lad? You're so bloody far up on the moral high ground, you can't see what it's like for us ordinary people down here."

"What, you're on Mark's side now?"

"What do you mean, 'now'? When did I ever say I was against him?"

"Mum, you didn't have to *say* it."

"Well, maybe I've noticed you looking a lot happier since you've been with him. And well, what's fourteen years, when all's said and done? Age is just a number."

"Mum, I can't believe you're— You know what? Never mind. Just tell me this: do you think it's right he lost the country millions of pounds of tax on a regular basis?"

"Is that what he said?"

"Pretty much, yeah."

"He was probably exaggerating. And if he hadn't done it, someone else would have. He's not doing it now, is he?"

"No, just living off his bonuses from grateful corporate fat cats."

"Would you rather he gave it all back and had to live off benefits?"

"Mum, that's not the point."

"Look, love, I know you feel you've got to make up for your dad, but what he did, it's not on you. Not your responsibility. And, well, your Mark's all right, when you get to know him. Stepped right up to the plate at the SAPS meeting Thursday night, took on the job of treasurer, which poor old Bridget's been trying to get rid of for years 'cept she couldn't find anyone who'd admit to knowing what two plus two was."

Patrick narrowed his eyes. "You never said he was at the SAPS meeting."

"Don't have to tell you everything, do I? Course, if I'd known you were planning to have a strop and dump him on Friday—"

"I haven't dumped him, all right? I just— We just had words. That's all."

"Oh yeah? Had any since?"

"Well, no . . . I was busy with the fun run, wasn't I? I couldn't just leave."

"You could've dropped in on your way home. Checked the poor bloke's ankle really is just twisted, not broken."

"It's not broken, all right?" Patrick's conscience kicked him in the gut even as he said it. "Look, just give me a bit of time, yeah? I got stuff to think about."

Maybe he'd go round tomorrow, after work.

And hope Mark wasn't still too pissed off with him to listen.

CHAPTER THIRTY

Mark's ankle was still somewhat painful Monday morning, although it wasn't as swollen as he'd feared. It was the least of his woes, in any case. He still hadn't spoken to Patrick—it'd seemed too soon to call, what with Patrick presumably exhausted from the day's event. But he hadn't been able to keep himself from hoping Patrick might call *him*. Just to see how he was.

He was now trying to ignore that little shoot of hope lest it die from overwatering. But then, things *had* seemed a lot friendlier between them after he'd turned his ankle yesterday. Well, briefly, at any rate. Until Patrick had left him to his mum's tender mercies, and not looked back.

No, not too much danger of nurturing that budding hope to death.

Fen had actually suggested of her own accord that she should take the bus to school so he wouldn't have to drive, which had been considerate of her, but meant he was left on his own even earlier than usual to contemplate the mess his love life had become.

Mark made himself a mug of coffee and managed to hobble into the living room without spilling more than a third. It was a lot harder than you might think to carry hot drinks while limping.

He'd just made it to the sofa and set his coffee on the table beside him when the doorbell rang, which was just as well. If he'd still been en route, the entire mugful would have ended up on the floor, the way his heart clenched and he jumped convulsively. Could it be Patrick? He swallowed, heaved himself up, and limped to the door.

It was David, wearing a looser pair of jeans today, in ordinary blue, and a shirt that seemed to lack his usual flamboyance. This time, he'd brought what Mark could only assume was an ironic bunch of grapes. "I've come to cheer the invalid, languishing upon his sickbed," David said, handing over the fruit. "Although you seem to be rather more upright than I was led to believe."

Mark took the grapes mechanically, with misgivings, and tried not to look too unhappy to see his guest. God, what if Patrick came round *now*? "David . . . I'm not sure this is a good idea."

"No. It's fine. It's all fine." David thrust his hands into his pockets as he stood there. "I'm over you. Really. Well, not *really*, but I'm getting there. And I thought, you know what? It's just silly to avoid each other. To go out of our way so we won't bump into one another accidentally."

Mark's conscience pinched him, hard, at the reminder that he wasn't the only one with an unhappy love life. "David, you had to travel across London and then twenty-five miles out to get here. That's the very *definition* of going out of your way. Come in, anyway," he added, because, by his own argument, it'd be hardly fair to expect David to turn around and go straight back again.

"Oh, twenty-five miles here, twenty-five miles there." David slunk down the hallway with his usual catlike grace and flopped onto an armchair at Mark's gesture. "If we were in America, it'd be *nothing*."

"But you can't keep using up your days off visiting me." Mark eased himself back down onto the sofa, where the sight of his coffee cup on the table reminded him he was being a bad host. Damn it. Now he'd have to get up again. "Ah. Would you like a coffee?"

"No, don't get up. I'll make myself one in a minute." David sighed theatrically. "Work's horrible. Charles is horrible. I'm thinking of giving it all up and becoming a market gardener."

Mark coughed to hide a smile. "David, have you ever gardened in your life?"

"I grew some cress on blotting paper once. How hard can it be? You just plough the fields and scatter, and then sit back and wait for nature to do all the work for you. 'First the farmer sows the seed, then he sits and takes his ease.' We sang that in primary school. And I'd be a natural at the market part. Can't you just see me behind a stall, charming all the housewives and househusbands into sampling my wares?"

"I think you might want to look into it a little more deeply before you hand in your notice. Why not try another job in a similar field to what you do now first, and see if it's any better with a different boss? Maybe one who's a little more up-to-date in his attitudes?" Mark finally managed to take a sip of his coffee. It'd gone cold.

"God, I know. Charles is, like, a quarterback or something."

Mark blinked. "A throwback?" he guessed.

"That's the one. I *mean*. I don't remember anyone *ever* being that bad, even when I was a little gay-boy growing up. I heard him tell Ms. Ignield in Partnerships he didn't agree with women wearing trousers in the office—can you *imagine*?"

Mark didn't have to imagine. He could remember Ellen's first job interviews, and how much she'd agonised over whether a trouser suit would be acceptable, before playing it safe and putting on a skirt. "It's like you grew up in a different century to me."

David cocked his head. "Actually, if you define growing up as the period of your teens, I *did* grow up in a different century to you." He beamed.

Mark winced and took another sip of cold coffee without thinking. Ugh. He put his cup back on the table and nudged it farther from his reach. "Thanks for the reminder. But it's more than that. Look, how old were you when you first told someone you were gay?"

"I never *tell* people I'm gay. Not in so many words. They always seem to know. Ooh, ever since I was in short skirts, I suppose."

Mark stared for a moment, then forged bravely on. "And you've never felt the need to hide who you really are? Never felt the need to try to change?"

"Never felt the ability, so what would have been the point?" David cocked his head to one side. "So let me guess—you think my life's been all beds and roses because I'm so clearly gay?"

"No. No, I don't." Mark sighed. "All I'm trying to say is . . . we've had very different lives." He was silent for a moment, then thought, to hell with it. "What do you think about what we do?"

"Well, it depends what you're talking about. Gay sex in general, anal in particular—"

"Not that! I meant, for a *living*. Working for a firm that specialises in finding ways for clients to pay less tax."

"It pays the bills?"

"Yes, but—should it? It's not exactly socially responsible, is it? Don't you ever feel like you're cheating the country out of much-needed funds? After all, with the National Health Service in the state it is . . ."

"Well, if we didn't do it, someone else would. And, anyway, that sort of thing was all more your area, remember? I just did the paperwork." David leaned close to give Mark a suspicious look. "What is all this? I thought you'd *had* the midlife crisis already, sweetie."

"Just something someone was saying. It made me think. Some people seem to give so much towards the common good. Other people just take." Mark looked away. "It's been rather brought home to me that I've always been one of the takers."

"Just because you've always been a taker doesn't mean you can't be a giver if you want to be," David said sagely.

Mark had a suspicion he was talking about gay sex again, but nevertheless it sparked an idea within him. Maybe some grand gesture, such as running the London Marathon for charity, would win Patrick back? He was saved from having to comment when his phone rang.

Mark wrestled it out of his pocket, frowning to see it was the school calling. God, what had Fen done *now*? "Hello?"

"Mr. Nugent? This is St. Jude's," a sharp female voice informed him. "Just to remind you, all absences due to sickness need to be notified by a parent or guardian before ten o'clock the first morning of absence."

Why was she telling him this? "Er, yes, I'm quite aware of that."

She *humph*ed audibly on the other end. "So when can we expect Florence back at school?"

"Wait, what? What do you mean, 'back at school'? Where is she now?"

"That, Mr. Nugent, is something we'd rather hoped you would know. She certainly isn't in school."

"What? But she should have been there"—Mark glanced at his watch—"nearly two hours ago. She was catching the bus."

"So you're confirming this is a case of truancy, Mr. Nugent?"

"I, ah, wait . . . I've got to go," Mark gabbled and put the phone down quickly. Oh God. His insides were tied up in so many knots any Boy Scout worth his salt would have had to go for a lie down on witnessing them. He felt faint, and queasy with guilt and worry.

This was all his fault. God, how could he have been so selfish? He'd had one aim with Fen, and that was to give her a stable environment. And what had he done? Dashed her hopes of a new family not once, but twice. Was it any wonder she'd— God, what *had* she done? Where *was* she?

"David, you drive, don't you?"

"*Naturellement.*"

"Good. You're driving me along Fen's route to school. In case she missed the bus and is trying to walk it—although why the hell wouldn't she just call me?" Mark stopped dead as he realised what an idiot he was being, and he grabbed his phone again to dial Fen's number.

It clicked straight on to voice mail. Damn it.

"No answer, came the stern reply?"

"No. Or yes. Whatever. Come on, we need to find her." Mark's heart was thumping painfully now. Surely nothing bad could have happened to her?

Nothing bad ever happened in a place like Shamwell, did it?

CHAPTER THIRTY-ONE

"Thank God you're here," Mark said as David drove them along the road, scanning for any sight of Fen. How hard could it be to spot one not-overly-petite teenager in a bright fuchsia uniform? "Don't know how I'd have managed, with this ankle."

"Oh, you'd have been fine without me. You'd have called someone. Your *Someone Else*, perhaps."

Mark hesitated, not sure what to say. If David *wasn't* over him, he didn't want to give him false hope by telling him Patrick wasn't exactly his at the moment—and anyway, what did it matter? What mattered was finding Fen. "I'm still glad you're here," he said at last, resting a hand for a moment on David's thigh without really thinking it through.

"Um," David began.

They were coming up to a T junction. "Turn left here," Mark told him.

"*Muchas* grassy-arse, but that wasn't actually what I wanted to ask. Your *Someone Else*. How would you say things are going?"

Mark stared at him. "Is now really the time?"

"Um. Possibly. You see, I may have received a phone call from the little moppet yesterday—and by the way, how did you *think* I knew you were injured? Facebook stalking is a wonderful thing, but it can only get you so far."

"David, please, could we get to the point?"

"Well . . . she seemed a tad upset about the contretemps between you and a certain Mr. S. Else."

Oh God. This was all Mark's fault. "What did she tell you?"

"Well, she was *asking* me too. About your work, specifically."

"My work?"

"Mm. Did you know she went to see your young Monsieur Else last night?"

"Patrick. His name's Patrick," Mark said distractedly, still scanning the pavements and bus shelters as they drove. Then he realised what David had said. "And no, I had no idea. She said she was going to see Lex—that's a friend she's made here."

"Oh, I know all about *Lex*. Fen and I had an interesting discussion on employment law, actually."

They had? Mark boggled. "But what about Patrick? What did she say about him?"

"Well, it more or less boiled down to *He's being, like, so stupid*." David's voice rose into a fair imitation of Fen's breathy outrage for the last part. "Or, to be brutally accurate, *They're both being so stupid*."

Mark winced. And then despaired, as they reached the school gates for the second time, having searched two alternative routes and found no sign of Fen. He felt so helpless. She could be *anywhere*.

"Have you tried ringing people she might have gone to?" David asked, pulling in to the side of the road.

Mark struggled to think. Who might Fen have run to? It wasn't a long list—not that he knew of, anyway. David—who was here, so could be scratched off at once; Lex, who was probably at work anyway—and God, he didn't even have their number; Ellen—

Oh God. He was going to have to call Ellen.

No, wait. If Fen had turned up at Ellen's, she'd have called, wouldn't she? Unless of course she was waiting to see how long it'd be before he noticed she'd gone missing, of course.

Yes. Yes, that was it. Fen was safe with Ellen, who hadn't called because she wanted to teach him a lesson.

Heart thumping, Mark made the call.

"Mark? What is it? Is something wrong with Florence?" Ellen's voice was sharp. She sounded harried, and there was busy background noise.

"Are you at work?" Why the hell hadn't it occurred to him she would be?

"It's Monday. Of course *I'm* at work. What *is* it?"

Mark took a deep breath. "Fen didn't turn up at school today. Do you think she might have gone back to your house?"

Ellen's voice rose the predictable two octaves. "What do you mean, she's not at school? I thought you were looking after her! Don't you even know where she is?"

"Of course I don't!" Mark snapped, his nerves run ragged. "Why do you think I'm ringing you?"

He stared as David nimbly plucked the phone from his fingers. "Hello, Mrs. Nugent? This is David—you remember we met at the Christmas do? You were in a delightfully retro little frock in pine green. I know, this is all terribly trying, isn't it? But it really would ease everybody's minds if you could find some way of checking whether the little moppet has gone back to your house."

David listened for a moment. "Oh, goodness me, no. I'm merely here as designated driver, Mark being something of a wounded soldier right now. No, no—just an ankle. Sprained, not broken. Well, hardly even that. Twisted. But don't worry, he's got me to mop his fevered— Oh. Right. Silly me. Well, we'll look forward to hearing from you, then."

He hung up. "She's getting the next train home."

"Good." Mark grabbed his phone back and called Patrick.

"Yeah?"

Mark winced. It wasn't exactly a *great to hear from you* sort of tone. "Patrick, I'm sorry to bother you, but is Lex at work right now?"

There was a pause. "Why?"

"It's Fen. She never turned up at school this morning, and she's not answering her phone. I thought maybe she might be with Lex, but I haven't got their number."

There was another, longer pause. "Lex is here. Call you back in a mo, yeah?"

What the hell did that mean? "Drive back to the village," Mark instructed David, and busied himself clenching and unclenching his fists while he waited for the phone to ring. When it finally did, he nearly dropped it. "Patrick?"

"'Ullo, Mr. Nugent. It's me. Lex."

"Do you know where Fen is?"

"I don't *know*, but I got an idea. There's this boy, see."

"A boy?" Why the hell hadn't he known about this? "From the theatre group?"

"Nuh. From where she used to live."

"From Warton?"

"Yeah. Ollie. Been having a hard time at school, she was telling me."

Did Ellen know about this? "And you think she might have gone to see him? But how would she even get there?"

There was a pause. "We, um, we sorta looked it up. Yesterday. On our phones. I swear I din't know she was gonna bunk off school," Lex added in a rush. "But it's dead easy, cos it's all commuter lines. You just gotta get the train down to King's Cross, get on the Tube, and then another train out to Warton. Prolly only take 'n hour an' 'alf."

An hour and a half. She could have got off the bus a stop early, and she'd have been right by Bishops Langley station. That would have been at, what, around half past eight? Maybe earlier? And the school hadn't rung him until nearly eleven. What the *hell* did they think they were playing at, leaving it so long to call? Fen could have been halfway to Scotland by then!

Mark looked at his watch. It was eleven forty-five. "What's his address? This boy. Where does he live?"

"Dunno. Sorry. But I fort your ex-missus might?"

Ellen. Yes. "Thank you. I've got to go now." He hung up and quickly redialled Ellen.

She didn't bother with hello. "Have you found her?"

"No. Where are you?"

"On my way home, of course. I'm just about to go down to the Tube. Where are you?"

"Bishops Langley." Mark looked out of the car window and saw that was no longer accurate. "Wait a minute." He covered the mouthpiece with his hand. "David, where are we?"

"On the way to Warton. Obviously."

Right. Yes. That made sense. "We're on our way. But do you know anything about a boy named Ollie?"

There was nothing. *Damn* it. She must be underground, if not on *the* Underground. Mark looked at his watch again. The journey out from her office in Southwark to Warton wasn't a quick one—at least,

Ellen complained about it often enough—so the chances were they'd beat her there, using the road and cutting across country. Mark had the instinctive feeling that would be best for all concerned. "David, can you drive any faster?"

"Not without getting you speeding tickets. It's speed-camera city along here."

"Damn the speeding tickets! We need to get there before Ellen does."

There was a pause. "Because?"

Mark's stomach flipped over painfully. "Because if she gets there first and starts taking over . . ." He swallowed. "She might want Fen to go back to live with her."

"Oh, petal." David patted his thigh with one elegantly manicured hand. "We won't let the nasty woman take your daughter away."

Mark couldn't help feeling that was a tad unfair on Ellen.

He also couldn't help feeling he really didn't care right now.

CHAPTER THIRTY-TWO

Ellen's house in Warton, which she'd bought following the divorce, was a small, mid-terrace town house with next to no on-street parking nearby. Most of the occupants of the terrace had turned their pocket-sized front gardens into pocket-sized car ports for the first family car, and bagged their little patch of street to park the second. Which was something of a problem, as just as David and Mark drove past it trying to find a space, they passed Patrick's Micra coming in the opposite direction.

Mark grabbed his phone and dialled. "Patrick? What are you doing here?"

"'Ullo, Mr. Nugent. It's me again. Lex. Patrick's driving."

"What are you doing here? Never mind. Tell Patrick to go down Kenilworth Drive and turn right into Lammermoor Lane—no, left, if he's coming from that direction—and there should be some parking there." He hung up. "David, drive back past again and drop me off."

"And what? You'll hop into the house and start laying down the law?"

"Well, it's better than hopping three streets, for God's sake."

"I've got a better idea. What's the ex-Mrs. Mark's house number again?"

"Twenty-seven. That one, with the Peugeot in the drive." Ellen didn't use her car to get to work.

David swung the car around and shamelessly parked in number twenty-three's empty drive. "What? They're almost certainly out, and anyway, I'm going to leave a note."

"Look, just stay with the car, all right?" Mark jumped out of the car, winced painfully, and hobbled the short way down the road.

This was madness. Here they were, all converging on Ellen's house, and for God's sake, Fen probably wasn't even there. He'd just hoped Ellen might have the boy's address or phone number, or at least some clue to where she'd stolen off to. He fumbled his key in the lock with a rush of gratitude to Ellen for giving him one, even if it had been only so he could water her plants when she took Fen on holiday last summer. *Calm down*, he told himself. *She almost certainly isn't here—*

"Dad?" Fen's shocked voice and decidedly guilty face greeted him in the hall. She was wearing jeans now, not her school uniform, which proved beyond all doubt that this was premeditated.

"Young lady," Mark said sternly, almost reeling with relief. "You are in *so much trouble* right now."

He advanced, and she backed into the living room—where, Mark saw, she wasn't alone.

The boy she was with was, to put it bluntly, not the sort of boyfriend Mark would have hoped she'd choose. His ripped jeans were the least objectionable part of his entire outfit. The inevitable hoodie, while intact, was emblazoned with what was presumably some pop culture icon making a rude gesture. Like Fen, he had pierced ears. Unlike Fen, he'd opted for the sort of wince-inducing cylindrical rings that stretched his lobes out so far you could drive a bus through them. He'd also seen fit to have a bar stuck through his left eyebrow, and the edge of a tattoo was just visible at his wrist.

He could have been used as an illustration for an article on teenage rebellion, although, if you asked Mark, the boy didn't look rebellious so much as dangerously feral.

"Is this Ollie?" he snapped.

Fen shot him a look of utter betrayal. "How do you know about Ollie?" She marched up to Mark, fists clenched at her sides. "Have you been stalking me?"

What? How the hell was *Mark* suddenly in the wrong? "Lex told me. And before you get all irate with Lex, this was after I rang up Patrick *worried out of my mind* because the school told me you hadn't turned up today. What the hell do you think you're playing at? And switching off your phone?"

"I forgot it was off. We always have to switch them off for school or they confiscate them," Fen said defensively. "And I told Serena to say I was ill," she added in a much smaller voice.

"And you really thought they wouldn't check with me?" Mark drew in a breath, then stopped as the boy—Ollie—stepped forward.

"Oi, leave 'er alone. 'S my fault." His voice was slow and thick, and as he walked forward, he seemed to stumble, bracing himself with a hand on the wall.

Mark couldn't believe what he was seeing. "What— Are you *drunk*?" Furious, he went to grab the boy by the shoulder.

Fen darted between them. "Don't touch him!"

Mark narrowed his eyes at her. Was her face flushed from anger— or alcohol? "Have you been drinking as well?"

"No. *Jesus*. He's not drunk, all right? He's got CP, so just leave him *alone*, all right?"

"CP? Is that some kind of drug?"

Out of nowhere, Patrick grabbed Mark's arm. When had he got here? "Uh, Mark . . ."

Fen made an inarticulate, high-pitched noise, like an overly exasperated kettle. "Oh, for *God's* sake . . . *Cerebral palsy*." She enunciated it loudly, distinctly, and with withering contempt: SEH-REH-BRAL PALL-SEE. *Duh* didn't even begin to cover it.

Mark felt simultaneously hot and cold. A nasty little part of him wanted to bluster and rail that how the hell could he have known? A much larger part of him wanted to sink into the ground. He'd been an insensitive idiot. He'd been an insensitive idiot in front of *Patrick*. "God—I'm so sorry. I didn't mean . . ."

The boy shrugged, an awkward, lopsided motion. "'S all right. 'M used to it."

The silence was broken by Lex's cheerful voice. "I'm gonna put the kettle on, yeah? Fink we all need a cuppa."

They ended up all perching awkwardly on Ellen's three-piece suite in her tiny living room, matching mugs of tea in their hands. Well, Mark, Fen, Patrick, Lex, and Ollie did. David had tactfully taken his outside, "To keep an eye on the car." Patrick had asked Mark if he was all right with him staying, which Mark was hoping was a good sign. Lex had just stayed, which suggested they were feeling guilty about grassing Fen up and wanted to make sure Mark wasn't going to throw the book at her.

Or maybe Lex just hadn't discovered tact yet.

Mark cleared his throat, feeling absurdly self-conscious. "Now, Fen, I know you were upset by Patrick and me having a, ah, disagreement, but there was really no need for you to . . ." He trailed off at Fen's increasingly incredulous looks.

"What? This is *not* about *you*, Dad, all right?" She flushed. "I'm sorry I missed school, but it was *really important*, all right?"

It *wasn't* about him? "What was?"

"*Ollie.* See, there's these kids at school, that's like my old school, right, you know, Waverley High, and they're like total bastards to him, and it's *not fair*, and they're always calling him spaz and crip and stuff, and—"

Out of the corner of his eye, Mark noticed Ollie's flinch, barely perceptible before he reverted to hands-in-pockets, am-I-bovvered type. God, poor kid. "Fen! Slow down." Mark tried to make soothing gestures. "Come on, calm down."

"But it's *not fair*. And I know what you're gonna say, right, and it's just *rubbish*."

Mark looked at her for a couple of beats before speaking. "What's rubbish?"

Fen's chin remained up. "You're gonna say talk to a teacher, aren't you?" She waited.

"That was going to be my advice, yes. Is there any particular reason why you can't?"

"You're not *listening*. We *did*, okay? *Ages* ago. We talked to Mr. Hayes about it, who's our form teacher, and he just did, like, *nothing*, and then we heard him talking to Mr. Smith about Ollie like he's a *problem*, and Mr. Smith, he's the PE teacher, he made this *joke* about Ollie playing football in games, and that's why we keyed their cars . . ." Fen's voice trailed off a bit towards the end, as well it might. Then she rallied. "And now Mr. Smith's saying Ollie shouldn't do PE at all, cos it's not fair on the other kids having to make allowances, which is *rubbish*, and it's only gonna make his legs worse and make everyone say stupid crap about him even more."

Mark glanced at Ollie, whose ears must be burning if their colour was any indication, and bit back a knee-jerk comment about the vandalism. That was in the past. More importantly, if any teacher had disparaged *his* child like that, he'd most likely have been egging the vandals on and handing them a knife so they could slash the tyres as well.

"Yes, well, there are ways and means to tackle these things," he said finally.

Patrick was nodding. "Yeah, mate." He spoke to Ollie, not Fen. "Can you get your parents, or your guardians or whatever, to make a written complaint? Far as I know, you wanna go to your head teacher first, or if they're not likely to help, you can go straight to the school governors, then the local authority, and after that there's the Special Educational Needs and Disability Tribunal. Chances are it won't get that far, though. Not something like this. The law's pretty clear on indirect discrimination."

Ollie was staring at Patrick. "How'd you know all that?"

Patrick shrugged. "Work for a charity for the disabled, don't I? It's adults, the one I'm with, not kids, but you learn stuff anyway. If you want, I'll have a word with your mum and dad—will they be at home now?"

"Nah. They both work. It'll just be me bruvver there now, less he's gone out."

"No problem. I can come round one night, or at the weekend. Unless you reckon they wouldn't be interested? Did you try talking to 'em about it, and they didn't listen?"

Ollie hung his head. "Nah . . . 'S just, 'm not a little kid anymore, right? Fed up with everyone treatin' me like I'm a problem."

"You're not the problem, mate. It's that git of a teacher who's the problem. And trust me, even grown-ups need a bit of help sometimes to solve their problems." Patrick glanced at Mark as he said it. "C'mon. Let's get you back to your house, yeah? Cos chances are *your* mum and dad are going spare too cos the school's told 'em you never turned up."

"Nah, we got an INSET day today. No school." He sent Fen a glance that was equal parts accusing and admiring. "You never told me you were bunking off."

She went pink. Mark could feel a stern lecture on the perils of Doing Things to Impress Boys coming on.

Later. Once he'd got her home, safe and sound. Mark was beginning to see the virtues of those doorless towers fairy-tale princesses always seemed to be locked in.

"Am I grounded?" Fen asked sadly. Mark's heart melted. "We'll see, okay? Let's just get you home for now. Ollie, do you need a lift back to your house?"

"Nah. 'S just round the corner. I can walk." The steel in Ollie's eye and the stubbornness in his tone seemed to hint that anyone thinking of suggesting he might not be up to the walk could avail themselves of the message on his hoodie.

"Right then," Patrick said briskly. "Just give me your number, and I'll sort something out with your mum and dad, yeah?"

Mark waited while they exchanged details. "Fen, you'd better say good-bye to Ollie now," he instructed gently.

She bit her lip and looked down at her Doc Martens. "Bye, Ollie."

His ears went pink again. "Yeah, see ya."

Mark rolled his eyes. Kids.

When they left the house, they found David outside, talking animatedly to the most enormous man Mark had ever seen. Si and Alasdair would look like a couple of Hobbits next to his Gandalf—no. Next to his Smaug. (Fen had discovered to her horror recently that Mark hadn't seen *any* of the Hobbit movies, and had insisted on rectifying that with the aid of a box set of DVDs and an industrial-size bucket of popcorn. He'd quite enjoyed them, actually.)

The giant wore a black leather jacket that appeared to be a close cousin to Lex's metal boots, slung over smart blue overalls embroidered with the logo of Langley Locksmiths. That, and the Harley Davidson currently obstructing the pavement went a long way to reassuring Mark that David wasn't about to be flattened by the irate tenant of number twenty-three.

Lex let out the most high-pitched noise Mark had yet heard from them and flung their slight body at the biker. "Rex! You din't 'ave to come."

Mark shot Patrick an incredulous glance. "Lex and Rex?"

He shrugged. "Maybe it's how they got talking? Someone said Lex, and he thought they said Rex? Who knows?"

"What's he even doing here?"

"Lex rang him—they were s'posed to be meeting for lunch today, so they had to let him know what was going on. Looks like he's the protective sort."

"Course I come, din't I?" Rex was saying, looking down—way, way down—at Lex like they were the only person in the world. "Weren't gonna leave you on your own to get in trouble when it ain't even your fault."

"Rex, this is Patrick, yeah? My boss?"

Rex smiled at Patrick through his immense beard, and held out a paw. "All right, mate? Listen, me and the lads are having a bit of a bash at me mum's house at the weekend, fort you might wanna come along? So Lex'll know someone else there apart from me? Bring your bird or your bloke if you got one."

Patrick nodded, but sent Mark a quick glance that made his stomach flip. "Let you know on that one, all right? But yeah, I'm definitely up for it."

Mark decided there and then he could face making small talk with the entire British arm of the Hells Angels if it meant he was back with Patrick again.

At that moment, a red-faced and breathless Ellen turned the corner, carrying a briefcase and walking fast in unsuitable heels that looked like they pained her. She stared at the seven of them milling around outside her house.

Mark gave her a beaming smile. "Ellen! Nothing to worry about, after all. It's all sorted out now. You might as well go back to work."

CHAPTER THIRTY-THREE

"Think we need to talk," Patrick said in Mark's ear. Ellen had stomped off back to the station after a short but impressive blow-up at Mark that'd stopped just short of flattening him with her briefcase. Which, in all fairness, he'd probably deserved. Patrick just hoped someone had thought to put the dirty tea mugs in the dishwasher or she'd be pissed off all over again when she got back home tonight.

Mark looked torn. "I really need to get Fen back home. And forge a sick note for her."

David gave them a saintly smile. "Not to worry. I'll get the little moppet home for you. You two lovebirds can take the scenic route." He heaved a dramatic sigh.

Patrick gave David a sharp look, but Mark just said, "If you're sure you don't mind?" and waved them off.

Lex had already roared off on the back of Rex's Harley.

"Right, then," Patrick said. "Car's this way."

He helped Mark in, and they drove in silence for a while, Mark apparently as reluctant to break the silence as Patrick was.

"Yeah, so," Patrick said in the end, staring straight ahead through the windscreen. Had to keep his eyes on the traffic, didn't he? "Think you might have noticed already, but I got a bit of a temper. Get it from my dad, much as I'd like to think I'm sod all like him. And yeah, well, adding a few drinks into the mix generally isn't such a great idea."

There was a silence. Shit. "'S okay, I get it," he carried on, his chest feeling hollow. "Not the sort of thing that's much fun to be around. Prob'ly best you found out sooner, yeah?"

"Wait—what?" Mark sounded genuinely confused, so Patrick risked a glance over to him. He looked baffled and all. "You're apologising to *me*?"

That . . . that was sounding a lot more hopeful. But Patrick didn't wanna count his chickens too soon. "Well, yeah. Shouldn't have gone off on you like that. 'Specially not in front of everyone else. Not cool, and I'm sorry."

"No. It wasn't exactly pleasant to be on the receiving end of. But . . . a lot of what you said was true. Well, not the bit about me having everything handed to me on a plate," Mark added.

Patrick winced. "Yeah. I knew it while I was saying it, you know? It's just—sometimes I open my mouth and shit comes out."

Mark gave him a funny look, halfway between a grimace and a laugh. "You *are* aware that's a really unappealing image? Especially for someone who's kissed you."

Patrick had to laugh then. "Yeah, but it kind of proves my point, doesn't it?"

"Possibly. No. It wasn't . . . shit . . . what you said." Mark huffed something like a sigh. "I just need to know how much of it you really meant."

That was the clincher, wasn't it? How much *had* Patrick actually meant? Trouble was, what with the beers and the heat of the moment, he wasn't totally sure he was even remembering it right. "Which bits?" he asked cautiously.

"I mean, if you really think my work as a tax advisor is fundamentally immoral, we might have a problem."

Shit. "Look, I just— There you were, boasting about your bonuses, and I—"

"I was *not* boasting. That's ridiculous."

"No? Cos it sounded a lot like it to me. In fact, that seemed to be the main point of what you were saying."

"You just heard what I said to Si, took it out of context, and didn't give me a chance to explain."

Patrick's hands tightened on the steering wheel, and he made a conscious effort to ease back on the accelerator. "So go on, then, explain."

"Well . . . have you ever thought that tax loopholes might be the one thing keeping a company in this country, rather than taking all the jobs elsewhere? And some of those corporations make sizeable donations to charity. I'm not going to pretend they do it for anything other than the PR value, in a lot of cases, but the end result is the same." Mark drew in a heavy breath. "And . . . the other thing that was said. I'm sorry, but I *do* think people have to take responsibility for their own finances. And there are some people in this country who take advantage of the welfare state. Maybe you're right, and companies should pay more tax. But equally, there are some people who claim benefits they're not entitled to, or who just sit back and let the state pay their bills instead of bothering to get a job."

Ouch.

"You don't agree?" Mark asked after a long moment of silence.

Patrick swallowed. "Yeah, see . . . I told you a bit about my dad, didn't I? Well, that's him, basically. When he's not in jail. So . . . I guess it felt like a bit of a dig, when you said all that." Christ, it was like ripping off a scab.

The silence prickled. Then Mark spoke, his tone a lot different from before. "Patrick . . . You're not your father. You're a much better man, and I would *never* throw what he's done in your face." He huffed. "At least, not now I know about it. I'm so sorry you've had all this to deal with, and I think you're doing a bloody marvellous job."

Mark reached over to grip Patrick's thigh, and Patrick took his hand off the wheel to cover Mark's hand with his briefly. God, that felt good. Like things were back how they ought to be, finally.

"I think you might have noticed already," Mark said after they'd driven on for a bit, his tone apologetic, "but I can be a little pompous and self-satisfied on occasion."

"And defensive," Patrick teased, because his heart was flying somewhere up in the clouds and yeah, he was a bastard.

"Now wait a— Oh. Yes, I suppose so." Mark paused. "But the thing is, I *do* see your point. It's just . . . Things aren't always so cut-and-dried."

"Yeah. Yeah, Mum's been telling me that and all. And Fen, come to that. Came round my house last night to read me the riot act. "

"Ah. Yes. She does that."

"Think it's a female thing. They probably learn it in the Girl Guides or something."

Mark nodded. "They have a badge for everything these days. Not that Fen stayed long enough to earn any." He took a deep breath. "So are we all right? Because—" He broke off as his phone buzzed.

He looked at the screen and winced.

"Something wrong?" Patrick asked.

"No—well, not really. A text from David: *Little moppet about to expire from hunger. Taking her to lunch at Pizza Express.* I'm fairly certain that's not what Teenager Taming would recommend as the ideal way to impress upon her that skipping school is *not* to be repeated."

They were almost in Shamwell now. Patrick made a split-second decision to turn right instead of left when they got there. "Teenager Taming?"

Mark flushed. "It's a website."

Still sensitive about his parenting abilities, then, poor sod. Patrick wished he was in a position to give the bloke a hug. "Bit late to worry about it now, I guess. It's pretty good of him, really," he added after a pause. "He fancies you, doesn't he?"

"He, um, did seem to at one point. But he and Fen get on like a house on fire."

"Still pretty decent of him to give us some time together." Patrick wasn't certain *he'd* be so generous in similar circs. "He knows we're together, right, you and me? What am I saying? He's mates with Fen. He probably knows more about our relationship than we do."

"So . . . we do still have a relationship?" Mark asked, sounding so hopeful, Patrick would have reached over and squeezed his knee if they hadn't been going around a roundabout at the time. "It's not a total deal-breaker, then, my profession?"

"Do you want us to still have a relationship? Not too pissed off at me for the way I went off on you?"

"God, yes. I mean no—"

Patrick cut him off with a laugh. "Then yeah, we got a relationship."

"Oh, thank God for that. I won't have to run the London Marathon after all."

"What?"

Mark's face went red. "It was just an idea. I was going to run the London Marathon for charity, to prove to you I can be a giver as well as a taker."

Patrick was glad they'd got to his house, cos it meant he could pull up at the kerb and turn to give Mark the incredulous stare that deserved. "Mate, you barely made it twenty-six feet in the Shamwell Fun Run. I'm not sure you ought to be tackling twenty-six miles anytime soon."

"Well, that was one idea. I'm open to suggestions. Actually, I thought I might do a bit of volunteering at the Citizens' Advice Bureau. Help people with their taxes, their money, whatever—you know, people who can't afford to pay an accountant."

Swallowing down a lump of emotion that was threatening to get stuck in his throat, Patrick turned and cupped Mark's face with his hand. "Yeah, that'd be good. Long as you're doing it cos you want to. You don't have to prove anything to me. Now come on, let's go inside."

Mark unbuckled his seat belt, then paused, frowning. "Oh—we're at your house."

Patrick nodded. "It's a good house. Got a nice little garden, doesn't cost too much to heat, and most importantly, Mum's out at work until five, so we've got it all to ourselves. Coming?"

"Oh God, yes."

CHAPTER THIRTY-FOUR

Mark's mouth was dry as he followed Patrick into the house. This was it. *Finally* he was actually going to get to have sex. Gay sex. With a man. With *Patrick*. "Are you sure your mum's at work?" he couldn't help asking, looking around as if she might be hiding somewhere, ready to jump out and catch them in flagrante.

"Positive. It's Monday, and her car's gone."

Mark felt like a teenager again. It was like the one and only time he'd dared to sneak Ray into his house, and they'd spent the whole time paranoid Mark's dad would burst in on them. "I keep getting this awful feeling something's going to happen again to interrupt us. Your mum will decide to take the afternoon off. David will bring Fen up here. The house will spontaneously combust."

"Nah, trust me. It can't keep happening like that. Third time lucky, yeah?"

"Or is it bad things always come in threes?" Was that a movement off in the living room?

Patrick slipped his arms around Mark's waist and pushed him gently against the wall. "Look at it this way. As long as we keep trying, there's gotta come a time when we actually manage it. Basic laws of chance, innit?" His kiss was sweet and dirty. "Bed?"

"God, yes."

They hurried upstairs, Patrick pulling off his shirt as they went. His bedroom was larger than Mark had expected, all in deep blues that made his eyes darken as he turned back to Mark. "Like it?"

Mark swallowed. "Big bed."

"Yeah. Well, I need a bit of room for all my conquests—" He broke off laughing. "God, your face. Trust me, the number of blokes

I've had in here is a *lot* lower than you think. I don't invite just anyone back here. Mum reckons I'm overcautious. What do you think?"

"I think you're just cautious enough." Mark unbuttoned his shirt, desperate to get skin-on-skin with Patrick.

Patrick was way ahead of him, already stripping off his trousers. Unable to resist touching him long enough to get his own clothes off, Mark pulled him close. Patrick felt amazing, all lean muscle and hot, hot skin. *If I licked him, would he sizzle?* Mark thought deliriously, hardly knowing where to touch first. Patrick's hands were at Mark's belt buckle, a frustrating obstacle to Mark's goal of pressing them so close together, they'd merge into one.

"Hey, gimme a bit of space here," Patrick muttered, getting Mark's trousers open even as he said it. They fell to the floor, and he pulled Mark close again, their groins meeting with only thin cotton layers between them. "That's better. You wanna fuck me?"

Oh God. He just threw it out there, like it was no big deal . . . Mark couldn't catch his breath immediately, most of his higher thought processes entirely off-lined by the way his erection felt pressing against Patrick's matching hardness.

"Or not, you know," Patrick carried on, mistaking his hesitation. "However you wanna do this. I'm versatile, yeah?"

"No. I mean . . ." Mark closed his eyes for a moment. "I mean, yes, I'd like that."

"Cool." Patrick broke away and sprawled on the bed to grab a couple of foil packets from the bedside drawer. Lube and a condom. He tossed the condom over to Mark, then quickly stripped off his boxer briefs and lay there on the bed, knees up, fully naked.

God. Mark's hands shook as he stripped off his boxer shorts, and it took him a couple of goes to get the condom on properly. He knelt on the bed, hoping nothing was sagging too obviously in comparison to the golden young man laid out before him, and watched, dry-mouthed as Patrick ripped open the lube and started fingering himself.

By some kind of miracle, he found his voice. "Let me do that," he begged.

"No problem." With a wicked smile, Patrick handed over the lube and wiped his greasy fingers on Mark's condom-clad dick, sending electric jolts right through Mark's body and up to his brain to kill off any remaining thought processes. It was all he could do not to just throw himself down on Patrick and rut to completion there and then, but he somehow managed to restrain himself and even to lube up his fingers without making *too* much of a mess on the sheets. Then he reached down to touch Patrick's most intimate area, circling his hole with one shaky finger, then slipping gently inside.

Had he thought Patrick's skin was hot? Inside, he was an inferno. Mark groaned, moving his finger in and out.

"Go on, gimme another," Patrick urged. "I can take it."

As Mark did so, there was a loud bang from somewhere in the house. Mark froze. "What was that?"

"Bathroom window . . . in the wind. Don't stop," Patrick gasped.

Mark bent back to his task, and soon Patrick was telling him he was "Ready, damn it, get inside me now." Barely believing this was actually going to happen, Mark lined up and pressed the head of his cock against Patrick's hole. He pushed, hesitating when he met resistance.

"Not gonna break," Patrick muttered, sounding strained.

Mark pressed, gently but firmly, and finally, *finally* he made it past the ring of muscle and was inside Patrick. It was the most incredible feeling he'd ever—

There was another bang, followed by a crash. Mark's heart jumped around three feet. "What the *hell*?"

Patrick grimaced. "Stuff on the windowsill falling in the bath. Or next door's cat's got in again. Keep going."

A little uncertain now, Mark pushed in farther and farther until, oh God, his balls touched Patrick's body, and they were joined, one flesh, deep and perfect and utterly, completely overwhelming. He had to wait, he remembered dimly. Give Patrick's body time to adjust—

"You can move," Patrick told him, and that was it.

Mark leaned down to kiss Patrick, the angle awkward but the sensations incredible. Pulling back, he ran his hands over Patrick's perfect chest, pinching his nipples in turn and being rewarded with blissed-out moans. Then he gave up on all hope of coordinating his movements and just moved in and out of Patrick's body, each thrust taking him higher and higher. He was in heaven, this was the best, the most wonderful thing that had ever happened to him, and any minute now he was going to—

There was a loud creak of hinges. Mark leapt, pulling out of Patrick like he'd been forcibly ejected, and spun, heart racing, to face the door.

There was no one there. He turned back, frowning, to find Patrick laughing helplessly. "Sorry," Patrick got out eventually. "It does that if you don't shut it properly. Swings open in the wind."

"This is *not* funny," Mark snapped, and he then threw himself back down on the bed and was laughing too. "Oh God," he gasped. "It's like a play by Samuel Beckett, and we'll keep trying and hoping and we're never, ever going to get to finish—"

"Bugger that," Patrick said, grinning, and pulled him close again. "C'mon. Third time lucky, remember? Now get back inside me."

"I've heard about pushy bottoms," Mark said, getting back up on somewhat wobbly knees. He lined himself up again and pushed back in. God, that was good. Even hotter than he'd remembered, and so, so tight.

"Yeah? What have you heard about 'em?"

"That you have to be very, very *firm* with them." Mark punctuated the sentence with a hefty thrust that had him seeing stars.

Patrick groaned aloud. "Fuck, yeah. Just a bit higher—oh Christ, yeah. Just there. Fuck, don't stop." He grabbed his dick with a hand and started jerking himself raggedly. Mark stepped up the pace to match, hoping to God he wouldn't peak too soon, but God, it felt so *amazing* . . .

Nothing, *nothing* had prepared Mark for the sight of Patrick convulsing beneath him, his face screwed up in ecstasy as he spattered his chest with thick, white spunk. It was the most erotic sight in the world, and Mark felt as if he bestrode the world. "God, I love you so much," he breathed, and then he was coming almost before he knew it, his orgasm hitting with the force of a ten-ton truck.

Panting, he collapsed on the bed half beside Patrick, half on top of him, and they lay there in a sweaty tangle of damp sheets, holding one another.

As his breathing calmed and his mental powers slowly returned, Mark became aware that he'd done the unforgivable. "Um. What I said just then—"

"Nah, don't worry about it. No one takes stuff you say during sex seriously."

"No—I mean, that's not it." Mark's stomach was horribly fluttery, but he stared up at the ceiling and forced himself to go on. "I meant, I'm sorry I said it then. For the first time, I mean. But, well, I do. Love you." He flushed. "And I realise saying it just after sex isn't much better, but I—I wanted you to know."

Patrick pushed himself up on one elbow to look down at Mark. "Yeah?" he said, his deep blue eyes twinkling.

"You don't have to say it back," Mark said quickly, feeling suddenly flat, as if someone had just dumped a large, damp, sex-scented mattress on top of him.

"I know I don't," Patrick said, leaning over to kiss him. "And yeah, I love you too."

The mattress of depression turned into an air bed and floated away, almost taking Mark with him, he felt so light. "That's good," he managed.

"Yeah," Patrick agreed with a chuckle. "Handy, innit?"

"Absolutely," Mark said, laughing back at him.

Half an hour later, they still hadn't moved, although Mark was aware they couldn't put it off indefinitely. After all, Fen was really quite fast at eating pizza. And Patrick's mum would be home in a matter of hours.

Time was passing quickly, just holding each other and talking about all sorts of things.

"Still got Lex to worry about," Patrick was saying. "Well, the job, anyhow. Looks like we needn't have worried about the boyfriend after all." He sighed. "I could kill that bloody git Onslow."

Mark gave him a sharp look. "Onslow? Kenneth Onslow?"

"Yeah, he's the one who's been trying to convince the trustees Lex oughta go. You know him?"

"Not exactly. He's a member of the SAPS, but he wasn't at the meeting I went to. But I do need to talk to him. I've taken over as treasurer—apparently it's not a good idea to ever admit to having an accountancy qualification at this sort of thing."

Patrick chuckled. "Yeah, Si's been trying to offload that gig for years."

"Well, anyway, I've spent some of the last few days looking over the accounts—trying to get a feel for them, pick up any potential problems, that sort of thing. And I've found a whole stack of *very* dubious expense claims from your Mr. Onslow. Now, obviously I won't be able to permit anyone to, shall we say, take advantage of the society while I'm treasurer, but I might be open to persuasion to take the view that what's done is done. If, say, I were to be convinced that he's the sort of person who has everyone's best interests at heart."

"You're gonna blackmail him?"

"Um. That's a very strong word. But basically, yes. I, um, I hope that's not going to run counter to your principles?"

"People are more important than principles." Patrick smiled, warming Mark's heart to ridiculous levels. "Well, some of 'em are, anyway. The ones I love are, definitely."

"Good," Mark said firmly. He ran a hand down Patrick's hard, youthful chest, feeling certain stirrings that suggested maybe thirty-nine wasn't as old as all that. Did they have time, though?

Oh, to hell with it. Fen was perfectly safe with David, and Patrick's mum didn't seem the sort to be easily shocked even if she did come home early. He smiled. "Feeling up to testing whether fourth times are lucky too?"

Patrick grinned and rolled over on top of him. "You're my sort of bloke, Mark Nugent."

EPILOGUE

A month or so later, during the May half-term holidays, they were sitting in Mark's living room, Mark and Patrick side by side on the sofa but not actually touching in deference to their guest. Fen had been *quite* clear on that before he'd arrived. "Dad, it's got nothing to do with homophobia. It's just, like, parental PDAs are *so gross*."

Ollie, slumped awkwardly in the armchair opposite them, looked like he'd probably prefer a bit of old-people-snogging to the current atmosphere of excruciating politeness.

Good, Mark thought. Let him suffer. That'd teach him to dare to date *Mark's* little girl. Mark had been firm on them not disappearing up to Fen's room, despite her pleas that they weren't, like, going to *do* anything.

Mark had one rule, *one*, regarding significant others in Fen's life, and he was damn well going to enforce it.

Patrick, by contrast, had been spending quite a bit of time in Mark's bedroom lately, to the satisfaction of all concerned. Ellen, although not precisely supportive of the new openness in their relationship, had declared her grudging acceptance after a particularly heartfelt rant from Fen, which Mark had been only too glad not to be on the receiving end of.

Patrick stirred now and broke the silence. "Hey, you're never gonna guess who my mum's started going out with."

"You sound like you actually approve of this one," Mark said, giving Patrick an intrigued look.

"Well, I'm not sure I'd go that far, but he's not a complete no-hoper. Quite. It's Rory from the Spartans."

"Rory?" Mark stared.

"Yeah, they got talking after the fun run—you know he was running the bouncy slide? He let her have a few goes for free after all the kiddies had gone home."

"Well, top marks to him for the novel chat-up," Mark said thoughtfully. "Although I'd have thought she could do better, looks-wise." He smirked. "At least someone her own height. And with hair."

Patrick reprimanded him with a dig in the ribs, which descended into a mock fight, which was what Mark had been aiming for.

"That's baldist, that is. And heightist," Fen said, coming in with two glasses of orange squash and causing Mark and Patrick to spring apart guiltily. She handed one glass to Ollie, making certain he had hold of it before letting go, gave him a soft smile, and sat down in the other armchair, tucking one leg underneath her. "You know what would make this really perfect?"

Mark sighed. "Let me guess: it's got four legs, whiskers, and a tail?"

The Campaign for Really Cute Cats hadn't lost any momentum in the Nugent household, especially since the campaigner-in-chief was no longer distracted by having to fix her father's love life and Ollie's problems at school. Patrick's advice hadn't resulted, as the children had hoped, in the PE teacher's dismissal, but he *had* been compelled to give Ollie a written apology, and there was a pretty solid rumour that, humiliated, he was now looking for another job.

Fen grabbed her phone and jumped up. "There's this little black-and-white kitten on the RSPCA website, and he's *so cute*—Dad, please can we go and see him?" She thrust the screen under his nose, displaying a picture of a worried-looking kitten that apparently rejoiced in the name of Snoop Cat. *Snoop Cat?* Mark wondered if he'd been taken away from his previous owners for mental cruelty.

"I said we'd get a cat in the summer, didn't I? *If* you're doing well at school." Mark had been trying to stave off his inevitable surrender a while longer. At least until the memory of his frantic worry over her truancy had faded a little, and he'd no longer feel like he was *actively* rewarding bad behaviour.

"But he might be gone by then." Fen slumped back into her armchair and sulked for a solid minute. Then she spoke again. "Dad, can I still be a bridesmaid when you and Patrick get married, even though there won't be a bride?"

Mark spluttered on his tea.

Patrick slapped him on the back, which didn't help, and answered for them both. "Bit soon to talk about marriage, yeah?"

Fen sent him a serious look. "You do know Dad's gonna be forty in October, right?"

Patrick laughed, the traitor. "Yeah, but I reckon he's got, oh, at least another decade in him. So no need to hurry."

"Yeah, but if you got married in September, he'd still be in his thirties and that'd look better, wouldn't it? I mean, you're twenty-five, Dad said. So you marrying a fortysomething, that's gonna look well weird. And anyway, that'd be a good month to get married in. So he wouldn't think about marrying Mum that time of year."

Mark coughed. "No, darling, your mother and I were married in May."

Fen snorted. "Yeah, right." She and Ollie sent each other matching scornful looks.

"Fen?"

"Dad, I worked it out in *primary* school. That wedding photo you used to have on the wall? You and mum standing in front of that bush with the big orange flowers? We had one of those in the school garden, and it *never* flowered before we broke up for the holidays. It was always out when we came back in September. I even asked Miss Cromwell about it, and she said there aren't any that come out in May, they're all late-flowering. *And* you could see Mum had a bit of a bump in some of the other pictures."

Oh God. "Darling, I'm sorry we, well—"

"Lied to me about it, like, *all my life*."

Mark swallowed. "Um. Yes. You know we were only thinking of you."

Patrick slung his arm around Mark's shoulders and gave him a gentle squeeze of support.

She glared at them both. "You're supposed to be able to trust your parents, you know. I could get a complex about it. Have all kinds of trust issues and stuff. I could need, like, *years* of therapy or something."

Ollie, the little sod, was grinning.

"So, Dad?" Fen went on with an evil smile that was all her own. "When are we going to see Snoop Cat?"

Explore more of *The Shamwell Tales* at:
riptidepublishing.com/titles/universe/shamwell-tales

Dear Reader,

Thank you for reading JL Merrow's *Out!*

We know your time is precious and you have many, many entertainment options, so it means a lot that you've chosen to spend your time reading. We really hope you enjoyed it.

We'd be honored if you'd consider posting a review—good or bad—on sites like **Amazon, Barnes & Noble, Kobo, Goodreads, Twitter, Facebook, Tumblr,** and your blog or website. We'd also be honored if you told your friends and family about this book. Word of mouth is a book's lifeblood!

For more information on upcoming releases, author interviews, blog tours, contests, giveaways, and more, please sign up for our weekly, spam-free newsletter and visit us around the web:

Newsletter: tinyurl.com/RiptideSignup
Twitter: twitter.com/RiptideBooks
Facebook: facebook.com/RiptidePublishing
Goodreads: tinyurl.com/RiptideOnGoodreads
Tumblr: riptidepublishing.tumblr.com

Thank you so much for Reading the Rainbow!

RiptidePublishing.com

ALSO BY JL MERROW

The Shamwell Tales
Caught!
Played!
Spun!

Porthkennack
Wake Up Call
One Under (coming March
2018)

The Plumber's Mate Mysteries
Pressure Head
Relief Valve
Heat Trap
Blow Down

The Midwinter Manor Series
Poacher's Fall
Keeper's Pledge

Southampton Stories
Pricks and Pragmatism
Hard Tail

Lovers Leap
It's All Geek to Me
Damned If You Do
Camwolf
Muscling Through
Wight Mischief
Midnight in Berlin
Slam!
Fall Hard
Raising the Rent
To Love a Traitor
Trick of Time
Snared
A Flirty Dozen

ABOUT THE AUTHOR

JL Merrow is that rare beast, an English person who refuses to drink tea. She read Natural Sciences at Cambridge, where she learned many things, chief amongst which was that she never wanted to see the inside of a lab ever again. Her one regret is that she never mastered the ability of punting one-handed whilst holding a glass of champagne.

She writes (mostly) contemporary gay romance and mysteries, and is frequently accused of humour. Her novel *Slam!* won the 2013 Rainbow Award for Best LGBT Romantic Comedy, and several of her books have been EPIC Awards finalists, including *Muscling Through*, *Relief Valve* (the Plumber's Mate Mysteries), and *To Love a Traitor*.

JL Merrow is a member of the Romantic Novelists' Association, International Thriller Writers, Verulam Writers and the UK GLBTQ Fiction Meet organising team.

Find JL Merrow on Twitter as @jlmerrow, and on Facebook at facebook.com/jl.merrow

For a full list of books available, see: jlmerrow.com   or JL Merrow's Amazon author page: viewauthor.at/JLMerrow.

Enjoy more stories like
Out!
at RiptidePublishing.com!